1/09

Praise for the novels of Cathie Linz

Big Girls Don't Cry

"The characters spring to life, and readers will be thrilled to
find th... ... ...t
like o... ...o
looks and ... like a ... woman." —*Booklist* (starred review)

"[A] sweetly charming, splendidly funny, and supremely satisfying contemporary romance." —*Chicago Tribune*

"Another winner." —*Fresh Fiction*

"Another keeper." —*Contemporary Romance Writers*

"Definitely one for the keeper shelf." —*Genrefluent*

Bad Girls Don't

"A humorous tale . . . The secondary characters are comical
and outrageous . . . You won't want to miss *Bad Girls Don't*."
—*Romance Reviews Today*

"Cathie Linz gives her beautifully matched protagonists lots
of sexy chemistry and some delightfully snappy dialogue, and
the quirky cast of secondary characters gives *Bad Girls Don't*
its irresistible charm." —*Chicago Tribune*

"Linz, known for her fast-paced, snappy romantic comedies,
once again sparkles in this heartwarming, funny tale. And
her secondary characters . . . make an already excellent story
exceptional." —*Booklist* (starred review)

"Linz's characterizations are absolutely wonderful. I fell in
love with the protagonists from the first page of this book . . .
We've watched Ms. Linz's writing develop and grow over the
years. It has always been a pleasure to read her books, but I
must say that this one is a fantastic novel!" —*Rendezvous*

"Totally delightful." —*Fresh Fiction*

cont...

EVAN...

W9-BUV-582

Good Girls Do

"Humor and warmth . . . Readers are going to love this!"
—Susan Elizabeth Phillips

"Cathie Linz is the author that readers of romantic comedy have been waiting for. She knows how to do it—characters with depth, sharp dialogue, and a compelling story. The result is a charming, offbeat world, one you'll hate to leave."
—Jayne Ann Krentz

"Sometimes even good girls need to take a walk on the wild side. Linz deftly seasons her writing with her usual delectable wit, and the book's quirky cast of endearing secondary characters adds another measure of humor to this sweetly sexy, fabulously fun contemporary romance."
—*Booklist* (starred review)

"Sexy, sassy, and graced with exceptional dialogue, this fast-paced story is both hilarious and heartwarming, featuring wonderfully wacky secondary characters and well-developed protagonists you will come to love . . . A winner that will leave readers smiling long after they have turned the final page."
—*Library Journal*

"Lively and fun, and you won't be able to put it down."
—*Fresh Fiction*

"A fun contemporary romance . . . Fans of *You Can't Take It With You* who like romantic romps will enjoy this funny family tale."
—*The Best Reviews*

Smart Girls
Think Twice

· · · · · · · · · · · · · ·

Cathie Linz

BERKLEY SENSATION, NEW YORK

THE BERKLEY PUBLISHING GROUP
Published by the Penguin Group
Penguin Group (USA) Inc.
375 Hudson Street, New York, New York 10014, USA
Penguin Group (Canada), 90 Eglinton Avenue East, Suite 700, Toronto, Ontario M4P 2Y3, Canada
(a division of Pearson Penguin Canada Inc.)
Penguin Books Ltd., 80 Strand, London WC2R 0RL, England
Penguin Group Ireland, 25 St. Stephen's Green, Dublin 2, Ireland (a division of Penguin Books Ltd.)
Penguin Group (Australia), 250 Camberwell Road, Camberwell, Victoria 3124, Australia
(a division of Pearson Australia Group Pty. Ltd.)
Penguin Books India Pvt. Ltd., 11 Community Centre, Panchsheel Park, New Delhi—110 017, India
Penguin Group (NZ), 67 Apollo Drive, Rosedale, North Shore 0632, New Zealand
(a division of Pearson New Zealand Ltd.)
Penguin Books (South Africa) (Pty.) Ltd., 24 Sturdee Avenue, Rosebank, Johannesburg 2196,
South Africa

Penguin Books Ltd., Registered Offices: 80 Strand, London WC2R 0RL, England

This is a work of fiction. Names, characters, places, and incidents either are the product of the author's imagination or are used fictitiously, and any resemblance to actual persons, living or dead, business establishments, events, or locales is entirely coincidental. The publisher does not have any control over and does not assume any responsibility for author or third-party websites or their content.

SMART GIRLS THINK TWICE

A Berkley Sensation Book / published by arrangement with the author

PRINTING HISTORY
Berkley Sensation mass-market edition / January 2009

ISBN: 978-0-425-22648-3

BERKLEY® SENSATION
Berkley Sensation Books are published by The Berkley Publishing Group,
a division of Penguin Group (USA) Inc.,
375 Hudson Street, New York, New York 10014.
BERKLEY® SENSATION and the "B" design are trademarks of Penguin Group (USA) Inc.

PRINTED IN THE UNITED STATES OF AMERICA

10 9 8 7 6 5 4 3 2 1

For my agent, Annelise Robey, a very smart girl who wants to move to my towns of Rock Creek and Serenity Falls. Your enthusiasm and belief in me have kept me going through good times and bad. Thank you from the bottom of my heart.

For my editor, Cindy Hwang, who gets so excited about my books that I keep replaying her voice-mail messages to me over and over and over again.

You both made my dreams a reality!

Acknowledgments

Gobsmacked Knob, Rock Creek, and all the people and places in this book existed only in my imagination and would have stayed there without the encouragement of a lot of people. Thanks to:

Fellow writer and good friend Jayne Ann Krentz, who said, "You can do it!" from day one.

My Chilebabe buddies—Susan Elizabeth Phillips, Lindsay Longford, Margaret Watson, and Suzette Vann—who have been lifesavers on more than one occasion. I'm honored and blessed to have you in my life.

Fellow writer and good friend Jennifer Greene, who shares retail therapy with me along with so many other things.

My best friend since I was five—De Patch all the way up in Alaska—for always being there for me no matter what. You are a sister to me and I love you.

All the SEPPIES online, especially Lizzie, Ann, Lynne, Lynda, Teble, Tracey, Carolyn, and Jeanna.

My family for understanding what deadline dementia really means and loving me anyway.

Special kudos to the great people at Berkley including assistant editor Leis Pederson, who never laughs at me when I beg for books; art director George Long, who gives me such awesome covers; and PR guru Julia Fleischaker, who likes my PR photo and works hard on my behalf. You all rock!

Last but never least, my readers and the hundreds of book-sellers (especially the crew at my hometown store, Anderson's!) and librarians who spread the word about my books and make my day by e-mailing me saying how my stories have touched them. You're the reason I write.

Chapter One

· · · · · · · · · · ·

Emma Riley's arrival in her hometown of Rock Creek, Pennsylvania, was quiet and uneventful—just like her life up to that point. Emma wasn't the kind of person who made a splash and that was okay with her.

It clearly wasn't okay with her older sisters Sue Ellen and Leena, who were standing before her in the living room of the mobile home in which they'd all grown up. Her sisters were eyeing her outfit with varying degrees of disapproval.

"What?" Emma adjusted her glasses to look down at her khaki skirt and blue polo shirt. "What's wrong?"

"You look like a librarian," her sister Leena, the former plus-size model, said.

Emma found nothing wrong with the comparison. "Yeah, so?"

Leena and Sue Ellen shook their heads in unison.

Emma was used to her family shaking their heads at her. Leena, the pretty one, was only two years older than

Emma. Sue Ellen was the oldest. Both her sisters were getting married this summer, but that was another story.

Right now Emma was focused on other matters—like walking into the local bar in search of a man. And not just any man, but the sexiest guy in town.

"You'll never get him to say yes wearing that," Leena said.

"You need to show some cleavage." Sue Ellen reached out to undo the top four buttons on the polo shirt. "And some leg. I could cut that skirt shorter—"

"Forget it." Emma hurriedly took a few steps back. "I'm not trying to get the man to propose to me. You two are the brides-to-be."

Emma should never have told her sisters about her plans for the afternoon, but she was so excited about her research project that she'd just had to share. Big mistake. Where she saw academic possibilities, they saw sex.

As a sociologist, Emma knew that family relationships were complicated. And her family's dynamics were particularly thorny. Even though she was twenty-seven, her sisters still viewed her through the lens of their childhood.

"You need to walk into Nick's Tavern from a position of power," Leena said. "And you can do that by feeling confident about yourself."

"Right," Emma noted wryly. "And you two tearing down my appearance is a surefire way to boost my confidence."

"We're just trying to help you."

"Well, stop it. I've got to go." Emma grabbed the keys to her blue Prius and left the mobile home.

Emma had been back in town only two days, and already she was feeling the gnawing affects. That had to stop. She knew her sisters loved her. But they didn't get her.

Looking at her reflection in her Prius's rearview mirror, she said, "You are a strong and capable woman." The affirmation would have been more powerful had she not laughed at the end of it.

Emma couldn't help it. No matter how hard she tried, she couldn't seem to get the affirmation thing down pat.

Yes, she was here for professional reasons, and yes, she was here for her sisters' weddings. But Emma had also returned to her roots to figure out who she was. Somehow she'd gotten lost along the stressful academic fast track she'd been on for the past ten years.

There was a name for what she was feeling. Quarter-life crisis. So called because it usually hit twenty-somethings who were a quarter of the way through their life when they started doubting themselves. A boatload of fears, doubts, and insecurities had Emma second-guessing all the choices she'd made so far. Plus she was stuck with student loan debt that she often felt would take her two or three lifetimes to pay off.

While it was true that Emma loved her work, she wasn't as sure about her actual job as an assistant professor at a very small college. Her salary was certainly nothing to brag about, and she constantly had to prove herself. Publish or perish was very much a reality for her.

Which was why this research project was so incredibly important. She had to make it work. She'd only been teaching for a year. As the last one hired in her department, she'd be the first one laid off. The job she had was definitely preferable to no job at all.

Glancing again in the rearview mirror, Emma belatedly realized she hadn't refastened the buttons on her polo shirt that Sue Ellen had undone. She waited until she'd pulled the Prius into a parking spot in downtown Rock Creek before fixing that. She wasn't so desperate that she had to use what little cleavage she had to get what she wanted. At least not yet.

Even considering such a thing was very unprofessional. And Emma prided herself on being professional. Not that pride would pay off her remaining student loans.

She paused to unfasten the top two buttons on the shirt, telling herself she was only doing so because it was a warm June day.

Taking a deep breath, she pulled open the door to Nick's Tavern and entered. The darkness inside made it difficult for Emma to see at first. The place seemed like the Batcave compared to the bright sunlight outside. Once her eyes adjusted to the change, her gaze traveled over to the bar and the man standing behind it.

She'd heard that bartender Jake Slayter was a bad boy "hottie," but even so Emma wasn't prepared for her reaction to him. The guy's wow factor was clear off the charts! So was her response. Her heart beat faster, her palms became damp, and her womb tightened. All classic signs in the science of attraction.

Ordinarily she wasn't into ogling men. There were no calendars of naked males on her bedroom walls. That was her sister Sue Ellen's thing, not hers. Emma's few relationships with the opposite sex had been with guys who were more geeky than hunky. The most recent had been Ted Howser, who had a master's degree in information technology and in his spare time had edited a trivia book on the BBC television series *Doctor Who*.

She and Ted had recently agreed to call things off but remain friends. The truth was that their six-month-long relationship hadn't been all that passionate to begin with. He'd never even given her an orgasm.

Jake Slayter was the kind of man who instantly made a woman think of orgasms.

Emma drank him in—his dark brown hair, wide shoulders, and golden brown eyes. Brooding eyes. A black T-shirt revealed a thorny tattoo on his right upper arm.

Rumor had it that Jake had made a name for himself in extreme sports, but a climbing injury had put an end to that. A quick search on Google had confirmed that information. But no one knew what he was doing in Rock Creek, and apparently no one was brave enough to ask. Until now.

"Are you going to stand there by the door all day or come on in?" he growled impatiently.

"I'm, uh . . ." Emma cleared her throat and tightened her hold on her navy blue North Face backpack. "I'm here to interview you."

His expression instantly turned stone cold. "I don't speak to the press."

"I'm not a reporter." She nudged her glasses higher on the bridge of her nose. She didn't really need them except for reading, but she thought they made her look more serious. Hiding behind glasses might be a cliché, but hey, it worked for her. She never claimed to be perfect. Far from it. "I'm a sociologist. I'm interviewing all the newcomers to Rock Creek for a research project I'm doing—"

Jake cut her off. "I'm not interested."

"But I haven't even told you about my project yet."

He glared at her. "What part of *not interested* do you not understand?"

Emma refused to give up. This was too important. She was a woman on a mission. Wearing smart-girl glasses. "Maybe we should start over." She climbed up onto a bar stool, tugged her conservative khaki skirt over her knees, and then placed her backpack on the stool beside her in order to remove her ever-present laptop. "I'm evaluating the resurgence of Rock Creek over the past year. And why so many people have been drawn here recently."

"Don't care. Still not interested."

Okay, the guy's attitude was beginning to aggravate her. It's not like she was asking for anything outrageous here.

He could at least give her a fair chance. "I won't take much of your time."

"You've got that right."

Even though Emma's job was studying people and their behavior, she often felt awkward around them. Not that she let it show. She couldn't afford to. "If you'd just let me explain—"

"See that?" He pointed to the NO SOLICITING sign next to the register.

"I'm not trying to sell you anything."

He folded his muscular arms over his broad chest. "Do you want a drink or not?"

"I don't suppose you have a nice California Riesling?"

"We don't serve wine."

"Right." She paused a moment to consider her options. Not just in the drink department but in her approach to Jake. She hadn't expected him to be so grumpy. Maybe she should try something else. Her coworker and buddy Nadine Parsen had an adolescent son who was a huge fan of Jake's and longed for his autograph. Maybe she should have started out by asking him about that.

Eyeing his grim expression, Emma decided that topic of conversation wouldn't be any easier to tackle. Instead she took a moment to study her surroundings. The grungy paneled walls of Nick's Tavern had definitely seen better days. Unlike most of the rest of the town, no attempt had been made to upgrade or update anything here. Jake was by far the best looking thing in the place.

Which brought her back to the man with the incredible wow factor. She wasn't about to give up on Jake. Not because of her intensely physical reaction to him. She needed him in order for her research study to be successful. This was strictly professional. She couldn't afford to be a wimp.

"There must be some way I can convince you," Emma said.

He leaned closer. "Is that an offer?"

She couldn't reply, momentarily distracted by the fact that he had the thickest lashes and most intense eyes she'd ever seen. Dark and mysterious. Irish poet eyes. Orgasm-promising eyes.

"Go ahead. Try me," he said huskily.

Her eyes slid to his mouth. She licked lips suddenly gone dry. Images of him bare chested and begging to pleasure her suddenly filled her mind.

Yeah, like that was ever going to happen.

But, oh, it was a powerful fantasy. Especially since her romantic reality had been so lacking lately.

"Forget about him. Try *me* instead," a man drunkenly slurred in her ear as he grabbed her derriere and squeezed hard. "Or better yet, I'll try you."

Her gasp of outrage was instantly followed by a sinister glare from Jake. "Back off, Roy," he growled.

"Or what, pretty boy?" Roy taunted. "What ya gonna do about it? You think you can claim every woman in this town, even the ugly ones?"

Emma saw red. For once in her life, she didn't think; she just acted. A moment later, Roy ended up on the floor, his hands protectively cupping his family jewels.

"No one touches me without my permission, and no one calls me ugly." She sent a warning glance to the remaining handful of patrons in the bar. "You got that?"

They all nodded.

Emma could tell Jake was impressed. That certainly hadn't been her intention. He now eyed her with newfound respect along with a dose of masculine curiosity. "Who are you?"

"I'm sorry." Her voice shook, so she paused to clear her

throat and regain some calm. "I should have introduced myself in the beginning. My name is Emma Riley."

"Riley?" a pot-bellied man with a John Deere cap said. "Are you related to Sue Ellen Riley?"

"Yes. She's my oldest sister."

He nodded sagely. "That explains it. Those Riley women are downright crazy."

"I don't appreciate being called crazy," Emma said.

"Where did a sociologist learn moves like that?" Jake asked her.

"Self-defense classes. I live in Boston. I'm only here for the summer doing my research." She awkwardly climbed back onto the bar stool. Inside she was shaking like crazy, frantically trying to keep the panic at bay. *You're okay, you're okay, you're okay. You're safe now. You're safe.*

Deere-cap Man helped Roy to his feet and guided him out. Before leaving, Roy paused at the door to look back at Emma. The venom in his stare made her tremble even more.

How had things gotten so out of hand so quickly? Her sisters Sue Ellen and Leena were the ones who caused chaos. Emma was the one who studied mayhem from afar and dispassionately analyzed its cause and effect.

But being groped like that brought back bad memories and Emma had just reacted instinctively. Not her proudest moment. She clasped her shaking hands together in her lap.

"So you're a kick-ass sociologist," Jake said.

Yeah, right. "I should have gone for a more peaceful resolution, using words instead of force."

"Roy was in no mood to listen to anything you had to say."

"Even so, I shouldn't have stooped down to his level."

"You were protecting yourself."

"I should have reasoned with him."

"Yeah, that would have worked," Jake noted in a mocking voice.

"It might have. I didn't even speak to him. Give him a warning before—"

"Busting his nuts?"

Emma put her hands to her flushed face. "Maybe I should go after him and apologize."

"Are you crazy?"

She lowered her hands and glared at him. "I believe I've already stated the fact that I do not appreciate being called crazy."

"Yeah, well, how would you describe a woman who walks into a bar and stirs things up?"

"I'd describe her as having a very bad day. Stirring things up was never my intention. I leave that to the rest of my family," Emma muttered.

"Here." He poured her a stiff drink. "You look like you could use this."

Emma eyed it cautiously. She was totally out of her element here. She was an academic who was more at home in a university library than a bar. So what was she doing starting a brawl like some biker babe?

Okay, so she hadn't actually *started* it—Roy had done that by grabbing her and squeezing her derriere. He'd trapped Emma between his body and the bar and she'd panicked. Plus he'd called her ugly.

Apparently those Managing Assaultive Behavior classes she'd taken on campus had worked better than she'd expected.

Not that she'd ever attack someone merely for saying she was ugly. Emma knew all too well that she was no beauty. Her sister Leena got the pretty genes. Emma got the smart genes—along with mousy brown hair, a face that was a tad too wide, and plain brown eyes.

Jake nudged the glass a little closer. "Drink."

She did and almost choked.

"You're supposed to sip it, not gulp it in one go," he said.

She was too busy coughing to answer him.

"Next time you'll know better. Live and learn."

Emma was better at the learning part than the living part. Always had been.

"You could have warned me," she said once she could finally speak again.

"How was I supposed to know that you were so . . . inexperienced?"

"I only drink the occasional glass of wine. Do I look like the kind of woman who's a pro at belting shots of whiskey?"

"No, but then you don't look like the kind of woman who can kick ass either."

"I already told you that I regret doing that."

"I don't believe in regrets."

"Really?" Emma said wistfully. "That must be nice."

"I don't do nice either."

"You stuck up for me when Roy grabbed me. That was nice of you."

Even Jake's grimace was brooding. "Yeah, right. You didn't need my help. You nailed him on your own."

"Oh, but I do need your help," she assured him. "The success of my entire project rests on your participation."

"You don't give up easily."

"Not where my work is concerned, no."

"Why me?"

"Because I need your demographic. You're the most recent arrival in Rock Creek and the only one in your subset."

"Just lie and say someone else is the most recent arrival."

"I don't lie."

"Everybody lies," Jake said.

"I don't."

Jake stared into her wide brown eyes and wondered if this chick was for real. She seemed younger than she probably was. How long did it take to be a sociologist anyway? She looked like an academic with her smart-girl glasses and sedate blue polo shirt tucked into her prim khaki skirt. Not that he had much experience with that kind of woman. He was more accustomed to babes than bookworms.

She had great legs, though. From what he could see of them. Imagining her kicking ass in stilettos and black leather got him hard and hot. He'd clearly been without a female for far too long.

Time for some sex.

But not with smart girl Emma Riley.

Jake didn't need any distractions in his life right now. He had his own reasons for coming to Rock Creek. *Private* reasons he wasn't about to share with anyone.

Not that he was a man who made a practice of spilling his guts. Not in this lifetime. He'd learned early that showing any vulnerability was the kiss of death. Growing up in the foster care system, being moved from place to place, had taught him early to be self-sufficient. No one else was going to look out for him. No one else was going to protect him. The tougher he was, the better.

Not so Emma. He had her pegged as a total heart-on-her-sleeve type, mixed in with a big dose of intellectual nerdiness. His total opposite. Having sex with her was definitely not a smart idea.

All very logical, but Jake was an adrenaline junkie and a rebel. There was no satisfaction in playing it safe. If he had played it safe, he wouldn't have survived the climbing accident that had ended his career.

The more he told himself that he should send Emma packing, the more tempted he was to keep her around.

"Why are you studying newcomers to town?" he said.

Her entire face lit up as she leaned closer. "It's part of my project about the rebirth of Rock Creek. I'm conducting a study on the recent societal influences and changes here. In the past year the town has gone from a past-its-prime location to becoming a New Age center for the arts."

Jake couldn't help wondering if her face lit up like that when she was having sex. He wasn't really paying attention to her words, but he still said, "Tell me more."

"Sure." She beamed at him. "I'd be delighted to."

"Start at the beginning."

"Well, as you probably know, sociology is the study of human society and social behavior. Sociologists are mainly interested in social interaction. You know, how people react."

Jake sure knew how he was reacting. It didn't take a sociologist to figure out that his body was primed and ready for hers.

"What's going on in Rock Creek is a social phenomenon of sorts," she continued. "I'm here to observe the facts and events, to examine group behavior, to unravel the hidden meanings behind the human actions. Are you with me so far?"

"Oh yeah." The human actions he was picturing were all X-rated and probably illegal in several Southern states.

"I can show you more if you'd like."

He imagined her showing him plenty—undoing the buttons on her polo shirt, shimmying out of her prim skirt before stepping up onto the bar and doing a striptease just for him, showing him every inch of creamy skin on her entire body.

"As I said," Emma continued, "what's going on here is very exciting."

Oh yeah. Jake was past excited at this point and rapidly approaching ready to launch.

"What made you pick Rock Creek?" she asked. "Do you have family here?"

Emma saw the change that instantly came over Jake's face. She also saw her chances of getting him to agree to participate in her study slipping away before her very eyes. Why, oh why had she asked him that personal question? It was too soon. She should have stuck to facts and figures. She'd totally messed up and he'd totally shut down.

Just when Emma thought things couldn't get any worse, they did: her mother sauntered into the bar and plunked herself onto the stool beside her.

"Sweetie, what are you doing in here?" Maxie, aka Maxine Riley, asked. As a retired hairdresser, she prided herself on the style du jour she devised for herself. Today's version featured seashell combs holding her artfully colored red hair atop her head. The combs matched her seashell top and cropped pants. Maxie eyed Emma with disapproval. "Why are you hanging around a bar in the middle of the day?"

Emma felt like sinking through the floor. She wasn't a child requiring parental supervision. "I'm working, Mother."

Maxie leaned toward Jake. "She only calls me 'Mother' when she's really peeved with me. Otherwise it's always 'Mom.' But you can call me Maxie," she told him before returning her attention to Emma. "I overheard some inebriated man outside claiming you beat him up. Is it true? Is that part of your job, Emma? I didn't think sociologists were supposed to assault people."

"They're not. He started it." Great. Emma momentarily closed her eyes. Now she *did* sound like a nine-year-old.

"Hmm." Maxie switched her attention back to Jake. "I'll have a Diet Coke with a slice of lime, please."

"What are you doing?" Emma said, her eyes popping open to gaze at her mother in horror.

"Ordering a drink," Maxie replied.

"You can't stay here," Emma said a tad frantically.

Maxie turned and eyed her from head to toe. "I thought your sisters were going to help you with your outfit."

"I don't need their help."

Maxie's raised eyebrow indicated otherwise. She smiled at Jake as he placed her Diet Coke and lime in front of her. "You may have noticed how tan I am. That's because I live in Florida. I'm up here for my daughters' weddings. Not this daughter, of course." She tilted her head toward Emma.

Emma wondered why the *of course*. Was it so far-fetched that she would find the man of her dreams and tie the knot?

"I mean my other two daughters," Maxie blithely continued. "They're both getting married. Only two weeks apart, can you believe it?"

Emma had to stop this runaway train somehow. "Mother, I'm sure Jake isn't interested in the family's wedding plans."

"You should come," Maxie told Jake. "We really don't have enough good-looking men attending. You could be Emma's date."

"She's kidding," Emma quickly assured Jake. She had to get her mother out of there before she said or did anything else to embarrass her. "Come on, Mother, we've got to go."

"Go where?" Maxie protested. "I'm not done with my drink."

"Yes, you are." Emma tugged her mother off the stool and put a five-dollar bill on the bar. "We'll talk again soon, Jake."

"Of course you will. He's bringing you to the wedding," Maxie said. "Right, Jake?"

"Don't answer that," Emma told him.

"I raised her to have better manners," Maxie told Jake.

"I'm sure you did," he said solemnly.

Maxie shook her head. "Emma has never been a troublemaker before."

"She's having a bad day," Jake said.

"A *very* bad day," Emma muttered.

"A very bad day, hmm? So what are you going to do about that?" Maxie aimed her question at Jake.

His smile was deliciously wicked as he said, "Why I'm going to take Emma to the weddings, of course."

Chapter Two

. . . .

Emma glared at Jake. "That's not funny," she said.

"I wasn't trying to be funny," Jake said. "What makes you think I'm not serious?"

"Why would you want to take me to my sister's wedding?"

"Why not?"

"Because you hardly know me, for one thing."

"I know you're a kick-ass sociologist with a mom who likes Diet Coke with a slice of lime," Jake said.

Smiling widely, Maxie inserted herself into their conversation. "You'll have to excuse my daughter. She's not a pro at accepting invitations from handsome men."

Gee, thanks, Mom. Could you make me sound any lamer? "No, I'm not a pro at *accepting* invitations from handsome men. I'm a pro at turning them down." A total lie but at least it made her sound like less of a loser. Only a few minutes earlier she'd assured Jake that she didn't lie, yet here she was, bending the truth completely. Where her work was concerned, she was honest, but when push came to shove, she apparently lost that quality where her personal life was concerned.

Emma's glare at Jake was intended to send the message that she no longer wanted to continue this line of conversation.

Being a male, he totally ignored her visual request. He clearly wasn't about to give up the chance to have some fun at her expense and his gotcha look told her so.

Maxie looked from Emma to Jake and back again. "Uh, maybe I should leave now and let you two work things out."

"That would be a good idea," Emma agreed. She waited until her mother had actually exited the bar before telling Jake, "Forget everything she said about the wedding."

"Why? Was she making it up?"

"No, my sisters are getting married. Two weeks apart. But that's not your problem."

"Is it *your* problem?"

What, Jake was suddenly turning into Dr. Phil on her now? Why was he asking her stuff like that? "I just meant that you don't have to worry about me taking your comment seriously."

"Which comment exactly?"

"The one about taking me to the weddings."

"Why do you have a problem with that?"

"I already told you. You don't know me."

"Taking you to your sister's weddings is a good way of fixing that."

"Why would you want to know me better? Never mind." She hurriedly stuffed her laptop into her backpack. "I shouldn't have asked that."

"Why not?"

"Because it was a personal question."

"You don't think asking me why I came to this town is a personal question?"

"Not in the same way."

"Why not?"

"Because I was asking you out of professional curiosity. No, *curiosity* isn't the right word." *Come on, Em,* she told herself. *Get your act together here. Be coherent. Be precise. Be the totally in control academic you pretend to be.* "I was asking as part of my study." When he said nothing, she added, "What I mean is my interest in you isn't personal."

"What if mine is?"

She frowned in confusion. "What personal reason could you have in wanting to go to my sisters' weddings?"

"Are a lot of people coming?"

"Yes."

"Then it's a chance for me to get to know some of the citizens of Rock Creek."

She looked at him suspiciously. "You don't strike me as the kind of man who is a people person."

"Bartenders have to be good with people."

If that was the case, then why had he growled at her when she'd first walked in the bar? Not exactly the mark of a friendly extrovert.

"Why that look?" he said. "You don't think I'm good with people?"

Far be it from her to make that judgment call. She was a bit of a social misfit herself. Okay, maybe more than a bit. She'd definitely gotten all the nerdy genes in her family. "You're probably great with people," she said.

"Probably?" He leaned closer and fixed those intense Irish poet eyes of his on her. "Sounds to me like you have some doubts on the matter."

Emma was unable to reply given the fact that her tongue

suddenly seemed stuck to the roof of her mouth. He was like some hottie scrambling device that messed up her internal communication system.

He raised one dark eyebrow. "If you don't think I'm the type to be a people person, what type of guy do you think I am?"

The type to make a woman think of orgasms. Not that she could share that extremely intimate opinion with him.

"I don't know." That would apply to orgasms as well. She was no expert in that department.

"Aren't you interested in finding out?"

"I, uh . . ." Could she possibly sound more tongue-tied? The problem was she absolutely was interested in finding out more about him . . . and orgasms.

"I'm interested in finding out more about you," he said. "You definitely managed to get my attention."

Probably because she'd kicked Roy in the bar. Dumb move on her part. She was still unsettled from that incident. Maybe that's why she was feeling so susceptible to Jake's sex appeal. "I don't want your attention, I want your demographic."

"Then accept my invitation."

"Are you saying that if I let you come with me to the weddings, you'll agree to participate in my research study?"

"I'll agree to consider it."

"Only consider it?"

"That's my best offer. Take it or leave it."

She desperately wanted to leave it. She couldn't figure out Jake's motivation in wanting to come with her. She wasn't buying his story about wanting to meet more citizens of Rock Creek. He had a reason that had nothing to do with her. And he wasn't about to tell her what it was.

She certainly didn't believe that he was interested in

her. Hotties like him never went for plain-Jane brains like her. No, he had some other agenda.

She was dying to ask him what made him go from not interested to a possible yes. Was he just stringing her along? Probably. But again, she didn't have much choice here. She needed him. His participation was pivotal to her research. And he had seemed to pay attention when she'd been talking about the details of her study. Which reminded her . . .

"Listen, before I forget, my friend's son is a big fan of yours," she said. "You're one of his heroes or something. Would you be willing to sign an autograph for him? His name is Liam."

Slam. Jake's expression closed up tighter than a drum. "I don't do autographs." His tone was downright rude.

"Fine." He made her feel like pond scum for asking the question in the first place. She returned her laptop to her backpack and pointed at the five-dollar bill still on the scarred bar. "How much do I owe you for my mom's drink?" Her voice was almost as curt as his had been.

His expression was stone-cold. "Is this study of yours some kind of smoke screen to get me to do an interview?"

She narrowed her eyes at him. "What?"

"You heard me."

She chose her words carefully. Otherwise she'd singe his sexy eyebrows off with her anger. "Do you want me to be completely honest with you?"

"That would be a good idea."

"Then the truth is I'd never even heard of you before I started the research for my project. You may be some big extreme sports guy in your world, but it's not like you're a quarterback for the Steelers or anything. You're not from PA or you'd know this is football country. Liam just happens to follow that extreme sports stuff for some reason. I don't know why. He also likes the music of The Roots and Vampire Weekend. I don't know much about them either."

"How do you know I'm from out of state?"

"I looked you up online. Just for the basics. You grew up in California, as I recall. I only got the bare minimum on you and then stopped, because I didn't want any preconceived notions ruining my research. The bottom line is that I don't care how many races you've won or trophies you have. I'm only interested in you in regard to Rock Creek and your reasons for being here."

Jake had no intention of telling her his real reason for landing in Rock Creek. He was here on a personal mission—to track down his biological mother. He'd taken a temporary job as the bartender at Nick's Tavern while trying to put together a list of likely female suspects who might have given birth to him. The only clue he had was that she'd lived in Rock Creek. The private investigator he'd hired hadn't given him much else to go on. The adoption had been a private one, the records sealed. The agency that had handled it had gone out of business after a fire destroyed most of their records. So here he was, scrounging for information.

Trust had never been an easy deal for him. Not given his background. None of the information about him online said anything but the briefest of references to his years in the foster system, and he liked it that way. There was no mention of his running away at seventeen, of crossing the border into Mexico to work as a bartender for a summer when he turned eighteen, of his returning to the States a few months later, returning to the slopes and snowboarding.

Jake's love of snowboarding had been ingrained in him at a young age, before those dark years in foster care. He'd had loving adoptive parents back then; his dad had given him his first snowboard when he was four. Both his parents loved the mountains around Lake Tahoe, and he'd spent his early childhood flying down those trails, the wind in his face, the exhilaration of freedom in his veins.

Those days had abruptly ended with his parents' death in a car accident one icy night. Snowboarding wasn't in the foster care system's program so he made do with a used and battered skateboard instead. But he'd always known he'd return to the mountains someday. And he had.

He'd become the Tom Brady of extreme sports, from snowboarding to mountain biking to developing new ways to fly faster down a mountain. He'd dominated his competition. He was known as Slayter the Slayer. He was invincible, always in search of the ultimate thrill.

"Do you want me to show you my sociology degree?" Emma's exasperated question brought him back to the present.

"Do you carry it with you?"

"No. But I have my business card. Will that do?" She slid it across the bar to him.

The card was as prim and proper as she was. So were her fingers. No fancy manicures for her. Yet there was a fire beneath that controlled exterior that made Jake wonder what she'd be like in bed.

It wouldn't be the first time that his curiosity had gotten him into trouble. Hell, he'd wondered what climbing the southern slope of that mountain peak in the middle of the Andes would be like and he'd found out—almost losing his life in the process.

His entire life had been one big risk after another up to that point. Only after coming back from the jagged edge of death had he started questioning things in his past. His curiosity had never extended to his own background before. Until now.

Which meant he had enough on his mind without getting distracted by a woman. She was no babe on a bar stool. But she could well be his ticket into the behind-the-scenes stuff in this town.

If it cost him an autograph, so be it. No big deal. "What was that kid's name again? Liam?" He reached for a pad of paper near the cash register and scribbled his name. "Here."

He could tell by her expression that she wanted to tell him to go to hell. But he suspected that she was too polite to do that. He could practically see her weighing the pros and cons—but in the end she took the autograph as he'd known she would. She wouldn't let her friend's kid down. Just as she wouldn't refuse to have him go with her to her sisters' weddings. Because he had something she wanted. And for once, it wasn't his body she was after. Yet.

But he could change that. And he would. Because he wanted her body, and Jake had a way of getting what he wanted.

* * *

Late that afternoon, Maxie stared at the suitcases Emma had gathered by the mobile home's front door before giving Emma a mother-knows-best look. "Are you moving out because I asked that handsome man to accompany you to your sisters' weddings?"

"No. I told you that I was subletting a furnished studio apartment in town."

"I don't remember you saying that."

No surprise there. Her mother didn't register half of what she said. Instead her focus was on the two upcoming weddings. Which was fine by Emma. She certainly didn't want her mom interfering with her own personal life any more than she already had by involving Jake at the bar today.

"The apartment wasn't available until this evening," Emma said.

"But you don't need it. You can stay here in the trailer with me. Sue Ellen is practically living with her fiancé and so is Leena. Living with Cole, I mean, not that Sue Ellen and Leena are both living with Donny."

Emma ignored her mom's convoluted comment and stuck to her guns. "It'll be easier if I have my own place for the summer."

"That's just it. You'll only be here for a few months. So why waste money paying rent on an apartment?"

Because I'd suffocate if I stayed here. "I need to work in a quiet environment," Emma said.

"I can be quiet. It's your sisters who are rowdy."

"Are you talking about us behind our backs again, Mom?" Sue Ellen demanded as she walked into the trailer with several shopping bags dangling over each arm. Leena was right behind her.

"What did she say?" Leena's voice reflected her suspicion.

"I was just commenting to your baby sister that I do know how to be quiet," Maxie said.

Leena rolled her eyes and waited until Sue Ellen and their mom had retreated to a back bedroom before she told Emma, "Don't believe a word she says. No way can Mom be quiet. Did I ever tell you about the time she came to visit me on a photo shoot in Chicago? Mom swore up and down that she wouldn't say anything. She promised me that no one would even know she was there. And do you know what happened?"

Emma shook her head.

"She made so much trouble bossing the hair and makeup people around that she got me kicked off the photo shoot along with her."

"She came to the bar today," Emma said.

"She did?" Leena shook her head and gave Emma a commiserating hug. "I told Sue Ellen not to say anything about your trip, but you know how she is. She takes after Mom."

And who do I take after? Emma wondered. She wasn't outgoing and rowdy like Sue Ellen. And she wasn't confident and feisty like Leena. Both her sisters had gotten their emotional approach to life from their mom. Maybe Emma was more like her father. Not one to wear his heart on his sleeve. A man of few words. No, she wasn't really like him either.

"Is Dad coming to the wedding?" Emma asked.

"Whoa, where did that question come from?"

"Well, you and Sue Ellen haven't talked about it. Is Dad giving Sue Ellen away? Is he giving you away?"

"No way."

"Why not?"

"Look, we're not as close to Dad as you are."

"Because of his drinking?"

Leena shot her a look of surprise. "You knew about that?"

Emma nodded. "I have some vague memories. But Dad hasn't had a drink in twenty years."

"I know that. He's just not a touchy-feely kind of guy, you know?"

"And that's why you don't want him giving you away at your wedding?"

"What do you mean you're not having your father give you away?" Maxie said from the hallway as she walked toward them.

"Sorry," Emma mouthed to her sister.

"I'm a big girl now," Leena said. "I don't need anyone giving me away."

"You've always been a big girl," Maxie said. "Large boned. But I don't see how that has anything to do with your father giving you away. Are you saying that if you weren't a size sixteen, you would have him in the ceremony?"

"No, that's not it at all," Leena said.

"Then what's the problem?" Maxie turned to Emma. "Do you know what this is about?"

"I, uh . . ." Emma tried to think fast. "I believe what Leena means is that she doesn't feel the need to have anyone give her away because she's her own woman."

Leena nodded. "That's right. I'm my own woman. A successful businesswoman. Since our website was picked out and featured on *Oprah* a few months ago we've gotten half a million hits per month. Advertisers are clamoring for our attention."

"You know about Leena's website, right?" Emma said to their mom. "She and her partner started it last fall as a place for women to learn how to increase their self-esteem. They offer all kinds of help—from blogs to message boards to tips from guest speakers. They have sections for all age groups and ethnic groups. The website has really become a big deal in a short period of time."

Leena grinned. "Who knew empowering women would be so popular?"

Maxie wasn't impressed. "I don't see what any of that has to do with your wedding. At least I can count on Sue Ellen to do the right thing? Right, honey?"

"Huh?" Sue Ellen looked up from the pair of sundresses she had in her hands. "Which color do you like better? This one?" She held a cherry red one in front of her. "Or this." She switched to a lemon yellow one.

"The yellow," Maxie said. "And I was just telling your sisters how you'll do the right thing and have your father give you away."

"I, uh . . ." Sue Ellen looked around as if searching for an escape route. "I think I'm gonna barf." She ran for the bathroom.

"Maybe you shouldn't pressure Sue Ellen right now," Emma told her mom. "She's already under a lot of stress."

"Is she okay? I'm supposed to leave now to meet Donny's mother so we can go over some last-minute things about the wedding and bridal shower," Maxie said.

"Then you'd better go."

"Okay." Maxie grabbed her seashell-covered purse. "But we'll continue this conversation when I get back."

"Not if I can help it," Leena muttered as their mom left.

"I won't be here when Mom gets back," Emma said. "I'm moving into a studio apartment in town tonight."

"Chicken."

"Absolutely," Emma readily admitted. "Do you think Sue Ellen is really okay?" The sounds coming from the bathroom were not pleasant ones.

"She's fine. She's just pregnant."

"*Pregnant?*" Sue Ellen a mother? Emma couldn't quite wrap her mind around that image. Her big sister had never even taken care of a pet let alone an infant. "Does Mom know?"

"No, and you're not gonna tell her."

"Of course not. You're sure Sue Ellen is okay?"

"She's just peachy."

"Why didn't she tell me?"

"She had to tell her fiancé first."

"How's he taking the news?"

"The same way Sue Ellen is. They're both totally, almost obnoxiously thrilled."

"Who's obnoxious?" a pale Sue Ellen asked as she plopped onto the living room couch.

"Emma knows you've got a bun in the oven," Leena replied.

Sue Ellen frowned. "You know I can't bake. Except for cupcakes. Donny taught me. Ohhh." Emma could almost see the lightbulb go on over her oldest sister's head. "You mean she knows I'm pregnant. Why did you tell her?" Sue Ellen smacked Leena's arm. "I wanted to do that myself."

"I told Emma because she was worried about you puking in the john."

"It's morning sickness. The doctor says it will pass. Otherwise I'm healthy and so is the baby," Sue Ellen said.

"How far along are you?" Emma asked.

"Four months. I was afraid that I'd already reached my expiration date. Or that my eggs had. You know, you two aren't getting any younger either. Neither are your eggs."

Emma ignored that comment. "When are you going to tell Mom?"

"I haven't decided yet. Maybe after Donny and I have left on our honeymoon. I could leave her a letter. Or a card. A 'Congrats, you're gonna be a granny' card. Do they sell those?"

"I have no idea," Emma said, still struggling to picture her oldest sister raising a baby.

"They should. Maybe I should design one. I could probably make a bundle on it."

"The only bundle you should be focusing on is the one you're gonna be delivering in five more months," Leena said.

"Do you know if it's a boy or a girl?" Emma knew she was asking a lot of questions but she couldn't help herself.

Sue Ellen shook her head slightly. "No. Donny and I want to be surprised."

"You realize what this means, don't you?" Emma said to Leena. "We're going to be aunts."

Sue Ellen grinned. "Auntie Leena and Auntie Emma. Sounds cute."

"If it's a girl, I can dress her in cute outfits," Leena said.

Sue Ellen's smile turned dreamy. "They do have the cutest outfits for little girls. But there are some adorable ones for little boys too—like onesies with the Steelers logo. Donny is a big football fan."

"So Donny wants a son?" Emma asked.

"He says he'll be happy with either a son or a daughter."

"How do you think Mom is going to take this news?" was Emma's next question. Her older sisters both eyed her suspiciously. "I'm not going to tell her," she assured them.

"You better not. Or Dad either. Oh no, what if I barf on my way down the aisle?" Sue Ellen demanded. She tipped over until she was semireclining on the couch, her hand dramatically draped over her forehead like a Victorian heroine.

Leena wasn't impressed. "I told you that you should have eloped like your friend Skye did with her fiancé, Nathan."

Sue Ellen glared at her. "You only said that because you didn't want me taking your spotlight."

"You were originally supposed to get married in the fall, not right before I get married," Leena said.

"Pregnancy issues changed that," Sue Ellen said,

"Pregnant!" Maxie stood in the doorway to the trailer. "Who's pregnant? And before you answer, it better not be any of you!"

Chapter Three

. . . .

Uh-oh. Emma hurriedly stood up and headed straight for her suitcases. Time for her to leave. The faster the better.

"Where do you think you're going?" Maxie demanded.

"I told you I was moving out," Emma reminded her.

"Not until we get this settled." Maxie pointed to the couch. "Go sit down."

Emma wanted to rebel. She also wanted peace and an end to global warming, but it didn't appear that any of those things were about to happen anytime soon.

The sad truth was that she had very few rebel genes in her. Her older sisters had gotten them all. She sat on the couch.

"What are you doing back here, Mom?" Leena asked. "I thought you were meeting somebody to pick out a dress."

"I forgot my cell phone. I left it here on the charger." Maxie calmly unplugged the phone and put it in her large seashell purse. "What's going on, girls?"

"We're not girls anymore," Leena said. "Sue Ellen is thirty-six, and your baby Emma here is nearly thirty."

Stung, Emma said, "I'm only twenty-seven."

Leena shrugged. "Like I said, nearly thirty."

"You will always be girls to me," Maxie stated firmly. "Now tell me what's going on, and one of you had better start talking pronto." She glared at Leena, who glared right back.

Emma felt the situation slipping away from her and it drove her crazy. It was like waiting for a train wreck to happen. "Perhaps I should moderate this discussion," she suggested.

"Why do you do that?" Leena's glare shifted from their mom to Emma. "You never use a little word when a big word will do. Is it to prove how smart you are? There's no need. We already know you're the one with the fancy degree. The one Mom likes best. The one who never messes up."

"Which means she's not the one who's pregnant," Maxie said.

"Hold on a second." Emma held up her hand like a traffic cop. "I never said I don't mess up."

Leena waved her words away. "You don't have to say it. Mom says it all the time."

"Then get angry at her, not me," Emma said.

"If anyone has a right be angry around here, it's me," Maxie said. "My own daughter didn't tell me she's pregnant."

"You just said two seconds ago that none of us had better be pregnant," Emma replied.

"I was upset. In shock. What mother wouldn't be?" Maxie took a moment to compose herself. "So it's Sue Ellen, right? That's why she tossed her cookies."

Emma avoided her mom's eagle eye. She certainly didn't want to be accused of revealing secrets because she blinked at the wrong time or something. She already felt guilty that her mom had overheard them all talking.

Maxie stomped her foot, a sure sign she was losing her patience and her temper. "Who's pregnant?"

"We both are," Leena said.

"*What?*" Emma's mouth dropped open. So did Maxine's and Sue Ellen's.

Sue Ellen recovered first to say, "You can't be pregnant. I'm pregnant."

Leena shrugged. "You haven't cornered the market on being pregnant."

Sue Ellen pointed an accusatory finger at Leena. "You're only doing this because I'm pregnant and you have to do everything I do!"

"Hardly," Leena retorted.

Emma edged closer to her suitcases once again. Her sisters and mom were the drama queens. Emma liked things calm and orderly. "I, um, think I'll let you three work things out."

"What, you're not part of this family now that we're pregnant?" Sue Ellen said. "Nice to know where your loyalties lie."

Emma resented that accusation. "Hey, I'm wearing that Pepto-Bismol pink bridesmaid's dress with the dumb-looking butt bow and stupid puffy sleeves to your wedding. I think that proves my loyalty."

Leena nodded her agreement. "My bridesmaids' dresses are much better than Sue Ellen's."

"See, that's what I mean." Sue Ellen glared at Leena. "This is just a competition to you. The weddings, having a baby. All a competition."

"Hey, I've had my wedding date set for ages," Leena said.

"Yeah, well my proposal was more romantic than yours," Sue Ellen retorted. "And Donny makes more money than

Cole the veterinarian does. Smiley's Septic Service is a gold mine."

"You know the concept of sibling competition is an interesting one," Emma began, hoping to stave off any further escalation in their argument. "So is the part that birth order plays in character development . . ."

Her attempt at playing peacemaker was not greeted with appreciation. Instead both her sisters turned to her and shouted, "Shut up!"

"You shut up," Emma shot back. "I can be as messed up as you both are."

"Are you going to tell me that you're pregnant too, Emma?" Sue Ellen demanded.

"No, but—"

"Having a baby trumps everything else," Sue Ellen stated.

No surprise there. Her sisters had always demanded their place in the spotlight, leaving Emma standing on the sidelines. A mixed metaphor maybe, but an apt one. Their crisis du jour had always been more dramatic than anything Emma could come up with.

Not that Emma was vying for that kind of attention. She wasn't. She never had. Even as a kid, she'd always been the observer. The one quietly in the corner with her head in a book, off in another world.

Her mom patted her shoulder. "Ignore them, honey. They're just jealous that you are an important professor."

"Your daughters tell you they're pregnant and all you do is think of Emma." Sue Ellen's voice held more than a tinge of bitterness. "Figures. No surprise there."

Maxie turned to her oldest daughter. "Now what are you talking about?"

"The fact that Emma has always been your favorite."

"She's a good girl." Maxie gave Emma another approving pat on the shoulder.

We're all good girls, Emma wanted to say but somehow couldn't. She wasn't sure her older sisters would appreciate her attempt to stick up for them. Maybe they didn't want to be good. Maybe they liked being nonconformists.

Emma's uncertainty underlined the fact that she didn't know her sisters all that well anymore. She'd always felt closer to Leena, who was only two years older. But now . . . Emma didn't know what to think.

And that wasn't like her. Emma usually had her thoughts in order. Under control. Sure, she sometimes brainstormed and random ideas would hit her when she least expected it—like when she was in the shower or right before she fell asleep. Lately those ideas had all revolved around her project about Rock Creek's revival. Had she been deliberately avoiding thinking about her family's dynamics and the impending weddings? Probably.

She'd certainly walked into a hornet's nest here. Emma had no idea that both her sisters seemed to think that their mom favored Emma as the baby in the family. Yes, her mom seemed proud of Emma's academic accomplishments, but she'd seemed equally proud of Leena's modeling successes as well.

As for Sue Ellen, well she had lead a colorful life and their mom had worried about some of Sue Ellen's choices. Sue Ellen had married right out of high school against their parents' wishes. And gotten divorced soon afterward. Emma had barely been in middle school then, so her memories of that time weren't exactly fresh.

But Sue Ellen seemed to have chosen a good guy this time around. Emma had met Donny the first evening she'd been in town. He'd seemed really nice and he clearly adored Sue Ellen.

Your sisters have their lives mapped out before them and where are you? Lost in your own underachieved goals.

Unsure of your choices. Still searching in vain for your own place in the world.

"Yeah, we all know Emma's a good girl. Yada, yada, yada," Sue Ellen was saying.

"I love all my daughters," Maxie said defensively.

"Sure you do," Sue Ellen said before adding the kicker, "just not equally."

"You're pregnant." This time Maxie patted Sue Ellen's shoulder. "Your hormones are talking, not you."

"How typical," Leena muttered. "This family never talks about anything. You're all in total denial."

Maxie shot a look at her watch. "I've got to go. I'm late for meeting Donny's mother."

"Sure, Mom, take off and avoid the situation. You too." Leena turned her accusing look toward Emma.

Maxie hurried out but Emma stayed.

"Notice she didn't say how she felt about becoming a grandmother," Leena said.

"I'm not avoiding any situation," Emma said, defending herself. "What's the deal with you both saying I was Mom's favorite? That's not true. Yes, she's proud of me, but she's proud of you too, Leena. And if anyone is her favorite, I think it's Sue Ellen."

"Me?" Sue Ellen looked stunned. "How do you figure that?"

"She always calls you first and more often than she does either one of us."

"Because you two are harder to reach."

"No, it's because you know Mom better. You stayed in Rock Creek when Leena and I left," Emma said.

"I moved to Serenity Falls for a while."

"Which is the town right next door. You've always been here for Mom," Emma pointed out. "I'm sure she appreciates that."

"She's never said so."

"That doesn't mean she doesn't feel that way."

"I'm no mind reader like you."

"It's not mind reading. It's basic psychology."

"Now is not the time to point out how smart you are," Sue Ellen growled.

"I just meant that Mom shows you how she feels instead of telling you. She's always sending you articles about things she knows you're interested in, like scrapbooking."

"She does that for everyone."

"Not for me," Emma said.

"Me either," Leena said. "Not that I'd want her to."

"And Mom's done nothing but talk about your weddings for weeks now," Emma added. "Why she even left Dad to come up here to help you guys out ahead of time."

"She just likes weddings," Leena said. "Did I tell you she wanted to do my hair with some upswept style held in place with fake birds?"

"I liked that idea," Sue Ellen said. "I've got dibbies on that."

Leena waved her hand. "Hey, it's all yours."

The room was still filled with a prickly energy that made Emma uneasy. She didn't like confrontations. They left her feeling wrung out and weepy for some stupid reason. So she tried to calm the waters. "I think you're both probably stressed out about the wedding, and of course there are definite hormonal changes when you're pregnant. I can't believe you both are going to have a baby."

"I'm only about two months along," Leena said. "And I only found out earlier today. Cole is over the moon. He knew before I did. I thought I had a stomach bug and sent him out to get some club soda and then called him on his cell phone to add squirty cheese and a mango to the list."

"You hate mangoes," Emma said.

"I know. That's why Cole brought home a pregnancy test. I mean, the man is a doctor after all."

"An animal doctor," Emma said, but her sisters ignored her.

"When the stick turned pink, Cole did this macho dance."

Sue Ellen nodded. "That's the macho my-swimmers-are-da-bomb dance. Donny did it too. So you've started with the food cravings?" Sue Ellen asked Leena.

"Yeah, jalapeno peppers and Cheerios."

Emma watched her sisters sitting on the couch, heads together as they laughed and compared their weird food choices. She felt like an alien in a strange world. An outsider in her own life.

She doubted Sue Ellen and Leena would even have noticed she'd left had her suitcase not bumped into the side table on her way out the door. As it was, they gave her a preoccupied wave and then resumed their sharing.

It was time for Emma to make it on her own.

* * *

Jake watched Sheriff Nathan Thornton walk into Nick's Tavern. "I've been expecting you," Jake said. He'd been in town only two weeks, but he knew how fast word spread about stuff like fights in the bar.

"Really? Am I getting that predictable?"

Jake just shrugged. "Heineken, right?"

Nathan nodded and slid onto a bar stool. "It's quiet in here."

"Yeah." Jake placed a napkin on the counter, then set the beer down on top of it.

"There a reason for that?"

Jake shrugged again. "Who knows?"

"I think you know what I'm talking about. I heard there was an . . . altercation in here earlier today."

"An altercation?"

"Yeah."

"Did someone file a complaint?" Jake asked.

"No."

"Then what's the problem?"

"You haven't been in town very long."

"Is that a problem?"

"I don't know." Nathan took a sip of his beer. "Is it?"

"You always answer a question with a question?"

"Do you?"

"Pretty much."

"Yeah, me too." Nathan took another sip of his beer. "So how are you enjoying your time here in town?"

"So far, so good."

"You plan on settling down here?"

"Do you ask all newcomers these questions?"

"Nah, just the ones who won the King of the Mountain trophy three times in a row."

Jake made no comment.

Nathan said, "Rumor has it that you might be interested in opening a sports resort around here."

"Do I look like a resort kind of guy to you?"

"Maybe that was a poor word choice. How about a sports training center for extreme sports?"

"What if I was? Is there some law against that?"

"No. So that's why you're here?"

"I didn't say that."

"No, you don't say much."

"Neither do you."

"True."

Jake watched as Nathan took another sip of his beer before asking, "Is there any reason why I should be concerned about you or your reasons for being here?"

"Nope."

"Would you tell me if there was?"

"Probably not."

"I had that feeling."

"I'm not planning on committing any crimes, if that's what you're worried about."

"Would you tell me if you were?"

"Good point. Guess you'll just have to trust me."

"My wife tells me I have some trust issues."

"I've been told the same thing about myself," Jake said.

"You've got a wife?"

"No. I'm not the marrying kind."

"Too busy traveling the world?"

"Something like that."

"And how does Rock Creek compare?"

Jake shrugged. "It seems like a nice small town."

"And I'd like to keep it that way."

"Understood."

"So do you like being a man of mystery?"

"I like minding my own business and having others do the same."

"See," Nathan drawled, "that's a problem in a small town. Everyone knows everyone else's business sooner or later."

Jake's gut tightened. He didn't want anyone knowing about his private business, not until he was ready. And he still wasn't even sure that time would ever come. Not that he planned on hanging out here indefinitely. He'd never been the type to put down roots in one place.

He'd been called a loner, a rebel, and an adrenaline junkie. He'd also been called much worse, starting in the foster homes when he was twelve. A misfit, a bastard, a troublemaker.

He was here for a reason, and it was time to get off his butt and start taking action instead of just brooding about it. He was on a personal quest more intense than any he'd attempted before. But this search wasn't about physical accomplishments. This was about finding his birth mother.

He'd first gotten the idea when he was lying in the hospital in Peru, groggy from the morphine they were feeding him intravenously, ravished by the pain of his injuries and consumed by the nightmares of what had occurred on that mountain.

Three men had gone up and only two had come back alive. Jake still had a hard time accepting that reality. Why him? Why had he survived when his best buddy Andy hadn't? Why had Jake suggested climbing that freaking mountain in the first place?

They said that near-death experiences changed a man. Reshaped him. Transformed him into something more or something less than he'd been before.

Jake had survived close calls before but none as horrific as that deadly day on that killer mountain.

The nightmares still consumed him. He couldn't beat them or forget them. And he hated that. But not nearly as much as he hated the fact that his best friend was dead. He didn't care about many people, but when he did, they died. What kind of sick life lesson was that?

"You've been rubbing that same spot on the counter for five minutes now," Nathan noted.

"You timing me?"

"Just noticing details. An occupational hazard."

"Yeah, I know all about hazards."

"I'm sure you do. And I'm equally sure you have no intention of sharing those stories. Am I right?"

"What do you know about Emma Riley?" Jake asked abruptly.

Nathan showed no surprise at the sudden change of subject. "Why do you want to know?"

"She's not a reporter or anything is she?"

"Emma? Hell, no. Last I heard, she was a professor in Boston. She's home for her sisters' weddings."

"Yeah, I know. I'm going with her."

"Going with Emma?" Now Nathan did look startled.

"To the weddings. Never mind." Jake wanted to bite his tongue off. Why had he shared that bit of info with the local sheriff?

"What made you think she might be a reporter?" Nathan said.

"She asks a lot of questions."

"So do I. And I sure as hell am no reporter."

"Right. She asked for my autograph. Said it was for a friend of hers."

"So?"

"I don't do autographs anymore."

"Is that what caused the altercation in here earlier?"

"No."

"Are you saying that you think Emma is a groupie or something?"

"No."

"Then what are you saying?"

"Damned if I know," Jake muttered in frustration.

"It sounds like Emma got to you."

Jake clamped his mouth shut. No way was he responding or even acknowledging that comment. Instead he left Nathan to his beer and helped another customer.

But Nathan didn't give up that easily. In fact, he seemed to call in reinforcements as two guys joined him at the bar—one a big black guy who looked like he could be a defensive lineman, and the other a tall white guy with a ready grin. "Cole here is one of the grooms at one of the weddings you're going to," Nathan told Jake as he walked by to get a new bar towel. "Jake is taking Emma to your wedding."

Cole looked at Jake and said, "You're a friend of Emma's?"

Jake just shrugged.

"He doesn't like answering questions," Nathan told Cole.

"I don't blame him," the black guy said. "You two are nosy. Not me. I'm Algee Washington, owner of Cosmic Comics down the street." Algee stuck out his ham-sized hand and Jake shook it. "I've got another store in Serenity Falls. The main thing you need to know about me is that I like my beer cold and my women hot."

"Don't let Tameka hear that," Nathan said.

Algee just smiled. "I'm not saying anything she doesn't already know."

The three men were clearly good friends. They shared that same camaraderie that Jake had had with Andy. He and Andy had been convinced they were invincible. Extreme sports were all about attitude and pushing the envelope. Nobody did that more than he and Andy. They'd pushed that frigging envelope until it broke.

"Hey," a guy down at the other end of the bar yelled. "What's it take to get a beer around here?"

Jake gladly left Nathan and his buddies and pushed all personal thoughts aside. It was the only way he made it through the day. The nights remained a personal hell.

• • •

"Temporary home sweet home." Emma stood in her studio above the Health Nut health food store and surveyed her surroundings. The place was furnished with a futon couch that doubled as a bed, a table that doubled as a desk, two straight back chairs, and an armchair. The walls were painted a brick red and the floors were shiny hardwood. Oak she thought, but she was no expert.

In one corner was a postage-stamp-size bathroom with a toilet, a sink hanging on the wall, and a shower but no tub. The apartment had a small kitchenette along one wall complete with a compact sink, a stove that reminded her of the Easy-Bake Oven she'd had as a kid, and one of those small fridges like the one she'd had in her college dorm room.

At the moment the only thing in the fridge was her six-pack of Dr Pepper, which was minus the can she held in her hand. In her other hand she held a bag of Cheetos—the crunchy ones, not the puffs. Dr Pepper and Cheetos. Two of her guilty pleasures.

The room was stuffy in the June heat so she threw open the window and couldn't resist climbing out onto the fire escape to catch a little cooling breeze. At the last minute, she dragged a big pillow out with her and sat on it. Even though it was almost eight at night, it was still light outside.

Ah, this was the life. No sisters giving her disapproving looks. No mom giving her ulcers. No trouble . . .

Emma glanced across the narrow alley into the apartment directly across from her and saw him. Jake Slayter. Naked.

Chapter Four

. . . .

Jake naked. Emma almost choked on her Cheeto.

The windowsill covered his privates but barely. The rest of him was very bare. Arms. Shoulders. Chest. All muscular without being bodybuilding yucky. He looked so good she wanted to reach out and touch him. He seemed close enough to try.

Emma didn't realize she'd actually raised her hand until she spilled some of the Dr Pepper on her bare leg. Her cargo shorts and tank top suddenly seemed too warm and she wanted to strip them off.

Jake suddenly bent over, and his bare butt flashed in the window frame. The man mooned her. Was that a tattoo on his fine ass?

When he straightened, he had weights in each hand and was doing arm curls. Is that what they were called? Emma was no fitness expert. She'd once gotten a free month-long membership at a gym but never got around to actually going there. If she'd known there would be guys like this, she might have made more of an effort to get there.

Or maybe not. She'd never gone out of her way to see a pair of six-pack abs on a man. But then she'd never seen a man as hot as Jake.

Was she drooling? She raised her fingers to her mouth to check. Maybe that was Dr Pepper. She took another drink but kept her eyes on Jake.

He was in profile now. She could actually see his nipples. How narrow was that damn alley anyway that she could see him so clearly?

She knew she should look away but lacked the willpower to do so. Finally she reached into her pocket for her iPod and stuck the earbuds into her ears. Music blared. She now had a soundtrack to go with his arm curls. "My Favorite Mistake" by Sheryl Crow. *Ain't that the truth.* Thinking about Jake was a big mistake. That didn't seem to stop her, though.

Emma closed her eyes and let the residual images of naked Jake wash over her as the music pounded. So involved was she in this process that she didn't even notice there was someone on the fire escape with her until she opened her eyes and saw Jake right beside her. Not entirely naked but close enough as he was only wearing a pair of black running shorts.

"How did you do that?" she blurted out.

He shrugged. "Climbing your fire escape was a piece of cake." Catching her eyeing him, Jake matter-of-factly said, "My leg still looks pretty gnarly from my climbing injuries. It won't win any beauty contests but it holds me up just fine."

Emma thought he looked just fine. She hadn't even noticed the fine white line of scars from his left thigh down to his knee.

"What are you doing here?"

"I came over to ask you if you enjoyed the show."

"Were you putting on a show? I wasn't paying any attention."

"Yeah, you were. Avid attention."

"You're imagining things."

"Were you imagining things while you were watching me?"

"I was thinking about work."

"Right."

"I was."

"If you say so."

"I do."

Hunkering down beside her, he reached into her Cheetos bag and retrieved one. Instead of stealing it for himself, he held it up to her mouth and drew it around the curve of her bottom lip. "You can get addicted, you know."

She didn't know, but she was learning fast. He made addiction seem like a good thing.

Sheryl Crow continued singing in her ear while a secret excitement sang through the rest of her body. Jake was so close she could feel the heat emanating from his body, from his fingers holding that Cheeto and tempting her with it but actually tempting her with something even more appealing—himself.

He slowly moved closer, watching her reaction before erasing the remaining few inches between his mouth and hers.

"Mmm," he mumbled against her lips. "I've never kissed a girl who tastes like Cheetos and Dr Pepper before. I like it."

He licked her lips and she parted them, just like that.

Talk about guilty pleasures. This man put all others to shame. He was a trillion times better than Dr Pepper or Cheetos. The man was even better than Godiva dark chocolate truffles, and that was saying something. He braced his free hand against the back of her head while the hand holding the Cheeto that had started this whole thing was now running through her hair, sans junk food. His thumb brushed against her earlobe, and she shivered with heat, not cold.

He dislodged the iPod earbud, but she didn't care. The only thing that seemed to matter in that moment was that he continue kissing her. Which he did, blending one kiss into the next even deeper one.

Emma had never considered herself to be a particularly sensual being, but he was making her rethink that theory. Not that she was actually doing much thinking at all. None, really. This was all about feeling. All about the rush of heated pleasure that made her go up in flames.

She didn't even realize they'd rolled off the pillow and were now in a full body embrace until after it happened. By then she was enjoying herself far too much to question the wisdom of such a move. His bare leg was between hers. She allowed her fingers to linger on the small of his back, at the top of the waistband of his shorts.

He shoved her iPod aside and in doing so brushed his hands against her breasts. They responded, her nipples at full alert and begging for more attention.

He slid his hand beneath her tank top. He undid the front fastening of her bra with adept skill. The man was clearly no stranger to women's lingerie. Or to what moves made a woman melt.

Jake made the simplest caress of his thumb over her nipple seem like the most divine thing in the universe. This was nothing like the awkward gropings Ted had attempted. There was simply no comparison.

So this was what it felt like to be seduced by a pro.

Heaven. Sheer heaven.

Jake moved his hand down to the waistband of her shorts when a series of loud catcalls from the alley below ruined the moment. He rolled away from her to glare at the idiot down below. It was Roy.

Talk about a total buzzkill.

That fast, Emma scooted off the fire escape and into her apartment before slamming the window closed and locking it. She then lowered the blinds for good measure.

Jake leaned over the railing. The dangerous look he sent Roy's way was enough to make the jerk go running for safety.

Jake then turned his attention to Emma's window. Who knew a kick-ass sociologist could kiss like that? Unlike the bodacious babes who'd trailed after him most of his adult life, Emma had an element of freshness and fire that made for an unbeatable combination.

That discovery had Jake grinning. He knew better than to force the issue now, but he was definitely looking forward to picking up where they had left off real soon.

• • •

Jake was working a split shift—the afternoon shift when Emma had walked in and now the late shift from ten until closing at 2 a.m. Nick's Tavern was quieter than usual tonight. Not that he was any expert on the place. He'd worked there only two weeks, and he had yet to meet the owner. The manager had hired him.

A woman in her early fifties with platinum hair and artificially enhanced double-D-cup breasts shimmied onto a bar stool.

She looked like the hungry sort so he set a bowl of peanuts next to her. "Can I help you, ma'am?"

"Don't call me ma'am," she growled in the gravelly voice of a three-pack-a-day smoker. "The name is Nicole. Nicole Fabrizio."

Jake recognized the name as being on his list of possibilities in the birth-mom department. The private investigator he'd hired had e-mailed him the list to his iPhone a little while ago based on his mother's age at the time of his birth, a nugget of info the investigator had just now managed to dig up. The PI hadn't had a chance to do a profile on all the possible candidates yet.

"But you can call me Nic," the woman said.

"Nic?" Jake knew he sounded stupid, but damn he was more than a little freaked at actually meeting someone who might be his birth mother.

"Yeah. As in the owner of this place. Nick's Tavern. Why the stunned look? You thought Nick was a guy?"

"Yeah."

She laughed. "I used to be a guy."

It took a lot to shake Jake. The possibility that his birth mom was . . . hold on. That wouldn't work.

"Aw, I was just pulling your leg," Nic said. "I'm as female as they come. Hey, you don't look like you believe me. Want me to demonstrate?" she purred, running her fingers up his arm.

"No."

"You don't have to back up like that." She returned to her earlier growl. "And don't go thinking you can sue me with sexual harassment or any shit. I'll deny everything. I've got enough men trying to get my attention that I don't have to go chasing after anyone." She slid off the stool and posed before him. "A body like this doesn't come easy or cheap. You don't get a body like this by having kids."

"You never had any kids?"

"Do I look like I've had kids?" She lifted her stretchy black sparkly tube top to proudly display her tummy. "Do you see any stretch marks here?"

"Don't answer," a guy a few seats away advised Jake. "That's one of them trick questions women ask men. Like 'Does this outfit make me look fat?' Besides them plastic surgeons can do miracles these days. She could have had a dozen kids and had one of those lipo deals to remove all the evidence."

"No more booze for you," Nic growled.

"Nic, is that you?" The guy leaned closer and almost fell off his stool. "What happened to your flannel shirts and jeans?"

"I won a makeover in one of those contests."

"No shit." He moved closer. "You hardly ever come in here anymore. Not for years."

"Yeah, well, I decided to show off my new look. I was waiting for all the swelling to go down."

The guy's eyes were just about popping. "You're a real hot momma now."

Momma? The term took on a new meaning for Jake.

Turning his back on them both, Jake poured himself a shot of tequila.

"Are you drinking my booze?" Nic came around the bar to demand. "I should fire your ass." She eyed his denim-covered butt. "A damn fine ass it is too."

He sidestepped her pinching fingers.

"You sure are a jumpy one. I heard you were some kind of fearless extreme sports god or something. I guess that's just another one of those wild rumors."

"Hey, Nic." The greeting came from Sheriff Nathan. "You're not using that con again that you own Nick's Tavern to get free drinks, are you?"

Nic glared at him. "Anyone tell you that your timing stinks, Sheriff?"

"Does that mean that she's not the owner?" Jake asked.

Nathan just grinned. "Nic has a strange sense of humor."

"Yeah, I gathered that." He had yet to completely recover from her claim that she was a guy.

"What do her kids think of her humor?" Jake asked Nathan.

"What is it with you and kids?" Nic said. "I'm not a breeding machine. Those days are gone. And I really do own this place. Nathan is the one with the warped sense of humor. The tavern was my dad's before I inherited it. Nick Fabrizio." She made the sign of the cross. "May he rest in peace."

Peace was something Jake hadn't had much of in his life, and it didn't look as though he was going to find much of it here in Rock Creek.

• • •

The next day, Emma retrieved her laptop from her backpack and pulled up the file containing her notes about Skye Wright-Thornton, the owner of the Tivoli Theater she was about to interview. "Thank you for meeting with me—" Emma began.

Skye interrupted her. "So you're Sue Ellen's smart sister."

Emma grimaced.

Skye kept talking. "I've got a smart sister too. She's a librarian in Serenity Falls."

Emma had considered becoming a librarian. There were days when she wished she had continued those studies instead of pursuing her bachelor's and doctoral degrees in sociology. Just another decision of hers that she was second-guessing these days.

Emma used to scoff at the idea of a quarter-life crisis and thought it was just a lot of spoiled whining, but now that she was feeling some of the insecurities, she wondered if this was fate's way of laughing at her. But those thoughts would have to take a backseat for now. At the moment her focus was on her project. She'd set up several individual interviews, beginning with Skye.

"The revival of Rock Creek appears to have started

with your renovation of the Tivoli Theater," Emma said. "Did you anticipate that this would happen?"

"No way." Skye shook her head so vehemently her short red hair flew in various directions. "I don't plan that far ahead."

"What made you want to renovate this theater?"

"It called to me."

Emma stared at her blankly.

"You've never had a place call to you? Bonded with it? Felt that special connection? No? Well, I did."

"The town is beginning to make a name for itself as a center for the arts."

"And a center for female empowerment. Your sister Leena is responsible for that. She's a web celeb now. Her blog has really taken off. Of course, being recommended on Oprah's website didn't hurt. But you already know all that."

"Actually with the wedding preparations and everything, I haven't had a chance to sit down and interview Leena yet. I mean, I know about her blog of course and how successful it's been, but I haven't had a chance to discuss details about how it came to be. She's been busy getting ready for her wedding."

"I can't believe both your sisters are getting married within two weeks of each other. I told them both they should elope like Nathan and I did. We saved all that money that would have been wasted on a wedding ceremony. Instead we took off for the Smokies and got married in a little chapel near the edge of the national park and then spent the next week holed up in a log cabin." Skye smiled. "There's nothing like log-cabin sex."

Emma wondered what log-cabin sex would be like with Jake. She'd already imagined fire-escape sex with him. They'd come very close to it yesterday. She'd spent most of the night consumed with extremely realistic, extremely hot dreams about Jake.

"Yes, well . . ." Emma tried very hard to stay focused on her work. "Getting back to the theater. You've done a number of programs here on everything from comic book art to fabric art and weaving."

Skye nodded and launched into a long commentary about the importance of creativity and art and music and how local school districts were running out of funds and cutting art programs from the curriculum. Emma knew she should be paying attention, but she was still distracted by the thought of log-cabin sex with Jake.

The man was dangerous to her peace of mind. He'd be dangerous to most women's peace of mind. He had that dark and brooding thing going on that aroused her curiosity about the secrets hidden in the depths of those golden brown eyes of his.

The trouble was that Jake aroused more than her curiosity. He made her think about orgasms and fire-escape sex. These were not topics that Emma normally spent much time considering. Or *any* time considering. Until Jake.

"Don't you agree?" Skye said.

Emma quickly jerked back to reality and the fact that she'd missed much of what Skye had been saying. "I'm sorry, I got distracted for a moment there."

"You were thinking about sex."

Emma could feel her cheeks turning cherry red. She'd heard that Skye read auras. Was hers somehow X-rated or something? Was there a neon sign over her head flashing S-E-X in big letters like the displays she'd seen in the red-light district of Amsterdam? Not that she'd actually been there, but she'd seen a special on PBS about it. Or was it the Discovery Channel? She was so flustered she couldn't think straight. Apparently that was also evident to Skye.

"Don't panic," Skye said. "Sex is a good thing to think about. But I bet you're like Leena in that you don't talk about it. Sue Ellen is different."

"Yes." Sue Ellen had always been different. Definitely not the type of person to fit into a category or to draw inside the lines. "She's, uh . . . flamboyant."

"Now there's a word you don't hear much anymore."

Skye's comment reminded her of Sue Ellen's accusation that Emma used big words to prove how smart she was. Not that she considered *flamboyant* to be that big.

She needed to regain control of the conversation. "How would you describe the differences in Rock Creek since you opened the theater?"

"Well, I got married, for one thing. Something I never thought I'd do. I'm not exactly the conservative type, as you may have heard."

"I did ascertain . . ." Big words, big words. "Uh, yes, I heard."

"That's why Sue Ellen and I get along so well. We both have our own way of doing things."

Emma just nodded.

"As for the town, well it has a new Thai restaurant, which I'm thrilled about," Skye continued.

"Their spring rolls are awesome," Emma agreed. "And their pad thai is also great."

"We've got several new businesses all along Barwell Street. When I first opened the theater, there were a lot of vacant storefronts in town. Lots of FOR RENT signs. But you already know that. I mean, this is your hometown after all."

"I haven't had a chance to come home much for the past few years. Not since my parents moved down to Florida. I visited them down there for holidays."

"So what do you hope to prove with this study of yours?"

"I don't know that I'll prove anything. I want to try and

discover what triggered the rejuvenation here. See if it's unique to this town or if it could be utilized in other towns facing similar challenges." Emma went on to talk with Skye some more about Rock Creek before wrapping things up.

"Who else are you interviewing?" Skye asked.

"The mayor of Rock Creek and the mayor of Serenity Falls."

"The Serenity Falls mayor? Why do you want to interview him? I thought your study was about Rock Creek."

"It is but I can't ignore the fact that the town right next door was selected as one of America's Best Small Towns, yet that good fortune didn't spread here."

"Have you met Walt Whitman?"

"When I was a teenager." Emma had won second place in an essay contest the town had held for Memorial Day and the mayor had given her a certificate.

"Then you should know how obsessive he is. He's not that thrilled with what's going on here."

"Why not? I would think he'd like the improvements."

"He doesn't consider them to be improvements. He's not that fond of change for one thing. Or of creativity. He's definitely a by-the-book kind of guy."

"I heard your husband, the sheriff, was a by-the-book kind of guy."

"*Was* being the operative word there. I've wooed Nathan over to the dark side of chaos and creativity. Not that he'd admit that. You know how men are."

Not really. Sure Emma had studied male and female behavior in various classes she'd taken. And yes, she had some personal observations from her life at the university. But observations were different than experience. She definitely lacked experience. She had some, but it was limited to nerdy guys who were a subspecies all on their own.

She had no experience with a man like Jake. Someone who got to her on some basic "wham" kind of level. Not exactly a scientific description of her reaction to him and his Cheeto-laced kiss. Maybe it was just the junk food that had done it to her. And him licking and nibbling on her lips afterward had nothing to do with it.

Yeah, right.

"Mommy!" A little girl came skipping into the theater, wearing a pink GO GREEN top, shorts, and red cowboy boots. "Guess what we did in class today? We drew dragons."

"This is my daughter Toni," Skye said.

Looking at the cute little girl, Emma wondered what her niece or nephew would look like at six. Wow, in a few months she was going to be an aunt. She still had a hard time digesting that fact. "Hi."

"I have a cat named Gravity."

"I, uh, that's nice." Emma's experience with little kids was somewhat limited. Which is why she fell back on that old standard question, "What do you want to be when you grow up?"

"Korean."

Emma blinked. She wasn't expecting that response. But then she hadn't expected most of what had happened to her since she'd returned home.

"Toni's best friend in kindergarten is Korean," Skye explained.

"Who are you?" Toni asked Emma.

"I'm Emma."

"What do *you* want to be when you grow up?"

"Smarter than I am now," Emma said. "About a lot of things." Especially men who drove her crazy with just one kiss.

• • •

"Why are we meeting at the Dairy Queen to discuss your wedding plans?" Emma asked Sue Ellen later that afternoon.

"It's a favorite hangout of mine. And I didn't want Mom interrupting us every two minutes. I know she's not trying to drive me crazy, but she is."

"You could have come to my place."

"What do you have against the Dairy Queen?"

"Nothing. I was just saying . . ." *The wrong thing*, she silently continued. She seemed to be doing a lot of that lately where her sisters were concerned. And it left her feeling like an awkward dork. "What did you want to talk about?"

"You know the bridal shower is tomorrow afternoon, right?"

"Right. Saturday afternoon. For you and Leena both."

"We might have to change that."

"What?! Why?"

"Because we have totally different views on what the shower should look like."

"I thought you guys had this all settled."

"So did I. We're having it catered in the lobby of the Tivoli Theater."

"And there's a problem with that? I just came from speaking with Skye, and she didn't mention any trouble for the event tomorrow."

"The location isn't the issue. It's the decorations."

"What decorations?"

"Leena is using her engagement photos to put on the walls by her gift table."

"And?"

"She's a former model. It's hard to get a bad photo of her. Hard but not impossible. There was one shot a year ago for the Regency Mobile Home Sales that she hated, but that's another story. I don't have engagement photos to put over my table. I didn't like the way they turned out."

"Then put something else there. Flowers or bows or something."

"It won't look as good as Leena's table." Sue Ellen sniffed back tears.

"Look at me." Emma grabbed her sister's hands and made her focus instead of melting down in the middle of the Dairy Queen. "You're the one who has the interior decorating certificate on her wall. Remember, the one you got from the Internet?"

"Yeah, so?"

"So you know how to decorate. You can put your own stamp on things."

"My own stamp . . ." Sue Ellen thought a moment. "I know! My naked firemen calendars. I could put those up. They are very tastefully done. Nothing flapping in the wind, you know? Yes, I'll do that! Thanks, sis. You're brilliant." Sue Ellen tugged Emma to her feet and gave her a hug that nearly cut off her air supply. "Gotta run!"

Emma sank back onto her chair. She was so not looking forward to the shower this weekend, or Sue Ellen's wedding the following weekend. What kind of sister did that make her? Guilt nibbled at her. She should be so excited for her sisters. Instead she just wanted the madness over with. She had this tendency to want to make everything calm and controlled, and those two adjectives just didn't apply to Sue Ellen or Leena. Well, Leena was ultra-organized so that was a good thing. But not the same as controlled.

Emma also had this need to smooth things out whenever there was trouble. Both her sisters lived by their emotions. Emma preferred logic. She relied on logic. Required it.

"Dr Pepper again?" Jake slid into the seat Sue Ellen had recently vacated. "Are we looking at an addiction problem here?"

No, she was looking at another kind of yummy addiction. Jake. His effect on her was entirely too intense. Especially given the fact that she hadn't known him that long. As in two days. That wasn't logical at all.

Her fingers tightened on her drink.

Jake noticed. "Don't worry, I wasn't going to take your Dr Pepper away from you."

No, he was just taking her peace of mind away from her. Was he doing it deliberately? Was he trying to mess with her? Why would he bother?

No, Jake wasn't trying to gaslight her. This was an example of her hormones at work. A classic case of the science of attraction. In fact, she'd recently read a study in *Evolutionary Psychology* regarding the ways heterosexual men and women view first kisses. More than half of both men and women surveyed said they had been attracted to someone only to discover that, after kissing for the first time, they were no longer interested. Which seemed to suggest that there were unconscious mechanisms that had evolved to identify genetic incompatibility.

The study went on to point out that women were less likely to agree to have sex with a bad kisser than men, who were willing to have sex with just about anyone of the opposite sex. Men were opportunistic breeders—ready, willing, and eager to spread their DNA.

"Why are you looking at me that way?" Jake said.

"What way?"

"Like I'm a bug under a microscope."

She shrugged and looked down, nervously bouncing the straw up and down in her soda. "Occupational hazard, I guess."

"Sociologists see people as bugs?"

"No, although there are certain group dynamics in the insect world from which one could draw parallels." *Shut up, Em. You sound like such a nerd.*

He raised one dark eyebrow. "One could, huh?"

"Never mind," she muttered.

"Do I make you nervous?"

"No." Which was a lie, of course. Funny how she never

used to lie until she met him. "I've got to go. I've got a lot of work to do at home."

"I'll walk you there."

"You don't have to do that."

"I want to."

He held the door open for her and even held her backpack, making her feel like she was back in high school. Not that any guy had done either of those things for her in those days. She was always the brainy, geeky girl. She still was.

If she was so smart, she shouldn't be wondering if Jake thought she was a good kisser. The fact that he seemed ready to have sex with her on her fire escape didn't mean much according to *Evolutionary Psychology*.

When they reached her apartment, she mumbled, "Thanks. Bye." She grabbed her backpack and raced up the stairs as if the devil himself were chasing her. The indoor stairway ended in a shadowy hall on top. When a figure stepped out of the shadows Emma didn't think, she screamed.

Chapter Five

. . . .

"**Holy** crap!" Emma's father bellowed from the shadows. "You scared the hell out of me!"

Emma stood there shaking. *You're okay, you're okay, you're okay.* She silently recited the words as a mantra of reassurance to herself. The man was her father, not a mugger.

The sound of footsteps racing up the steps behind her had Emma turning, ready to face the next threat. When her father came up behind her and placed his hands on her shoulders, she jumped a foot.

"Get your hands off her," Jake growled.

"Who the hell are you to be telling me what to do with my daughter?" her dad growled right back.

"Your daughter?" Jake repeated.

"That's right. I'm Emma's father. And you are?"

"Jake Slayter. I heard her scream and I thought she was in trouble."

"She is in trouble for nearly causing her father to have a heart attack. Since when are you so jumpy, Sweet Pea?"

Her dad's gentle squeeze of her shoulders and use of her childhood nickname had Emma blinking away sudden tears. She was bombarded with the swirl of conflicting memories. The reassurance of her dad telling her a bedtime story about an Irish fairy named Sweet Pea. And the terror of hiding in the corner with Leena when her dad got drunk.

That terror was compounded by a more recent memory: not long ago, she'd been attacked in Boston. Maybe the residual fear from being mugged had drudged up that solitary image of fear from her childhood. She didn't remember much about her dad's drinking. She'd been only six or seven at the most. A huge majority of her childhood memories were good ones.

She wasn't afraid of her father. She was just afraid in general, and she hated feeling so vulnerable. First she'd leveled Roy in the bar, and now she was screaming like a ninny. She felt like a total idiot.

"Are you okay?" Jake asked her. His voice was unusually gentle.

She nodded, still too unnerved and embarrassed to speak. "Sorry," she croaked. She had to clear her throat before continuing. "I . . . um . . . I wasn't expecting to see anyone and my dad just startled me, that's all. I didn't realize he was in town yet."

"Arrived this morning. That was some scream," her dad said. "You've got a good set of pipes on you, Sweet Pea." He then turned his attention to Jake. "So are you a friend of my daughter's?"

"I'm her date for the upcoming weddings."

"Really? Her date, huh? Sounds serious. How long have you two been seeing each other?"

Since when had her normally nonverbal dad turned into

Mr. Chatty? He hadn't questioned her high school date to the prom this much.

Wait, she hadn't gone to prom.

"We haven't been seeing each other for that long," Jake replied, "but your daughter made a big impression on me the first time we met."

"She did, huh?"

"Yes, sir."

"Call me Bob." Her dad held out his hand, which Jake shook without wincing.

Emma knew her dad had the fierce handshake of a former Marine. He'd taught her as a kid to have a firm handshake and not a wimpy girly one that was like a dead fish. And when she'd get it right, he'd beam with pride. As he had when she'd graduated from college. He'd been so proud. Those were fond memories, not scary ones.

A majority of her memories were good, which was why that momentary flash of cowering in the corner was so disconcerting to her. She thought she'd come to terms with her past. It was her present that was giving her fits.

"Nice to meet you, Bob," Jake said.

"Same here."

"Well, if everything's okay here, I guess I'll leave you two alone then," Jake said.

"Why not come in for a spell?" her dad said.

Emma looked over her shoulder at her dad as if he'd lost his mind. Maybe he had. He never invited people in. He was not a people person. What was going on here?

"Invite the man in, Sweet Pea," her dad instructed.

"I, uh . . . would you like to come inside?" Hardly the most heartfelt of invitations, but hey, she was still wobbly on her emotional pins.

"Come on, Jake, we won't take no for an answer," her dad answered.

And so it was that Emma unlocked her door and ushered

the two men inside while mentally hoping she hadn't left anything in plain view that she shouldn't have. The small size of the studio apartment required her to be tidy. A quick scan of the room reassured her that the only messy place was the dining table she was using as a desk, where papers and books were spread out.

"And I thought the mobile home was small." Her dad shook his head. "I've seen RVs bigger than this."

"It's not that bad. I like it. Can I get either of you something to drink? I've only got Dr Pepper. The fridge doesn't hold much and I wasn't expecting company."

"Nothing for me," her dad said.

"I'm fine," Jake concurred.

Her dad gingerly sat on the futon, as if expecting it to collapse beneath his weight. "Your mom sent me over here to find out why you wouldn't stay with us at home."

Emma rolled her eyes. "I already told her I've rented this place for the summer while I do my work here. The research grant I got will cover the rent."

"Yeah, well, you know how your mom is." He looked around the room. "It doesn't seem like the flea-bitten hovel she made it out to be."

"She hasn't even seen it," Emma protested.

"You know how mothers are. Right, Jake?"

He just shrugged. Something about his expression caught Emma's attention and made her wonder at the momentary flash of emotion there. It was there and gone so quickly she couldn't even completely identify what it was— pain or anger?

"So are you from around here, Jake?" her dad asked.

"No, but I'm enjoying my time in Rock Creek."

"What do you do?"

"I'm a bartender at Nick's Tavern."

Her dad was not impressed. Emma was tempted to tell him that Jake was an extreme sports athlete, but it wasn't her place to reveal that information. And Jake chose not to, which didn't surprise her. She was surprised by the way he managed to change the subject, getting her dad to talk about himself.

"Uh-oh." Her dad glanced at his watch half an hour later. "I've got to go pick up your mom." He gave Emma a quick hug before hurrying out.

Emma closed the door after him and returned to the futon to face Jake, who stayed behind. "I'm sorry for overreacting the way I did, screaming like that."

"Something happened to you, didn't it?" he said quietly.

"With my dad?" Emma shook her head vehemently. "No, no, nothing like that."

"You're spooked."

"Not because of my dad." There was a moment of silence before she admitted, "Look, something happened back in Boston a few months ago. I was mugged. I was walking home after dinner out one night when this guy with a knife came out of nowhere. I wasn't raped or anything." Although she might have been had a neighbor not shown up and scared the assailant away. "He shoved me to the ground and took off with my purse. I signed up for self-defense classes the next day."

"Which you clearly excelled at, judging by the way you handled Roy in the bar."

"I'm not proud of that moment. I shouldn't have resorted to violence. It was just a knee-jerk response."

"Like you screaming when you saw your dad."

"I didn't know who it was when I screamed. I just saw a figure coming at me out of the corner of my eye and again I had a knee-jerk reaction. Please don't say anything about this to my family. I haven't told them about the mugging."

"Why not?"

"I don't want them worrying about me off in the big city of Boston on my own. I've always been the reliable daughter. The one that doesn't get in trouble."

He studied her for a moment. She wondered what he saw. Was he trying to read her mind or her soul? Could he tell how conflicted she was inside? How deeply she wanted him?

Finally he spoke. "I won't say anything."

"Thanks, I appreciate that."

"How much do you appreciate it?" His deep voice turned husky as he gently tugged her down onto the futon beside him. Cupping her cheek, he softly asked, "Are you afraid of me? Do I spook you?"

How should she answer that? On one level he did spook her. Not that she was afraid he'd physically injure her or attack her. She was nervous about the powerful attraction he held for her. Yet he also had the strange ability to make her feel gloriously alive.

Jake brushed his index finger over her bottom lip. "You're safe with me."

"Am I?"

"You don't feel safe?" He lingered a mere inch from her mouth, waiting for her reaction.

Emma wished he'd just kiss her and get it over with instead of tempting her this way, building the anticipation to unbearable heights until she leaned forward and placed her lips against his.

Making the first move wasn't like her, but she didn't care. They were kissing and that's all that mattered at the moment. She was consumed by the reality of his mouth on hers, of his tongue caressing hers as he took her face between his hands and kissed her fiercely.

There was nothing safe about their kiss. Its intoxicating potency sent a tremor of excitement through her. His lips were warm and bold as he tested and tasted each corner of her mouth and the full softness in between.

That first kiss on her fire escape hadn't been a fluke. Jake wasn't just an exceptional first kisser. He was a damn fine kisser, period. She'd never been convinced of the pleasures to be had from French kisses, but his expert tutelage made her a total convert.

The ever-fluid interplay of his tongue against hers was wickedly blissful. He devoured her with a forceful need. His mouth slanted ravenously atop hers, consuming all that was within her parted lips.

Bam, bam. It took Emma several moments to realize the sound wasn't her heart pounding in her ears. The pounding was coming from her front door.

"Come on, Emma, I know you're in there," Leena yelled. "Open up!"

"Ignore her and she'll go away," Jake said, nibbling on her throat.

Emma wished that were true, but knew it wasn't. She reluctantly moved away. The spell was broken. For now . . . "You don't know my sister. She's very persistent."

"Emma!" Leena yelled again.

Not in the best of moods, Emma marched over and yanked open the door. "What?"

"How could you?"

Emma bit her bottom lip, the one that Jake had just been kissing. How did her sister know she'd been making out with Jake? Had their dad suspected something and sent Leena to check up on her?

"How could I what?" Emma asked carefully.

"*Naked firemen* ring any bells?"

"I had no idea you were into naked firemen," Jake noted from the futon, where he eyed Emma with wicked speculation.

"I don't . . . I'm not!" Emma sputtered.

"Not her. Our sister Sue Ellen. At the bridal shower tomorrow."

"You're having naked firemen coming to your bridal shower?" His dark eyebrows rose. "Sounds like quite a party."

"Thanks for stopping by, Jake." Emma sent him a look. "I don't want to keep you."

"I'm not in any hurry," he said, settling himself more comfortably.

Emma narrowed her eyes at him. "My sister and I need to share some girl talk. In private."

He nodded knowingly. "To talk about the naked firemen."

"Among other things." She tugged him to his feet, no easy task given the fact that he had to be six foot two of muscular male who enjoyed making trouble. He seemed to also enjoy her attempts to get rid of him.

"You're not telling me you want me to leave, are you?" He pretended to look hurt.

"Yes."

He gave her a head to toe once-over that was hotter than the surface of the sun. "We'll finish this later." Reaching out, he tucked a wayward strand of her hair behind her ear before ambling out.

"Are you crazy?" Leena demanded.

"Probably," Emma muttered, closing the door after him before turning to face Leena.

"How could you tell Sue Ellen to post pictures of naked firemen at the shower tomorrow?"

"I didn't tell her what to put up. She was upset because she thought your table was going to look better than hers—"

"She's right. It will."

"—so I told her that she should make her table her own."

"Great. Just great. So what are you going to do about this mess?"

"Me?"

"Yes, you." Leena pointed at her. "You're the one offering dumb advice."

"It wasn't dumb, and I'm getting tired of being in the middle of this competition between you and Sue Ellen."

Leena responded by bursting into tears.

Sue Ellen might turn on the waterworks at the drop of a hat, but Leena rarely did. Emma felt awful for making her cry. "I'm sorry."

Leena just cried harder.

Emma was getting desperate. "I'll talk to Sue Ellen. Get her to put up something noncontroversial. Like pictures of sunflowers or something."

Leena hiccupped, her tears slowing, her face red. She wasn't a pretty crier.

"Here, sit down." Emma led her to the futon. "Can I get you a glass of water? Or Dr Pepper? I know. How about Cherry Garcia ice cream? It's your favorite, right?"

Leena nodded.

"Okay then." Emma retrieved the carton and two spoons and a box of tissues. They were just about to dig into the creamy dessert when there was a knock on the door.

Emma opened it to find Sue Ellen there. "I decided against the naked firemen," she said as she walked inside. "I'm not sure that Donny's mom would approve. And Leena has a nun coming."

"Cole's aunt is a nun," Leena reminded Emma.

"Right." Emma got another spoon.

She turned to find her sisters sitting side by side on the futon, digging into the Cherry Garcia together and waving their spoons as they brainstormed for an alternate photo display for Sue Ellen's table. Watching them, Emma felt a pang of . . . was it jealousy?

Leena had always been closer to Emma than to Sue Ellen. For one thing, they were closer in age, only two years apart. And while neither of her sisters really got her, Leena was the one Emma had talked to throughout their teenage years. Leena was the one who'd shared Emma's passion for Johnny Depp, who hadn't mocked her even though Emma was the only one in her freshman high school class who wasn't a fan of *Beverly Hills, 90210*. Leena was the one who'd encouraged Emma to take the job in Boston. To be her own woman and stand on her own two feet.

The newfound bond between Leena and Sue Ellen was unexpected and disconcerting.

Emma realized it was childish to feel threatened by this change in the sisterly dynamic. Rock Creek wasn't the only thing going through a change. Emma's own family was also going through a transformation. Her sisters would be married women soon. And they were both pregnant. Naturally they'd share a special connection during this time.

Suck it up, Em. Get over it. She pulled over a folding chair. There wasn't enough room on the couch for all three of them. Unable to get a word in edgewise, Emma just sat there and watched her siblings.

Leena was wearing jeans and a flowing empire-waist top with her customary élan. Sue Ellen was wearing blue cropped pants and a red knit top filled with tiny white stars, which were repeated on her neatly manicured fingernails. Leena had a beautiful French manicure. Emma looked down at her own unvarnished nails, her khaki shorts, and blue polo shirt.

"You need to go to Mai's Nails," Leena told Emma. "Before the shower tomorrow. Come on, we'll go now. My treat."

"I'll wait for you here," Sue Ellen said, hunkering down with the carton of ice cream. "I'm eating for two now."

"Two, not thirty-two," Leena said, taking the carton away, or trying to. Sue Ellen wasn't about to surrender easily.

"Dad's back," Emma said.

The news distracted her sisters enough that Emma was able to grab the carton and scoop out the remaining spoonful of ice cream for herself.

"Did he say anything about giving me away?" Sue Ellen asked.

"No." Emma scraped the spoon around the carton. "Was he supposed to?"

"Did he say anything about the wedding?" Sue Ellen asked.

"Only indirectly." Emma tossed the totally empty carton into the garbage.

"Meaning what?"

Emma admitted, "Jake told him he was my date."

"Your date? Jake? Did we know this?" Sue Ellen asked.

"Jake was here when I arrived," Leena said.

Sue Ellen licked her already clean spoon. "The guy moves fast."

"So I've heard. You be careful, lil sis. Don't get in over your head with this hottie," Leena warned.

Too late, Emma thought to herself.

* * *

Jake saw it all in gruesome detail. Felt it. Not the fear. That came later. Just the horror. And the utter helplessness.

He, Andy, and a buddy of Andy's had reached the summit and were making their descent. The snow-covered spires possessed a severe haunting beauty. It happened so fast. One second Andy was above him, the next he was consumed by a huge wall of ice, rock, and snow that rolled down the mountain without warning, swallowing everything in its wake.

Jake woke in a cold sweat. His stomach ached. His arms were trembling. The nightmare was never the same. Sometimes it was of the avalanche. Sometimes of the terrible aftermath of Jake trying to crawl off the mountain with his serious injuries, alone until he caught up with Andy's buddy. Sometimes the cold woke him. Sometimes the pain. But always the guilt.

Jake knew the drill by now. Knew he wouldn't be able to get back to sleep. So he went out running.

Jake had always had a need for speed. He could still remember how, as a real little kid, he'd been able to fly down the mountain. It was the fastest he'd ever gone. From that moment on, he was hooked.

He'd experienced it all—from the grueling pace of an XTERRA triathlon to the joy of heli-skiing. From hang gliding to bungee jumping. He'd even driven a Formula One race car around the track. But he always returned to the mountains.

There were no jagged peaks surrounding Rock Creek. Instead there were gentle hills interspersed with a few rugged ones. He'd explored a number of them in the short time he'd been here. They were child's play compared to the challenges he'd mastered before. But he wasn't the man he'd been before. He was scarred—inside and out.

The doctors had initially told him that he might not walk again, then that he'd always have a limp. He'd proved them wrong on both counts. Numerous surgeries over the past eighteen months had repaired much of his physical injuries but none of the emotional damage.

The nightmares were proof of that. There was no escaping them, no matter how fast he ran, or how long. He ran for one mile, then two . . .

"Woof!"

Jake slowed down at the nearby sound of a dog barking.

"Woof."

Jake stared into the darkness, trying to figure out where the noise came from. Everyone was sound asleep in their beds, probably next to their dogs. There had been no signs of life during his 4 a.m. run. Until now.

"Woof."

The bark was louder this time and sounded as though it was coming from behind him. He turned in time to see a row of sharp, glistening teeth charging right at him. *Shit!*

He backpedaled and fell on his ass in the grass along the road.

A half second later the dog was on him, licking his face and drooling all over him.

"Yuck." Jake turned his head to avoid the doggy spit. "Get off me, you big mangy ass."

"Woof."

"Whoa." Almost overcome by the bad doggy breath, Jake waved his hand in front of his face. "You need some mouthwash, mutt. Get off."

He shoved but the mutt ignored him.

So he tried something else. "Sit."

The mutt sat. Right on Jake's privates.

Swearing vehemently, Jake managed to dislodge the dog and scramble to his feet, although not as quickly as he would have under normal conditions. Gritting his teeth, he tried to walk it off, unable to stand straight for several minutes.

The dog sat and watched. The animal didn't seem to have any kind of collar or tags to indicate it belonged to someone.

"So you think this is funny, do you? Well, I don't. So get out of here."

"Woof."

"Do not follow me."

The dog immediately disobeyed orders.

Jake stopped.

The mutt stopped.

Jake started running.

The mutt ran alongside him.

"Woof."

"Shut up," Jake growled. "Do not talk to me."

The dog shut up but kept running beside him right to the door of Jake's building.

"Don't give me that look. You are not coming inside." Standing in the pool of light provided by the building's security lamp, Jake could see the mutt's ribs standing out.

Jake started running again, this time to the Gas4Less Mini-Mart three blocks away, open twenty-four hours. "Do you sell dog food?"

"Sure. Aisle two."

Jake bought a small bag with the few dollars he had on him.

"That your dog outside?" the male teenage cashier asked.

The mutt sat right next to the door, looking in at him. "No, he's not mine. Do you know who he belongs to?"

"Looks like he belongs to you now. Hey, aren't you that extreme sports guy?"

"No." Jake took the dog food and headed out, back to his apartment building. He opened the bag in the alley and then realized he didn't have a container to pour the dry food into.

No problem. The mutt stuck his head in the bag and started scarfing it all down.

"This doesn't mean we have a relationship or anything," Jake told the dog. "So don't go making more of this than it is. I'm not looking for a pet. I've never taken care of a pet and I'm not starting now. No ties for me. You've got the wrong guy here. Go find that vet guy Cole. I bet he'd find a home for you."

The mutt kept eating.

Jake slipped back inside the apartment building, refusing to look back. Looking back never solved anything.

Chapter Six

· · · · · · · · · · ·

Emma's morning ritual included her daily practice of tai chi, which she always did wearing her good-luck running shorts and navy Penn T-shirt. The exercise was meant to calm her, to start her day with the energizing and healthy effect of something that dated back two thousand years. It wasn't meant to make her think about sex.

Not just random sex. Specific sex. Sex with Jake.

She'd seen him twice since walking into Nick's Tavern. And both times she'd kissed him instead of asking if he was going to participate in her research study.

Emma wasn't researching the elements of first kisses. Or of outstanding kisses. Or of kisses that made you want to have sex. There was no reference whatsoever to kisses on the carefully crafted questionnaire she'd prepared for all the study participants. She was here to study the resurgence of her hometown, not to make out with the town's hottie.

She wasn't about to fall into a fit of dork mania over Jake the way Ted had at Comic-Con over that gray-haired actor who'd played Doctor Who for so many years. She wasn't a groupie. She was smart. Most of the time. So where had she gone wrong here?

She slowly changed positions into her next tai chi move. She was supposed to be meditating now. Not trying to analyze her illogical hormone-driven behavior.

The thing was, she couldn't seem to get Jake out of her mind. He'd taken up residency there come hell or high water.

Today was the bridal shower. Sue Ellen's wedding was only one week away. Emma's dress today was a favorite of hers—a floral jersey dress with a flared A-line skirt and ruching at the waist. The only reason Emma knew it was called ruching was because her fashionista sister Leena had told her before approving of her wardrobe choice.

Thinking of wardrobe choices reminded Emma of the over-the-top bridesmaid dress she had to wear to Sue Ellen's wedding. She only now realized that Jake would see her in that Pepto-Bismol pink dress with the big butt bow. That was so wrong on so many levels. Maybe she could change into something else at the reception being held at the Serenity Falls Country Club. The wedding ceremony was taking place on the stage of the Tivoli Theater, but Jake didn't have to come to that. He should just come to the reception.

Just thinking about standing on that stage in that nightmare dress almost made Emma hyperventilate. She had to do another half hour of tai chi before she calmed down. On her way to the shower, she realized her garbage can was full so she ran it downstairs and out to the alley. But first she grabbed her cell and clipped it to her waist, something she'd learned during her self-defense class.

Once Emma was out in the alley, she saw what looked like a big pile of dark rags on the far side of the Dumpster. Then the pile moved. It was a dog. A very skinny dog.

"Oh, you poor baby." Emma immediately reached for

her cell and called Cole. It was early enough that the animal clinic wasn't open yet, but she reached him at home.

He arrived within minutes. "What's going on?"

"This poor dog needs your help."

The dog didn't growl or snarl, but just barely lifted its head to look at them. Until the building door opened and Jake came out. Then the dog leapt to life as if it had been supercharged by the Energizer Bunny.

"Is this your dog?" Cole asked.

"Hell no." Jake was emphatic. "It's a stray. Followed me home during my run in the middle of the night. I gave it some dog food. I was just bringing it some water too."

"Looks like this guy likes you," Emma said.

"Yeah, women and dogs just fawn at my feet," Jake said with dry humor.

"Then you're the perfect guy to foster the dog until he regains some strength," Cole said.

"Trust me, he's plenty strong. I don't want any part of fostering. The foster system sucks."

"Actually people have saved a lot of animals' lives by fostering them until good homes can be found," Cole said.

Emma immediately noticed the change in Jake even before he spoke.

"And if good homes aren't found? If no one wants them? Then what?" Jake said. "Besides, I don't even know how long I'm going to be hanging around here."

That last revelation hit Emma like a 3 a.m. wake-up call. What was she doing kissing Jake when he could be gone tomorrow?

Maybe it would be best if he did leave, a little logical voice inside her head lectured. *Then he wouldn't rock your boat. You could return to the status quo. You wouldn't have to worry about convincing him to participate in your research study. And you wouldn't have to worry about him seducing you into his bed only to have him take off on you.*

Just because Jake kissed her didn't mean he wanted to have sex with her, although the fiery heat of his kisses seemed to indicate otherwise. But how many other women had he wanted . . . and gotten? How many other women had he kissed so expertly, so passionately? Dozens? Hundreds?

All the stress reduction her morning tai chi had accomplished was erased in a heartbeat.

Jake saw the way Emma was looking at him, with a new cynicism. And for some stupid reason that was all it took for him to back down and reluctantly agree to take in the dog.

"Come on over to the clinic with me and I'll look him over," Cole said.

The dog backed away from Cole, who then handed the collar and leash to Jake. "Here, you try it."

Mutt practically put the collar on himself, so eager was he to get close to Jake.

When Jake looked up, he expected Emma to look at him with respect and admiration after his heroic dog deal, but she was still looking a little cautious. Cautious was better than cynical.

Mumbling something about needing to get ready for a bridal shower, Emma turned and hurried away, giving him a nice view of her curvy butt in a pair of shorts. His first impression had been right. She had great legs.

"So Emma is bringing you to the weddings?" Cole said.

"Yeah."

"Providing you haven't left town."

"I'm not leaving before the weddings," Jake said.

"You and Emma seem to be getting along well in a short period of time."

Jake made no comment.

"Roy claims he saw you and Emma making out on the fire escape."

Again Jake made no comment.

"Look, here's the deal," Cole said. "I've been pressured into talking to you about Emma."

"Pressured?"

"Yes. By my fiancé-soon-to-be-wife. Emma's sister Leena. She's worried you might hurt Emma."

"So what did Leena tell you to do? Warn me off?"

"Just warn you to be good to Emma. She's from the academic world and doesn't have a lot of streetwise experience."

Jake didn't totally agree with that assessment. Emma might not have his kind of street smarts, but she was no naïve dummy.

"I think you're all underestimating Emma," Jake said.

"Just consider yourself warned," Cole said.

"Understood. And this dog deal is only temporary," Jake said.

Cole just grinned as if he knew better.

"Maybe the dog has some kind of chip or something that will tell you who his owner is," Jake said.

"I will certainly check that out."

Half an hour later, Cole's examination in the animal clinic was complete. "No chip. Other than needing food, he seems in good shape. We need a name for the dog."

"Mutt."

"We need a name for the mutt."

"No, that's his name. For now," Jake clarified. "Until he gets a real owner, I mean."

"Right."

"Woof."

Jake realized neither the vet nor the dog sounded convinced . . . he just wasn't sure what to do about it.

• • •

The good news was that since her sisters had combined their showers, Emma had to live through the experience only once. The bad news was just about everything else.

Okay that was a total exaggeration, but Emma was feeling pretty damn cranky. The party was actually going very well. The crab puffs made by Cole's cousin, who was catering the event, were delicious and hadn't made Sue Ellen hurl. The lobby of the Tivoli looked lovely. Emma hadn't really noticed the fine details when she'd interviewed Skye, but now she paused to appreciate the elegant ornateness of the architecture, the glistening pair of chandeliers, and the intricately inlaid marble floors. The center of the large lobby showcased a series of round tables covered in white tablecloths with floral centerpieces of pink and white roses along with small calligraphied name tents at each place setting.

No, the problem wasn't the food or the decorations. The problem was the bridal shower guests—and the things they were saying to Emma.

The first few times someone told her she was the "spinster sister now," Emma laughed politely and took the personal jabs like a big girl. But by the time the twentieth person said it, she was no longer even pretending to be amused. Instead she had her academic face on. Not that anyone noticed.

So she delivered a stern lecture to herself. She was good at lectures. *This is your sisters' day. A celebration. You're supposed to be having a good time. And if you can't manage that, you're supposed to look like you're having a good time. That's your job as part of the bridal party. That and wearing whatever stupid dress the bride picks for you. You're not supposed to complain about it. You're not supposed to wish you were somewhere else.*

She could be a team player. She *would* be, no more excuses. No whining. Even to herself.

After delivering that final stern self-reprimand, Emma returned her attention to the bridal shower. Everyone else seemed to be having a good time, without any major faux pas. No sign of naked firemen or naked males of any sort. The party was actually quite nice.

The conversation thankfully slowed while everyone sat down to eat their luncheon, which was served buffet style.

"Isn't this a lovely shower?" her mom, who was seated beside her and wearing a flowing pink gown, leaned over to say.

Emma nodded.

"Unlike that hovel you're living in."

"It's not a hovel. It's a studio apartment. Didn't Dad tell you he checked it out for you?"

"I don't know what you're talking about."

"Come on, Mom, I know you sent Dad over."

"Did he tell you that?"

"Are you saying you didn't send him?" Emma countered.

"I'm your mother. It's only natural that I worry about you."

"You shouldn't. You've got enough on your plate with the weddings."

"The weddings and the—" Her mom made a motion with her hand that Emma translated as "the fact that both your sisters are pregnant before they walk down the aisle."

Emma quickly put her hand over her mom's to indicate that she got the message and there was no need to speak the words aloud. "All good news. An abundance of good news."

"Yes, well, I'm afraid that Sue Ellen's . . . abundance . . . may be showing."

Emma frowned. "Why? Has anyone said anything to you?"

"They don't have to. I can read their minds."

Emma doubted that. Her mom didn't have a very good track record in that department. The most recent example had come just yesterday when Maxie read the mind of the clerk at Gas4Less and thought she knew the winning lottery numbers for that day.

"And before you say anything," Maxie continued, "my only mistake yesterday was in thinking the clerk knew the winning numbers. Had I been thinking straight, I'd have realized she couldn't have that information. See, I just read your mind, right?" Maxie paused only long enough to take a quick breath before barreling on. "Honey, I wish you'd let your sisters give you a makeover. They could make you look prettier than you are. Face it, you've only got a few good years left. Once you reach a certain age your chances of getting married are slim to none."

"Maybe I don't want to get married."

"Don't be silly. Of course you want to get married."

"Isn't it about time to start opening the gifts?" Emma looked around for an escape route.

"And frowning like that is just going to give you wrinkles."

Her mother was going to give her wrinkles—and an ulcer. Emma took another bite of her tiramisu dessert.

"If you eat too much, you're not going to fit into your bridesmaid dresses," Maxie said.

Which would be a blessing in disguise as far as Emma was concerned. She vehemently speared the dainty tiramisu, her fork hitting the dish so loudly that it seemed to echo around the lobby.

"If you don't want your sisters doing your hair, I could do it for you."

Maxie had experimented on all her daughters while they were growing up—giving them permanents, highlights, lowlights, haircuts. It was amazing that any of them had any hair left after all the chemicals their mom had poured on their heads.

Her mother's favorite customers when she'd been a hairstylist had been the over-fifty-five crowd. She'd once tried to bring in a younger crowd by giving Emma a mohawk the summer she turned eleven.

"I don't need you doing my hair, thank you very much," Emma said.

"But it's so flat."

Emma didn't even realize she'd raised her fork into a defensive move until her mom eyed it uneasily.

"Okay, okay." Maxie lifted her hands in the universal sign of surrender. "You don't want me making you beautiful. I can take a hint. I just thought you might want to look good for that handsome man escorting you to the weddings."

"I'm sure it must be time to open presents by now." Emma jumped from her chair and headed for the two brides-to-be. "We're opening presents now."

"Great idea." Sue Ellen practically clapped in anticipation.

"You have the lists?" Leena asked Emma.

"In my purse." Emma retrieved them. Leena, being the uberorganized one in the family, had done up a list of guests for both herself and Sue Ellen. All Emma had to do was enter the gift beside the name so her sisters could send thank-you notes stating what they'd received and personalizing their comments.

"Open mine first," Maxie shouted. "They're right in front on the gift table. The two beautifully wrapped ones with the pink bows. Wait. Before you do that, I want to propose a quick toast." She lifted her glass of wine. "To my daughters—may happiness slap you across the face and may all your tears be those of joy."

Sue Ellen looked as though she was on the verge of tears as she drank her sparkling grape juice, so Emma distracted her by shoving a large present in her lap. "Here. This is from Mom and Dad." Emma handed a matching present to Leena. "Ditto."

Their parents had gotten them each a nifty food processor as well as a tiered cupcake stand.

Emma handed her sisters another pair of presents. They eagerly ripped open the wrapping paper to find . . . a deviled-egg serving dish with ugly red chickens painted on them.

Emma made the notation beside the proper name.

And next came . . . another deviled-egg dish and more ugly chickens.

Leena smiled and beckoned Emma closer to whisper, "I registered online with Macy's bridal registry and there were no deviled-egg dishes on my list."

"I saw these at the dollar store," Sue Ellen leaned close to whisper.

"Who buys shower gifts at a dollar store?" Leena muttered.

Emma consulted her list. "Aunt Martha and Cousin Addie apparently."

"What did you get?" Maxie called out.

"Another deviled-egg dish," Emma replied.

"You can never have too many deviled-egg dishes," Aunt Martha said.

Which made Emma wonder how many more were hidden on the gift table. By the time all the presents were opened, they ended up with four sets each. All from family members.

Maxie was not pleased.

"Your father's side of the family." Maxie sniffed in disapproval. "My sister in Minneapolis sent you each the deluxe cappuccino machine from your lists, and she wasn't even coming to the bridal shower. And Cole and Donny's family all got you nice things as well. Those penny-pinching Rileys. Did I ever tell you what they got me for my bridal shower?"

"Many times," Emma and her sisters said in unison.

That didn't stop Maxie from continuing. "A Veg-O-Matic and a pair of rooster salt and pepper shakers. It wasn't even a real as-seen-on-TV Veg-O-Matic. It was a knockoff."

"Ladies, if I could have your attention please," Skye called out. "The entertainment has finally arrived."

She opened the door to the theater seating area to reveal two bare-chested men wearing firemen helmets and pants.

"Oh my stars!" Aunt Martha said. "Where's the fire?"

Chapter Seven

. . . .

"**I**s it just me or is it hot in here?" Skye said with a wicked grin.

Rip. Off came the firefighter pants, revealing black skintight bicycle shorts.

"Let's get this party started! Enjoy the show!" Skye stepped aside.

"Holy Toledo!" Aunt Martha pumped her fist in the air. "Take it all off, fellas!"

Emma took one look at her mother's astonished face before turning to see Leena's dismayed expression. Then Emma was distracted by the nearly naked fireman who stood right in front of her and shimmied his hips.

"Hey, bring those six-pack abs over here," Sue Ellen shouted. "I'm the bride-to-be, not her."

Emma gulped with relief as the guy obligingly turned his attentions to Sue Ellen. Then Emma's academic side came out. She'd never actually seen a male stripper before. He had a very nice body. Both men did. And they were good dancers, moving to the sound of Justin Timberlake's "SexyBack." But they were overly muscular in a beefcake sort of way that didn't really appeal to her on a personal or sexual level. Not like Jake's body.

They didn't make her feel the way Jake made her feel. Emma could admire the guys the way she'd admire a Greek statue, but they didn't ignite her inner fire. Until she imagined Jake standing before her, thrusting his hips at her. Whoa! Emma's response was instantaneous and intense. The aching yearning within her vagina had her crossing her legs tightly.

She had to get out of there before she had an orgasm or something. But her knees were too weak to support her just yet. By the time the men yanked off their cycling shorts, revealing a tiny thong, Emma was ready to douse herself with an entire pitcher of ice water. And all because of Jake, who wasn't even in the building.

Emma made her escape after their performance was over, slipping away from the lobby into the theater itself where she heard the muffled sound of someone crying. Once Emma got closer, she recognized Lulu Malick, one of her sister's bridesmaids. "Are you okay?"

"Do I look like I'm okay?"

She looked like a mom's worst nightmare. Her thick mascara was obviously not waterproof since it ran down her cheeks and neck to the leather dog collar around her throat. Her dyed black hair was tumbling out of one of her pigtails, and a pair of silver skeleton earrings dangled as she scrubbed the tears away, further messing up her makeup. An intricate cobweb tattoo was visible above the collar of her white shirt, tucked into a plaid skirt atop white leggings. She wore a pair of biker boots with chains. Emma had seen similar attire on a few of her more edgy students.

"I'm sorry, I didn't mean to interrupt." Emma turned to leave.

"No, stay." Lulu yanked her into the empty red velvet theater seat beside her. "You're the smart sister, right?"

"I, uh . . ." Emma stuttered. She should be glad Lulu wasn't calling her the spinster sister.

"Don't be modest. You're some kind of professor, right? A psychologist?"

"A sociologist."

"Close enough. What would you think about a mother who abandoned her kid and then years later shows up out of the blue?"

"Is that what happened to you?"

Lulu nodded. "She showed up at my grandfather's trailer two weeks ago. No warning, nothing. My grandfather raised me. He lives in the Broken Creek Trailer Park. His name is Jerry. You might have seen him around town. He has a lot of tats, tattoos. Rides a Harley."

Emma nodded. She had seen him.

"I'm living in Skye's old apartment above the theater here," Lulu said. "I've turned one of the bedrooms into a studio for my work. I'm creating a graphic novel. Not that that has anything to do with my mother. I shouldn't even call her that. She hasn't been a mother to me. I don't even know why she bothered coming back here after all this time."

"Did you ask her?"

"No. I don't want to know."

"Really?"

"I don't know." Lulu scrubbed away a fresh set of tears.

"Have you talked to Skye about this?"

"No. Skye would just tell me to kick some butt."

Emma's eyes widened. "She would?"

"I don't know. I didn't want to say anything and ruin the bridal shower for everyone. I don't even know why I'm crying. I don't do crying," she said fiercely. "Ask anyone. They'll tell you that I don't do crying. Ever. Do I look like someone who cries?"

"No."

"Damn right." Lulu wiped her nose with the back of her hand. "Crying is for wimps."

"Not necessarily. Crying can be a release for a build up of stress. It's the body's way of coping."

"Did they teach you that in medical school?"

"I didn't go to medical school. I'm a sociologist."

"Well, I never went to college, but that doesn't mean I'm stupid."

"Right."

"You're just saying that to be polite. You look like the type to be polite. Like Skye's polite librarian sister, Julia. You're a lot like her."

"Is she here at the shower?"

"No, she and Luke are on vacation with their daughter. Julia is a good mom. Unlike mine. My grandfather is the best, though. He used to be an electrician before he retired. He's always been there for me. He was my real parent, not her. And that's the bottom line here. It doesn't matter why she came back. Facts are facts. And the fact is that my grandfather is the one who deserves my loyalty and love. Not her. I don't owe her anything. It's so clear to me now. Thank you so much."

"But I didn't do anything."

Lulu laughed. "Now you're being modest. You probably learned that listening technique in college, huh? Letting me figure things out for myself. That was wicked awesome. I'm totally impressed."

"No, really I didn't do anything."

"Understood. That's what you're supposed to say. Got it. No worries. I'm not really into hugs, but if I was, I'd give you one."

"Uh, thanks."

"I've got to go put my warrior face back on. I'm not one of those emos who are always crying. I just want to make that clear."

"Understood." Emma's experience on the small campus where she taught hadn't put her into contact with many emos, but she'd heard the term before, referring to a lifestyle revolving around a certain type of music, clothes, and hairstyles.

"Not that I'm totally all goth all the time either," Lulu said. "I've got some emo in me. The truth is that I don't really fit into any one category. Like Sue Ellen. She doesn't fit either."

"Right."

"Not that I'm really like her. I just meant that neither one of us fits into a category. Neither does Skye. That's why we're all such great friends. Otherwise I'd never wear that Pepto dress for Sue Ellen. I wouldn't do that for anyone else. Except Skye, but she'd never ask me to do anything so stupid." Lulu looked at Emma. "What? You thought I was going to wear something like this to be Sue Ellen's bridesmaid?"

"It would be an improvement on the Pepto bridesmaid's dress," Emma said with a grin.

"You may be smart, but I like you anyway," Lulu said.

"I'm honored."

Now it was Lulu's turn to grin. "You should be."

* * *

Emma returned to the lobby to find her sisters and mother talking about her. "Poor dear, she was so embarrassed she had to leave," Maxie said. "You should be more considerate about your baby sister. You know what a sheltered life Emma leads in that little college of hers."

"It's a college, not a nunnery," Emma said.

"Of course it's not a nunnery," Maxie said. "If it was, you'd be a nun like Cole's aunt Sister Mary."

Emma gritted her teeth. It had been a long day. She had survived strangers calling her a spinster, her mother ranting about her looks, and a parade of nearly naked firemen. Well, that last bit had definitely been more enjoyable than the previous two.

The muscle-bound bodies of the stripping firemen made her think about Jake again and his sexy lean build. She remembered the way he'd looked in that black T-shirt when she first walked into Nick's Tavern. The sculpted muscles, the barbed-wire tattoo. He'd held her in those powerful arms when he'd kissed her on her fire escape and later on her futon. There was no escaping the memory of those moments.

But Emma could escape her family, and she did so by slipping out the front door while they were distracted. Emma was still thinking about Jake as she walked to her apartment a block away. That's why she didn't see the runner barreling out from the narrow alley until he almost rammed into her.

"Whoa." Jake steadied her. "Sorry about that. I didn't see you."

Yeah, Emma knew how that went. People frequently didn't see her. That had never bothered her before. It was starting to now.

Also bothering her in an entirely different way was the warmth of his hands on her upper arms. The floral dress she'd worn to the bridal shower was sleeveless. She could feel each of his fingers on her skin.

"Nice dress," Jake noted, his eyes wandering over her with blatant appreciation.

"Nice running shorts," she replied, her eyes wandering over him with discreet appreciation.

He was wearing more than the stripper firemen, but he

affected her ten times as much. Not that he was wearing that much more. His chest was bare, glistening with a fine sheen of sweat. She watched one rivulet trail down from his collarbone all the way to his navel.

He smiled in that slow sexy way that made her knees go weak. "I'm glad I ran into you. We still haven't settled on when I should pick you up for your sister's wedding. It's next Saturday, right?"

"Right. I just came from the bridal shower."

"And how did that go?"

"I survived it."

He brushed his right thumb up and down her upper arm. "I'm glad to hear that."

She shivered.

"Are you cold?" he asked, rubbing her arms.

Considering the fact that it was in the mid eighties she could hardly say yes.

"Is that better?"

She licked her lips. Better would be him kissing her senseless and peeling her dress off.

What was wrong with her? Why was she having these thoughts in the middle of town? With a man she'd only met a few days ago? Maybe she was having a meltdown. Maybe the stress of dealing with her sisters' impending weddings and her mother's constant nagging had finally fried her brain.

Emma clenched her hands to prevent herself from reaching out to him.

She looked over his shoulder to see her mom on the sidewalk in front of the Tivoli. Her mom flashing her the thumbs-up sign and motioning for Emma to get closer to Jake.

She leapt away from him as if he'd caught fire.

Her mom shook her head in vehement disapproval and made a shooing motion for Emma to return to her former position. Maxie then had the nerve to make a kissie face.

"I've got to go," Emma muttered, totally mortified by her mom's antics.

"What's wrong?" Jake looked over his shoulder to see what had caused the sudden change in Emma.

Her mother waved at him and came closer.

"Run for it." Emma gave him a shove to get him started. "Go. Save yourself."

"I'm not afraid of your mother," Jake said.

"You should be. Very afraid."

"Hello, Mrs. Riley," Jake said.

"I thought I told you to call me Maxie," her mother said coyly.

"Well, Maxie, you're certainly looking lovely this afternoon."

Emma did a combo eye roll and face scrunch. Jake tossed out compliments the way the Tastykake factory tossed out desserts. She'd be a fool to take any of them seriously. Or to take him seriously.

Maxie batted her triple-mascara-coated eyelashes. "Why thank you, Jake. We just finished up the bridal shower. The wedding is only a week away, you know."

Jake nodded. "Emma and I were just talking about that."

"You're not backing out, are you? Oh please, please tell me you're not backing out."

Just kill me now. Emma closed her eyes and bit her lip to prevent herself from screaming out loud.

"We were just talking about the details," Jake said.

"Yes, Mother, we were just talking about the details."

"Right." Maxie nodded knowingly. "The details. Maybe you should discuss the details somewhere private. But before I leave you two, I just have to say, Jake, that you look better than any of those male strippers we just saw." Having made that statement, she returned to the Tivoli.

Jake turned to Emma. "Male strippers?"

"It wasn't my idea."

"Did you enjoy their show more than you did mine?"

"Not really, no."

"I'm glad to hear that."

"Wait, I didn't mean that the way it sounded."

"No?" He reached out to cup her cheek before trailing his fingers down to the corner of her mouth.

Yes, yes, yes was humming through her entire body, a fire kindled by the touch of his hand. There wasn't a *no* molecule left inside of her.

"Woof."

Startled, Emma looked down to see Jake's dog sitting beside him. "Hi there. What's his name?"

"His name is Mutt and he's a pain in the butt."

"Woof."

"Surely not," Emma said. "He's kind of cute now that you've got him cleaned up."

"You must have a strange definition of cute."

"Yeah, I probably do." Physical appearance had never been a big deal to her. She did find odd things to be cute. Which was why her reaction to Jake was so unusual for her. She'd never been one to fall for a hunky guy. There wouldn't be any point in doing so, since they weren't the type to appreciate a plain Jane.

She really needed to dissect her attraction to Jake and work on overcoming it because there was no logic in continuing to practically melt at his feet. She might be something of a geek, but she did have her pride.

So no more kissing Jake, no more melting in his arms like ice cream on a hot day. From now on she was taking the cool, restrained approach. The newly revised, totally in control Emma told Jake, "I'll meet you at the Serenity Falls Country Club at five for the reception." And then she walked away.

You rock, her inner academic diva raved.
Don't stumble and fall, her inner dorky geek warned.

• • •

Monday morning, Jake checked his text messages to see if the private investigator he'd hired had any additional news. Dan had already answered his earlier message several days ago regarding Nic, who was indeed the owner of Nick's Tavern. As to her being his birth mother, well that was still unknown at this point.

Too much stuff was unknown. Like the reason Emma had gone all cool on him the other afternoon. All he'd said was that she must have a strange idea of cute. What was wrong with that?

There was nothing in his in-box—no new text messages. Just the last list that Dan had sent him with a narrowed down list of possible names for his birth mother.

One thing he had discovered yesterday was that he needed help with the mutt. That was his mission for today. He walked into Cosmic Comics and found her. Lulu.

A number of the rednecks who hung around Nick's Tavern spoke of her in respectful terms because of her granddad, who sported even more tats than she did and had the nickname Animal. Lulu was tough but fair. Bluntly honest. Or so he'd been told. He was impressed by the intricate spiderweb tat on her neck and shoulder. She wore a T-shirt with the words GOT BRAINS? on it and a pair of black jeans tucked into biker boots.

"I hear you might be interested in making some extra money," Jake said.

"Doing what?" Lulu asked suspiciously.

"Walking the dog when I'm at work."

"Your dog?"

"He's not really my dog."

"Then why are you willing to pay me to walk him?"

"It's only temporary."

"So is the planet Earth if we don't do something about global warming." She paused to snap her gum in aggravation. "So how much are you paying?"

Jake named an amount that made her pierced eyebrow rise.

"You must be rich. *You're* the new bartender, right?"

"Yeah."

"So why are you working as a bartender if you're the Bill Gates of extreme sports."

"I'm no Bill Gates. Are you interested in the job or not?"

"I need more info on my employer."

"Why?" Jake demanded.

"Because I'm nosy. Don't you have any friends who can walk your dog? Like Emma? I heard you two are friends."

Jake had no intention of asking Emma, not after she'd gone all weird on him the other day.

"Did you guys have a fight?" Lulu asked.

"No. Emma is too busy with her academic stuff to walk the dog."

"Yeah, right." Lulu gave him a speculative look. "I've heard about you and Emma."

"From Emma?"

"No way. She's—" Lulu made a zip motion across her lips. "I've just heard about you, picked stuff up around town. You used to be some kind of extreme sports competitor. I read on the Internet that you were a big deal until you were in a serious climbing accident in Peru. They're talking on the message boards about you, saying that you . . ." She paused at the look he gave her.

"Don't stop now," he mocked her.

"That you've lost your nerve. That you won't be back on the circuit. That you were one of the best. Always pushing the envelope. Until the accident that killed your best friend. Is it true that he died because of you?"

"Lulu!" Emma appeared out of the blue, stepping in front of Jake as if to protect him from the slings and arrows that the young goth might fling at him. "Leave him alone!"

Chapter Eight

. . . .

"I am capable of sticking up for myself, you know," Jake told Emma.

But Emma was clearly in fierce protective mode and wasn't about to back down. "I know, but you shouldn't have to."

"Not when I've got a kick-ass sociologist to protect me, huh?"

"I don't know about kick-ass, but Emma is a good listener," Lulu said. "I spilled my guts to her the other day, and she really helped me reach a decision. I had family issues."

"Who doesn't?" Jake said.

"You don't," Lulu said. "Your bio said your parents died when you were a kid and you grew up in the foster care system. It must be depressing not having any family. Although it can also be depressing having some people as family."

As if on cue, a woman walked into the comic-book store

and headed straight for Lulu, who clearly was not pleased to see her.

"What are you doing here?" Lulu demanded.

"I came to see you. Listen, Baby Doll, we need to talk."

"Do *not* call me that," Lulu growled.

"Why not? It's my nickname for you. Don't you remember?"

"I remember you walking out when I was five years old and never coming back," Lulu said.

"I'm back now."

"A decade and a half too late."

Tears welled in the woman's eyes. "Don't say that, Baby Doll."

"Maybe we should leave you two alone—" Emma began.

"Don't you dare." Lulu reached across the counter to grab Emma's arm and hang on to her. "Let me introduce you. This is Zoe Malick. My grandfather's selfish daughter."

"Your mother," Zoe said.

Jake had been watching the goings on with his typical removed attitude. But that name caught his attention. Zoe Malick was on his short list of PBMs—possible birth mothers.

"Right," Lulu scoffed. "A mother who deserted her only child without a word."

Her *only* child? Jake wondered. Or did Zoe have another one, a male baby she gave up for adoption? Him?

"I came back to make it up to you," Zoe said.

Lulu's eyes flashed with anger. "Don't you get that there is *no way* you can make it up to me?"

"I refuse to believe that, Baby Doll."

"Your problem, not mine."

Jake looked from one woman to the other. He could see some resemblances between the two of them. They both had the same upturned nose and similarly shaped eyes. Did he look like them? Hard for him to say since they were both females and he wasn't.

"Why are you being like this?" Zoe asked.

"Me? You're the one . . ." Lulu sputtered, temporarily unable to go on.

"Maybe it would be a good idea if you two got some outside help from a counselor to help you work out some of these very emotional issues," Emma suggested.

"You mean you?" Lulu asked.

"No, I'm not a therapist. I'm a sociologist. I came here today to give you your questionnaire for my research study, Lulu. And to leave one for Algee as well." Since Lulu still had a steely grip on Emma's arm, she reached into her backpack on the floor with her free hand and pulled out two manila envelopes. "I'm only here because of my research study."

"And to defend me," Jake added.

Zoe turned to face him. "Who are you?"

Your son. Maybe. Who knows?

"He's an extreme sports guy who wants me to walk his dog," Lulu said.

"I can walk your dog, Jake," Emma said.

"No way." Lulu released Emma's arm. "He asked me first and I accept."

"But I don't mind doing it—" Emma said.

Lulu interrupted her. "Yeah, well I mind."

Jake recognized Lulu's stubbornness. That was something they shared. That didn't mean they shared the same mother, though. Did it?

He'd been stupid to think that he'd somehow recognize his birth mother when he met her, or that she'd recognize him. A fool to think that there'd be some sort of bond there.

Maybe his birth mother was one of the other women on

the short list and not either of the two he'd met. Not Zoe
and not Nic. Fine by him. Both women seemed to be head
cases. Not exactly Mother of the Year material. Not that
Jake was looking for that. No, he was looking for answers,
and so far he was finding damn few of them.

• • •

"Do you think it's safe to leave the two of them alone in
there?" Emma asked Jake after he'd hauled her out of Cosmic Comics with him.

"I think we should mind our own business."

"Yes, but . . ."

"They don't need our help. And I didn't need you coming to my rescue."

"Fine." She yanked her hand out of his. "I won't make
the same mistake twice."

"Wait a second." He slid his hand down her bare arm to
twine his fingers through hers. "I didn't mean to bite your
head off."

Emma didn't reply because she was too distracted by
his touch. Did he know the effect he had on her? Did he
have this effect on *all* women? Why her? Why touch her?
She wasn't gorgeous or even close to beautiful. On her
best days, which today wasn't, she might be called cute.
On her bad days the description was just plain or nothing
special.

She was wearing jeans and a navy blue T-shirt. Hardly
seductive attire. So what was going on here? Why had she
leapt to his defense in that store? Yes, she had a track record of supporting the underdog, but Jake was hardly your
run-of-the-mill underdog. He wasn't your run-of-the-mill
anything.

Usually Emma was good at figuring out interpersonal
dynamics. But not when they involved her own personal

life. So how had Jake gone from being a sociological study participant to being part of her personal life?

When he kissed you on the fire escape, her inner academic diva replied.

"What do you know about Zoe?" Jake's unexpected question interrupted Emma's self-examination.

"Zoe? Not much."

"Is Lulu her only kid?"

"As far as I know. Why?"

"No reason."

She noticed Jake was looking down when he replied. Did that mean he was hiding something from her? Why should he care about Zoe? And why ask Lulu to care for Mutt instead of asking her?

Emma studied his profile and was again distracted. The man looked good from every angle. But she really didn't have time to stand here drooling over him. She had things to do, places to go, and people to interview. "I've got to go." She tugged free of his hold on her, at least his physical hold. Emma had yet to discover how to free herself from the sensual hold he had on her.

• • •

Emma had scheduled an interview with recently elected Rock Creek mayor Bart Chumley at his home in the Regency Mobile Home Community—formerly known as the trailer park. Her trailer park. Bart had bought it a few years ago when he'd retired after years spent as a circus clown.

Emma heard the familiar sound of classical music as she stepped out of her Prius. Bart sat out on the covered deck of his double-wide trailer with a pitcher of iced tea on the small table beside him. He had the build of a slightly thinner Santa Claus—short and portly. He was also bald, and he appeared to be conducting the music with one hand.

"One of Bach's cello suites, right?" Emma said.

He smiled. "Right. Played by my favorite, Yo-Yo Ma. Are you a fan of Bach?"

"I enjoy various classical composers. Bach, Mozart, Rachmaninoff."

"That's interesting."

"It is? Why?"

"Because the first two are more intellectual, while Rachmaninoff's music is passionate and emotional."

"Yes, well . . ." Emma set her backpack down and removed her laptop. She wasn't here to analyze her tastes in music. "I want to thank you for agreeing to speak with me this afternoon."

"No problem. Would you like some iced tea?"

Emma nodded. His deck was in the shade, but the June day was hot and humid enough to make her hair misbehave even though she'd tried to scrape it back into a ponytail. "Thank you."

After she took a seat across from him, Bart handed her a glass, the ice cubes clinking. "I love talking about my hometown, and I'm very proud of all the changes and improvements we've made over the past year."

"You were elected mayor two months ago, correct?"

"Yes. The changes in town started before then, however."

Emma nodded. "With the renovation of the Tivoli Theater."

"Yes. Since then, we've prettied up the downtown area with whiskey barrels filled with flowers in front of most of the businesses. You may have noticed them?"

"I did. The red, white, and purple petunias are very colorful."

"That was actually your sister Leena's idea, though she'd never admit it. Ditto for the new Rock Creek Community Park just north of town. Leena started that ball rolling by completing a grant application to a nonprofit organization that sets up parks and playgrounds in a weekend with community involvement. Those sisters of yours are real movers and shakers."

"Yes, I know."

"You must all be getting excited about the impending weddings."

"Mmm," Emma said absently as she typed info into her laptop.

"Not everyone in town is as excited about the changes in Rock Creek as we are," Bart said. "Traditionally, the citizens of Rock Creek have had the mindset of ridgerunners—they tend to be suspicious of flatlanders."

Emma grinned. "I haven't heard those terms in a while."

"Have you forgotten what they mean?"

"Not at all. Ridgerunners are born and bred in the hills of northern and central Pennsylvania. Basically everyone else is a flatlander."

"And flatlanders aren't really to be trusted."

"That's not unique to this area," Emma said. "The distrust of outsiders is a universal human social condition unfortunately. Both the Internet and satellite TV have broadened people's horizons in some cases, but there is still a sense of 'us' versus 'them' in many groups."

"Then you've heard that Roy and a bunch of his buddies aren't real happy with the recent changes?"

Emma already knew that Roy wasn't real happy with her, but she had no idea of his views on Rock Creek.

"Rumor has it that you and Roy got into a small confrontation at Nick's Tavern last week," Bart continued. "I hear he's been boycotting the bar ever since and getting his drinks at Buzzy's Liquor Store up by the interstate. He's also increased his complaints about the dangerous path this town is taking. He's not exactly a fan of the arts."

"Then he must not be happy about the Arts and Crafts Drive that Angel Wright has organized. I'm seeing her after I finish our interview."

"Roy and his buddies are not only unhappy, they've filled the direction signs for the drive with buckshot or painted over them. Basically they've done whatever they can to make trouble."

"What is the sheriff doing about it?"

"Everyone knows it's Roy behind the vandalism, but he hasn't been caught at it yet. There's no proof. He was quiet for a while there, but this past week he's been angrier than I've ever seen him."

"That's probably my fault," Emma said, feeling guilty.

"I didn't mean to make you feel bad," Bart said. "I'm a clown. Cheering people up is my specialty."

"Right. Well, getting back to the town, what plans do you have for continuing improvements?"

"We'd like to fill the few vacancies we have in the commercial space downtown. There has already been a huge improvement in that area in the past year to year and a half. You've no doubt seen the new health food store, the Thai restaurant, and the antique mall, among others. We've got a specialty tea shop opening soon. Even the Sisters of the Poor Charity Thrift Shop has received a facelift. Your sister Leena does the window display each month, and the shop has a very successful web presence. Speaking of the Internet, I'd like to see our town's website updated and made more interactive and welcoming. I'd also like to see everyone get involved with the town's future, with our citizens uniting rather than being divided."

"Did you plan on becoming the mayor when you returned to Rock Creek after so many years away?"

"No. But I could see the way the town was going downhill fast and I wanted to do something about it. That's one of the neat things about small towns. One person *can* make a difference. Not that I'm that one person. As I said, your sister has done plenty as have Skye and her mother Angel. I wasn't born to be a leader. I was born to be a clown. But I just happened to be in the right place at the right time to participate in this turnaround for my hometown."

Emma spoke with Bart a bit longer before concluding the interview.

"It's all about taking risks," Angel Wright said an hour later. She and Emma were seated in a screened-in side porch of the farmhouse called Nirvana. "Believe me, I know all about taking risks."

Which got Emma immediately thinking about Jake, the ultimate risk taker. That alone should have been a huge red flag for Emma.

It's not like I want to marry the guy. I just want to have sex with him.

Right. Like you make a habit of having sex with men for the hell of it.

There's always a first time.

Only if you're a risk taker . . . and you're not.

"Most of the risks I took ended in failure," Angel was saying. "There was Friendly Franks, a tofu hot dog stand in Fairbanks, Alaska. But there were too many carnivores up there for that endeavor to be a success. And garlic gelato was the downfall of another business that went bust. But one of my mottos is 'Fall seven times, stand up eight.' It's one of my favorite Chinese proverbs. Or to put it another way: perseverance is failing nineteen times and succeeding on the twentieth. Julie Andrews said that or something very close to it. I'm not the best at quotes. My daughter Julia, the librarian, is great at it." Angel frowned. "Where were we?"

"You were telling me how you started Angel Designs."

"And I was talking about taking chances and not fearing failure."

"My dad is a former Marine so I was raised with the concept that failure is not an option," Emma admitted.

"Oh, but that means that you're afraid of making mistakes and you shouldn't be. Mistakes can be a wonderful learning tool for you. You shouldn't be afraid."

The turn in the conversation left Emma feeling very uneasy. She didn't want to examine her fears. There were way too many of them for her to cope with at the moment. "Yes, well . . . getting back to Angel Designs and how it got started."

"It started with Ricky and Lucy. My two llamas. And then Nicole Kidman wore one of my crocheted designs and suddenly this was a big deal. My handmade scarves and shawls were really in demand. I expanded my collection and hired help. A while later I bought this farm and called it Nirvana. I got more llamas and some alpaca too. I networked with other llama owners as well as other fabric artists and weavers in the area. I have to say I was surprised at how many of them were located around here. I guess there's something about mountains that makes artists gravitate toward them. PA actually already has several artisan trails, along Route 6 and Route 15. And now we've got a talented and enthusiastic group starting here in Rock Creek. We've got artisans who do everything from photography to watercolor painting, from furniture making and leatherworks to glassblowing. It really is amazing."

"How many artisans do you have in the area?"

"Between forty and fifty and that's been in the relatively short period of time of the past year or year and a half. Of course, a number of them are people I know or have interacted with over the years. Gary the glassblower used to visit my gelato store in Seattle. Artisans are often good networkers with each other."

"A majority of them have agreed to participate in my research study and complete my questionnaire."

"They're good people, although you know, artists aren't into questionnaires," Angel warned her. "We don't do simple yes or no questions that well."

"I have plenty of space for additional comments."

"And I'm sure you'll get plenty. I suppose you've heard that not everyone is as enthusiastic about the addition of artisans to this area as you are."

"Yes, but they're not the majority."

"They don't have to be. They only need to use fear and intimidation to get their way."

"Have you received any threats?"

"Not directly, no. My significant other, Tyler, would scare off anyone who tried to come here to make trouble. But they don't have to step foot on Nirvana to create chaos. An organization called Americans for Rock Creek has put flyers on parked cars in town, saying that weirdos aren't welcome here, that we should all go back where we came from."

"I'm sorry to hear that."

"Yeah, so am I. They are creating bad karma for themselves when they wish ill on others."

Emma doubted that Roy and his group were worried about their karma.

• • •

"That was Mom." Emma closed her cell phone. They'd made it to Thursday, forty-eight hours before Sue Ellen's wedding, without any major family meltdowns. "She said she'd be a little late and we should wait for her before we start our spa experience."

"What can you say about a place called the Ritzee Day Spa?" Leena looked around, wrinkling her nose at the salmon and lime green paisley wallpaper that overpowered the tiny waiting area.

"They have coupons," Sue Ellen said. "Special discount

coupons for their grand opening this week. That's why Mom picked this spa."

"Which should have been our first red flag," Leena said.

Emma defended Maxie. "That's not fair. Mom is trying to do something nice for us before the wedding."

Leena shook her head. "There's always trouble when Mom tries to do something nice. Do you remember the Christmas that she put reindeer antlers on the roof of that green Pinto we used to have?"

"They weren't real reindeer antlers," Sue Ellen said. "She sewed them herself. And made the big fuzzy red nose on the hood."

"And drove us to school in the Christmas-mobile." Emma shuddered at the memory.

"Have you seen Sue Ellen's car?" Leena asked Emma. "The pink Batmobile isn't much better."

"At least it doesn't have antlers," Sue Ellen said, thumbing through an *In Style* magazine. "I saw on the Internet that there was a big fashion show in China where all the dresses were made out of condoms. Did you hear about that, Leena?"

"No."

"But that's your specialty."

"Condoms?"

"No, fashion."

Emma inserted herself into the conversation. "Just so you both know, I love you guys, but I am not wearing a condom dress for any of your events."

Sue Ellen tossed the magazine aside and focused her attention on Emma. "Change of subject. What were you and Jake doing before we came to your studio apartment last week?"

Emma felt her face go red. "Nothing."

"Did he kiss you? He did!" Sue Ellen said triumphantly.

"I can tell by the look on your face. Come on, dish. We want all the details. Where did he kiss you? Cheek? Lips? Chaste? French? Good? Bad?"

Emma tried not to look as mortified as she felt. "I am not discussing this when our mother could walk in any second."

"Why not?" Maxie demanded as she joined them. "Do you think I don't know about kissing and sex? Your father and I—"

Sue Ellen and Leena put their fingers over their ears and started saying, "La, la, la."

Emma couldn't help herself. She joined them. "La, la, la."

"What a bunch of prudes." Maxie shook her head. "Come on, let's get this spa stuff going."

Fifteen minutes later the four of them were seated in chairs getting their manicures done. "Emma, I bet Leena you'd get a French manicure," Sue Ellen said. "No bright colors for you."

"The bridesmaid's dress is bright enough," Emma said.

"And that florescent flamingo polish I showed you would have matched just fine," Sue Ellen said.

Emma scrunched her face in disapproval. "I don't want my nails to glow in the dark."

"Emma likes French stuff," Sue Ellen said. "French wine, French chocolates, French kisses."

"I hope you're not giving away the milk for free, Emma," Maxie said. "You're never going to catch a man that way."

"I'm not trying to catch a man," Emma said.

"Well, that's obvious by the way you dress. And your hair." Maxie did an eye roll. "If you'd just let me help you."

"With friends like you who needs enemies?" Emma muttered.

Maxie frowned. "What, hon? I can't understand you when you mumble like that. It's not attractive."

"I'll tell you what's not attractive," Emma said. "Those Pepto-Bismol bridesmaids' dresses. I'm going to look ridiculous."

"You're exaggerating. Tell her she's exaggerating," Maxie instructed her manicurist, who ignored them and focused on her job.

"I dreamt last night that someone stole the dress," Emma said.

"Who'd want it?" Leena said.

"Hey, at least it's not made out of condoms. Change of subject," Sue Ellen declared with a wave of her hand. "Oops, sorry about that," she told her manicurist as her nail polish smeared. "New topic. Did I tell you that Dad is going to walk me down the aisle? I need a strong arm to hang on to in case I feel faint or something. I faint a lot," Sue Ellen told the manicurist, who was looking more panicked by the second. "Not right here, not right now. Probably. Anyway, Dad seemed okay with the idea."

"Okay? He was thrilled, I tell you. Absolutely thrilled," Maxie claimed.

Sue Ellen wasn't buying that. "Yeah, right. I could tell that by the way he said okay and then went right back to watching his ball game."

Maxie defended him. "You know how your father is about expressing his emotions."

"Yeah, I know. He doesn't express them at all."

"He's not into all this girlie stuff like weddings and emotions," Maxie said.

"Maybe we should have invited Dad along to get his nails buffed." After making the suggestion, Sue Ellen giggled so hard she snorted, which got them all laughing so hard tears came to their eyes.

And they couldn't wipe them away, because of their just completed manicures.

Emma loved moments like this. It had been a long time since they'd had a group gigglefest. She missed having her entire family close by.

True, they could and often did drive her nuts, but they shared a special bond that couldn't be duplicated. This was why she was willing to wear the nightmare pink dress for Sue Ellen. Because she was her sister.

• • •

Emma tried to remind herself of those reasons two days later on Sue Ellen's wedding day as she stared into the full-length mirror at her reflection. "I hate you," she told Leena, who stood behind her. "How can you look good in something this awful?"

"It takes years of training," Leena said. "Trust me, I've modeled in worse."

"I find that hard to believe," Emma muttered. "Maybe if I took the stupid sleeves off . . . and removed the butt bow . . ."

"There's no time. We have to get Sue Ellen out of the bathroom and into her wedding dress."

"Maybe she should have put the dress on first."

"She was afraid she'd throw up on it."

"I thought the morning sickness was doing better."

"It is. She also had to pee, for the tenth time in the past fifteen minutes. Do you know how hard it is to pee wearing a wedding dress?"

"No, and I'm not real eager to find out," Emma said. This was her first time as a bridesmaid, and it was turning out to be more complicated by the second.

Their mother joined them to wail, "I look like I've got the measles!"

"You look fine." Emma patted her mom on the back, careful not to dislodge any of the colorful silk butterflies Maxie had strewn in her upswept hair.

Leena showed no sympathy. "I told you not to try a facial with new products right before the wedding."

"Where's your sister?" Maxie demanded. "Where's the bride? She's not leaving Donny at the altar, is she? You girls are going to be the death of me yet!"

Sue Ellen stepped out of the bathroom. "Let's get this show on the road."

"You need a dress unless you plan on getting married in your slip," Emma said.

"Right."

"Don't mess up her hair," Maxie warned them. "It took me two hours to get those silk birds placed in those curls just right."

Somehow, someway they were able to get Sue Ellen put together. She looked lovely in the elegant white satin princess-style dress with the full bustle skirt.

Leena consulted her list. "Something old? Mom's pearls. Something new? Pearl earrings from Donny. Something borrowed? Gold bracelet from Donny's mom. Something blue? The garter belt from me. Check, check, check. Okay, I say we're ready to go."

"Wait." Emma handed Sue Ellen her bouquet of pink and white roses. "Now we're ready."

Chapter Nine

. . . .

Fellow bridesmaids Skye and Lulu were waiting for them in the Tivoli Theater's lobby. Like Leena, they made the ugly bridesmaid's dress work for them. Lulu cheated by chopping off the billowing sleeves. Emma wished she'd thought of that. Unfortunately it was too late to rip them off now.

"Father of the bride, reporting for duty," Bob Riley said.

Emma had to admit that her dad looked great in his blue Marine dress uniform even though it was decades old. She was surprised it still fit, but their mom had admitted that he'd been watching his weight for the past six months just in case he would be "called upon."

This was it. The time had come. Emma was eager to get things started . . . until someone opened the door to the theater auditorium and she saw the crowd inside.

Had every man, woman, and child in Rock Creek come here today? There had to be at least three hundred people here. And the aisle looked as long as ten football fields. Panic, panic, panic.

Stay calm. Remember you spoke to a large crowd at that conference for sociologists, her inner academic diva reassured her.

Not wearing pink ruffles and butt bows, her inner geek pointed out.

Emma didn't even realize she'd done an about-face until Skye said, "The wedding is that way," and turned her back around.

"No deserters," her dad ordered. "Get a move on up there."

Leena had already started her walk with Donny's best man. But Donny didn't have as many groomsmen as Sue Ellen had bridesmaids so the remaining three of them were supposed to walk alone.

Which was normally fine by Emma. She didn't need a man's arm to lean on. She could stand on her own two feet.

She just couldn't seem to *walk* on them at this precise moment.

"Come on." Lulu came to her rescue, hooking her arm with Emma's and tugging her through the door and marching her down the aisle.

The next few minutes were a blur for Emma. Certain things stood out, like the reverberations of the theater's vintage organ playing the "Wedding March" and the fact that she didn't trip walking up the steps to the stage where the ceremony was going to take place. None of it seemed real. The rehearsal the night before had gone so smoothly that Emma hadn't expected that moment of panic at the size of the crowd.

She thought she caught a glimpse of Roy in the back row but couldn't be sure. She wasn't wearing her glasses for the ceremony. Maybe she needed those reading glasses more than she'd realized.

Why would Roy attend Sue Ellen's wedding? If he thought he could grab Emma's butt again as she walked back down the aisle, he was very mistaken. No, surely Roy wouldn't try something like that. Not with her dad, the former Marine, present.

So what was Roy doing there?

Maybe it wasn't even him. She shouldn't be thinking about him during the wedding ceremony. She should focus on positive things like Cheetos, Dr Pepper, and Jake. Was he out there somewhere too?

She'd asked him to meet her at the Serenity Falls Country Club for the reception instead of coming here for the wedding itself. But Jake wasn't real good at obeying orders. Not that she'd ordered him per se. She wasn't bossy, not when compared to her sisters.

It didn't take long before the minister said, "You may kiss the bride."

Donny did and the crowd applauded, hooting their approval. Then it was time to do the "bow-butt walking" thing back down the endless aisle. This time Emma accomplished it without Lulu's assistance.

I am kick-ass sociologist, hear me roar.

Before Emma could savor her newfound confidence, Sue Ellen grabbed her by the arm and frantically whispered, "Help me, I've gotta pee!"

At which time Emma reached the conclusion that while sociologists might rock, this bridesmaid stuff sucked.

• • •

Jake parked in the Serenity Falls Country Club parking lot and walked into the stately brick building. He wasn't a country-club kind of guy, but this one looked pretty much the way he'd expected. The place was packed with lots of people hanging around the lobby, dressed up in their wedding duds. He automatically reached up to make sure he'd put on a tie. Suits weren't his thing so he had to make do with a new pair of black pants, a black shirt, and a burgundy tie that was already choking him. Hopefully people would think that he'd ditched a jacket because of the unusually warm weather. Not that Jake normally cared what anyone else thought. But he didn't want to embarrass Emma.

Several strategically placed signs listed the various wedding receptions. He finally found the one for the "Riley-Smiley reception" and set out to find the Crystal Room. A nun greeted him at the door. "Welcome. And you are?"

"Jake Slayter."

"Right. Well, there is no formal reception greeting line so come on in. The bar is in that direction." She pointed to her right.

"Do you know where Emma Riley is?"

"I saw her around a short while ago, but it's hard to keep track of everyone. I'm sorry. I should have introduced myself. I'm Sister Mary." She held out her hand for a surprisingly tough handshake.

Jake knew who she was. One of his possible maternal candidates, Nancy Crumpler, was the nun's sibling.

"You're the extreme sports guy. I'm sorry but I don't know much about that subject," Sister Mary admitted. "I'm more into field hockey. I broke my leg three years ago in the regional championships. Those nuns from Sacred Heart are sore losers." She shook her head. "As for professional sports, I am a bit of a gearhead. That's NASCAR, you know."

"Right." If Nancy Crumpler turned out to be his birth mother, that would mean this nun would be his aunt. Jake thought he could live with that—a nun who was a gear-head. Awesome.

"You shouldn't hog time with our guest of honor." An older man joined them, directing his reprimand at Sister Mary.

"The bride and groom are the guests of honor," Sister Mary said.

"Sure. Whatever. I don't think we've been formally introduced," the man said. "I'm Walt Whitman, mayor of Serenity Falls. No relation to the famous poet. I wonder if I could have a moment of your time to speak to you about a matter of importance to us both."

"Certainly," Sister Mary said. "I'm always available for those in need of spiritual consultation."

"I was speaking to Jake." The man tugged Jake aside. "We're not so dissimilar, you and me."

"Really?" Looking at the older guy with the receding hairline and definite paunch, Jake didn't see any similarities.

"I've got an interest in extreme golfing."

"Extreme golfing? You're kidding, right?"

"Not at all. I'm surprised a man like you isn't more familiar with extreme golfing. Fearless golfers going to exotic locales to play the game."

Jake just shrugged. "That's not my thing."

"Yes, well, extreme sports are your thing and word has it that you're planning on building a resort of some kind in the area. I wanted to point out that Serenity Falls would be a much better location for such a venue than Rock Creek."

"Oh? Why's that?"

"Because we're one of America's Best Small Towns. I don't know if you're aware of that fact. Thousands of towns vie for the highly coveted title. And they don't make it. We did." The guy puffed his chest out, reminding Jake of a penguin. "And that's not all," Walt continued. "Maguire's here in town is a nominee in *Central PA* magazine's Readers' Choice awards for best restaurant. Their sweet potato fries are the best in the world. Adele has a secret recipe. She's a co-owner of the pub and married to our town sheriff. Not that you'd care about that, and I'm certainly not one to gossip. Anyway, I'm telling you the fries are not to be missed."

"I'll have to try them sometime."

"I can take you over there right now," Walt said eagerly.

"I'm kind of in the middle of something here," Jake pointed out. "A wedding reception."

"Yes, but it's not like you've known the bride a long time, have you?"

"No, but—"

"Then I'm sure they wouldn't mind if you left early."

"I think my date would mind," Jake said.

"Bring her along with you."

"She's part of the bridal party. The bride's sister."

"Leena?" Walt frowned. "I thought she was engaged to the veterinarian and getting married in two weeks."

"No, I meant Emma."

"Oh, the other sister. She's supposed to be the smart one, isn't she?"

"So I hear."

"You don't know? You don't think she's smart?"

"You don't think I'm smart?" Emma said from behind him.

Jake turned to face her. "That's not what I said."

"I was trying to tell your friend here how great the sweet potato fries are over at Maguire's."

"They are wonderful," Emma agreed.

"Walt wanted me to dump you and go with him right now to get some fries."

"Well, I wouldn't put it like that exactly," Walt said, turning red.

"Walt, are you making trouble again?" The woman who just joined them made the mocking comment.

Emma introduced him. "Jake, this is Nancy Crumpler, the owner of Crumpler's Auto Parts."

Also known as possible birth mother—PBM—number three.

"Nice to meet you," Jake said.

"So you're the extreme sports guy."

"Right. Are you a gearhead like your sister?"

Stupid, Slayter. Dumb question. But he was surprisingly nervous.

"How did you know that about my sister?"

"She told me a few minutes ago when I met her."

"Well, it's true. I'm more of a gearhead than she is."

"Is that why you got into the auto parts business?"

Nancy laughed. "No, that's because my fourth husband left it to me when he died and went to that great racetrack in the sky."

He knew Nancy had been married several times and had two kids by her second marriage. They were in their twenties now and had moved out of state.

"So it was just a lucky break. Not that my husband died, but that I got the auto parts store," Nancy clarified. "Are you a NASCAR fan, Jake?"

"I've seen a few races on TV." And he'd driven a Formula One race car around a track in Europe, but that didn't make him an expert at NASCAR.

"I can fill you in. Just stop by the store sometime. Uh-oh, I've got to go. Come with me, Walt."

Walt protested. "But I'm not done talking with Jake."

"Yes, you are." Nancy was adamant. "Leave him be. Can't you see that he and Emma want some time alone?"

Walt looked around in confusion. "But this room is packed with people."

"Don't you remember what it's like to be young?" Nancy took hold of Walt's arm. "Come along now. Don't make me get tough with you."

Walt reluctantly went with her, calling back to Jake, "We'll talk more later."

Emma took a page out of Nancy's book and took hold of Jake's arm. "Okay, I can't stand it another second." She tugged him into the back corner of the ballroom. "I can't wait any longer."

His wicked grin should have warned her what was to come. "Just say the word and we're outta here."

Emma frowned. "Why do we have to go somewhere else?"

"Fine by me." He lowered his head.

She put her hand on his chest. "Are you trying to kiss me?"

"You said you didn't want to wait."

"For your answer about participating in my research study. You said that if I invited you to the wedding, you'd agree."

"I said I'd *think* about it."

"That's not good enough." She snared a glass of champagne from a waiter's tray as he walked by and downed half of it in one gulp. "I am wearing the most atrocious dress on the planet and I need to hear some good news. Right now. So no more jerking me around, buster." She stabbed him in the chest with her French-manicured finger.

Jake raised an eyebrow. "Buster?"

"Just answer the question. Yes or no?"

"What's your hurry?"

"I thought extreme sports guys were into speed."

He traced his thumb along her lower lip. "Some things are better when you go slow."

"It would only take fifteen minutes of your time."

"What I have in mind would take much longer."

"Get your mind out of the gutter and say yes."

He laughed. "That's got to be the strangest invitation I've had in a long time."

"I am only inviting you to participate in my academic study regarding Rock Creek," she said succinctly. "Yes or no?"

"Okay, fine."

"Is that a yes?"

"Sure."

"Great." She hauled him out of the ballroom and down the hallway toward the main entrance.

"Are we going to celebrate now?" Jake asked hopefully.

"I stashed my bag in the coatroom . . ." Emma pulled him inside. Since it was in the high eighties outside, with matching humidity, the room was empty of coats, but there were a few tote bags. She dug around in one with UNIVERSITY OF PENNSYLVANIA printed on the side and yanked out several pages. "Here's your questionnaire on a clipboard so it's easy for you to fill out. And a pen. Look, there's a chair right over there. I'll leave you alone to complete the forms."

"Why can't you stay with me? What if I have questions?"

"I'll be right outside. The sooner you get started, the sooner you'll be done."

"Why this sudden need for speed?"

"I'm not having a real good day. I don't think I'm really cut out for this bridesmaid's job. But forget about that. Just concentrate on the questionnaire, please."

"This isn't your first time as a bridesmaid, is it?"

"What if it is?" She put her hands on her hips and glared at him.

"Sorry. Forget I asked." He picked up the pen and focused his attention on her clipboard instead of her cleavage. That dress was a monstrosity, but it did show off her breasts in a way that made him want to see more.

Emma stood outside the cloakroom and tried to regain some semblance of calm. Several latecomers greeted her as they walked by. One said, "Do you realize that if your sister hyphenates her name, she'll be Sue Ellen Riley-Smiley?"

"I hadn't really thought about it," Emma admitted. Did that make her a bad bridesmaid? A bad sister? Or both? No. No way. She was an exceptional sister and bridesmaid. She was wearing this awful dress and she'd helped Sue Ellen deal with a wedding dress that seemed bigger than a circus tent so that her sister could take a bathroom break. Several bathroom breaks. And the night was still young.

Emma hadn't considered the fact that Jake would see her in this mockery of a dress. Well, it was too late to worry about that now. She needed to focus on the positive, which was that he was filling out her questionnaire. That was a big thing. A huge thing.

"What are you doing out here, Sweet Pea?" her dad asked as he joined her. "Waiting for someone?"

"Jake."

"Is he late? It's not polite to make a young woman wait."

Hoping to distract him, Emma said, "You look great in your uniform."

"Marines have the best uniforms on the planet. I'm proud to have been a jarhead."

Are you proud to be a dad? she wondered. Despite the glass of champagne she'd consumed, she didn't have the nerve to actually voice the question. Instead she said, "Did you enjoy walking down the aisle with Sue Ellen?"

"It was okay. Having all those people staring at me was

a little nerve-wracking. Your mom is the people person, not me."

"Right."

"Well, speaking of your mom, I better get back to the reception. They're getting ready to serve the food. Donny certainly didn't spare any expense in footing the bill for this shindig. They've got steak and salmon. Good thing all those people at the church didn't come to the reception or Donny would be broke."

"Well, don't let me keep you, Dad. You don't want Mom to get upset."

"Right. And you'd better get back to the head table with the other bridesmaids."

"I'll be there real soon," Emma promised. Unless she made a break for it. The front door was only a few feet away and it was so tempting. Her dad was far enough away that he'd never see her leave . . .

"Thinking of making a run for it?" Jake asked.

"Of course not," she lied. She never used to lie. And this wasn't the first time she hadn't told the truth around Jake. What was it about him that brought out the hidden liar in her? That couldn't be a good thing.

He sure looked good though. He wasn't wearing a suit, but that didn't matter. His wow factor seemed to increase each time she saw him. And now she couldn't even sit with him because she had to be at the head table.

"I put your stuff back in your tote bag," Jake said.

"You completed the questionnaire?"

"Yeah." He tilted his head toward the front entrance. "So which is it going to be? Stay or leave?"

Emma sighed. "I have to stay. But if you want to leave . . ."

"I'm not going without you," he said.

"It could be a long night," she warned him.

"You're worth waiting for."

His husky words stayed with her throughout the evening, through the toasts, through the dancing, which she avoided. Finally the crowd started thinning out and Emma felt she could make her escape. She giggled as Jake hustled her out in a hurry. He led her to a black Jeep Grand Cherokee and helped her into the front seat. The champagne was making her world swim a little. Or was Jake responsible for that?

As they left Serenity Falls, she pointed to a sign on the side of the road. "The waterfalls that this town is named after are up that road. I used to skinny-dip there when I was in high school. You should visit the falls sometime."

Jake took the turnoff.

"What are you doing?"

"You said I should visit the falls. No time like the present."

She'd had just enough champagne that she couldn't find a logical argument to his comment. Or maybe she just didn't feel like voicing a protest. Twenty minutes later he stopped the Jeep inches from the chain barricading the entrance. Jake hopped out and undid the chain with the confidence of a man who'd done this before.

"The park is closed," Emma said.

"Not anymore."

He parked the Jeep in the space closest to the falls and the river it tumbled into.

"I haven't been up here in years." Emma knew she was breaking the rules. But what harm could be done by a quick midnight visit to one of her favorite old haunts? After all, skinny-dipping was hardly one of the approved uses for this area. So she already had a track record here. Her dyed-to-match pumps sank into the grass as she walked downriver to an area where a section of the water pooled off to the side creating a cool invitation on a hot night. "I used to dive in right here. It's deep enough with a sandy bottom."

Emma looked over her shoulder, hard to do with the huge bulbous sleeves on her bridesmaid's dress, to see if Jake had followed her. Not only had he done so, but he was also taking off his tie and then his shirt.

"What are you doing?"

"Getting ready to skinny-dip," he said.

"Now?"

"Right now." He kicked off his shoes and unbuttoned his pants.

She should have looked away. She really should have. A wiser woman would have.

But apparently Emma wasn't as smart as she thought, because she didn't turn away.

Of course it was dark and he was a few feet away. Not far enough, however, that she couldn't see how incredibly well-built he was. She'd already seen him across the narrow alley, but this was much more intimate. She tried to keep her eyes on his face or the waterfall in the distance, but that took more willpower than she possessed because her wayward eyes kept wandering back to his muscular chest and narrow waist and . . .

Her gaze skittered way down. He had nice feet. His body wasn't too hairy, which was a good thing. Okay, every inch of him was a good thing. Great, in fact. Awesome. Worrisome. Troublesome.

Jake was deliberately trying to get to her and he was succeeding.

"Enjoying the show?" he asked as he had before on her fire escape. He had his fingers hooked in his black briefs, ready to peel them off.

Emma's mouth went dry. Did she want him to stop or continue? While she was silently pondering that question, Jake went ahead and stripped before turning his back on her and diving into the water. She couldn't help but appreciate his fine backside. Which was how she got soaked with the splash he made when he hit the water.

"Come on in, the water's fine," he said. "Come on, I dare you."

She really shouldn't have had that third glass of champagne. Or was it her fourth? Because it gave her just enough Dutch courage to take him up on his dare. She stood behind a large bush nearby, kicked off her shoes, rolled off her pantyhose, and removed the horrible dress.

Should she keep her bra and panties on? Absolutely. She slipped into the water several feet away from him, partially protected by the branches of the greenery. She prayed she hadn't come into contact with any poison ivy.

Instead she came into contact with Jake. A naked Jake. Up close and very personal. He was treading water with the devil in his eyes. She was treading water in every way possible.

When he moved closer she lost her concentration and went under. He pulled her back up. Somehow her hands were gripping his shoulders and her legs were wrapped around his waist. Which put her into direct contact with his naked private parts. Her silky wet underwear provided little protection.

She instantly released him and went under again.

Again he pulled her back up. "I thought you said you skinny-dipped here before?"

"Not with a naked man."

He was pleased with this news. "So I'm your first, huh?"

"Is that a gun in your pocket or are you just glad to see me?"

"Oh, I'm very glad to see you." He moved closer to shore so he could stand on the sandy river bottom. "Can't you tell?" He rocked against her.

Emma tried to stand on her own, but he was taller than

she was so the water here was still too deep for her. Which he knew. He studied her closely. "Scared?"

"I should be," she muttered.

"I'm not going to mug you."

"I know that."

"I might seduce you, though."

"You can try," she countered, aggravated by his confidence. Of course, she was hanging on to him like a limpet. A limpet ready to mate. Did limpets mate? "You can let me go now. I'm ready. Ready to get out, I mean."

"I like you this way. I like the nude you."

"I'm not nude."

"Honey, trust me, you're as good as nude."

"You can't see me. It's too dark."

"I have excellent night vision."

"You do?" Glancing down, she realized the water had made her bra transparent. She broke away from him and swam closer to the shore.

Jake followed her.

"You stay right there," she ordered. "I'm getting out now and I need you to look away."

"Why would I want to do that?"

"Because I asked you to."

"And?"

"And it's the polite thing to do."

"Honey, I've never been known for being polite."

Okay, he was getting that dangerous look again. Not I'm-gonna-hurt-you dangerous. Temptation dangerous. We're-gonna-have-sex dangerous. And it's going to rock your world. Set it on fire. Light up the sky . . .

Wait. The sky really *did* light up. Lightning. "There's a storm coming," she said.

"That's one way to put it." He snared her in his arms.

"No, really. Look." She pointed, which lifted one breast from beneath the water.

"I'm looking," he assured her.

The heat in his voice let her know he wasn't staring at the impending storm.

Growling her impatience, she dunked him and then stalked out of the water. Okay, maybe it was more like scrambling, but she grabbed her dress and shoes and hightailed it back to the Jeep as thunder shook the vehicle's windows.

This is where planning ahead would have been a good thing. Her dress was wet and putting it back on would be difficult at best. And what was Jake going to wear? He wasn't going to drive the Jeep in the nude was he? He certainly was still naked as he confidently strode toward her, holding his clothes on his lap once he hopped into the Jeep.

"That was fun," he said, shaking his wet hair like a puppy.

"What now?" she asked.

A flash of lightning lit his wickedly wolfish grin.

"That's not what I meant," she said.

"What? I didn't say a word."

"You didn't have to. Your look said it all."

"Oh yeah?" He leaned closer. "What did it say?"

Instead of answering she reminded him, "I was asking about dry clothes."

"I probably have something in the back." He reached around, nearly dislodging the clothes hiding his privates from her view. "Here." He tossed a T-shirt at her. At her distrustful look, he added, "It's clean. Pretty much."

Emma didn't have much choice here. She tugged the T-shirt over her head, hiding her wet bra. "Stop looking at me as if you're judging me in a wet T-shirt contest."

"I've judged more than my fair share of those contests."

"I'm sure you have," she muttered.

"And you'd do quite well in that department. Just something to keep in mind in case this sociology gig doesn't work out for you."

"How reassuring. I'll be sure to keep that in mind as an optional career choice," she said tartly. "I think you need to get dressed and we should leave before you say something else that will get you in trouble and before this storm gets even worse."

Before Jake could reply, a bolt of lightning struck a huge oak tree nearby—severing it in half amid a fiery shower of sparks. The ground shook as part of the tree fell to the ground, blocking their exit from the parking lot.

Chapter Ten

. . . .

"**See?** That's what happens when you break the rules." Emma's voice was shaky. "You almost get struck by lightning."

Jake couldn't hear her because of the deafening noise of hailstones hitting the roof. Instead of looking concerned, he looked excited.

"Cool, huh?" he shouted over the din.

"Just peachy."

"What did you say?"

"Did you know that PA leads the U.S. in lightning damage?" Emma recited useless trivia in times of extreme stress.

Jake showed no such stress. "Awesome."

"How are we going to get out of here?" she yelled.

"Doesn't look like we are. At least not until daylight."

"No, that's not acceptable."

"Mother Nature says otherwise. No worries. I've got a

sleeping bag in the back, and there's enough room to lie down."

"No worries?" The hail didn't let up so Emma raised her voice even louder. "No worries?!"

"You're not afraid of storms, are you?"

The hail stopped as suddenly as it started. "Not unless I'm out in one and almost hit by lightning."

"Come on, that's an exaggeration. It wasn't that close."

"That's as close as I care to get."

Jake reached out to trace one finger over her mouth. "Are you sure about that? Getting closer sounds like a good idea. You seemed to enjoy our . . . closeness when we were skinny-dipping."

"That was an error in judgment."

"Have a lot of those, do you?"

"Very rarely."

"Yeah, I had that feeling."

The hail was replaced by a heavy downpour that beat almost as loudly on the roof. Leaning forward, she peered through the windshield. A flash of lightning revealed the thrashing branches as the wind picked up, forcing the rain sideways.

"Hey." Jake tapped her gently before slinging an arm around her shoulders. "Are you having fun yet?"

She remained silent.

"Maybe we need some music." He hit a button and the song "Over My Head" by the Fray blasted through the Jeep's interior. Emma had always liked the song and had it on her iPod, so she instinctively started swaying to the song and mouthing the words as she did when listening alone. Next up was "Is It Any Wonder?" by Keane.

Before Emma knew it she was jiving with Jake as they sat in their seats and moved to the music, singing along and grinning at each other like a pair of idiots. Which she supposed they must be to be acting like this.

But oh what fun it was—despite the storm raging around them, despite everything. Emma's damp hair slapped against her cheek as she rocked back and forth to Keane's sharp guitar riff. In her own version of do-it-yourself karaoke, she sang into her clenched fist as if it were a microphone. Jake leaned closer, singing into her fist · along with her.

Suddenly she was aware of his lips moving over her hand as he sang. She felt goose bumps rise on the entire length of her arm. The music stopped just as she pulled her hand away from the temptation of his mouth and dislodged his arm from her shoulders.

Jake laughed. "You look so cute when you're getting down with your bad self."

"Are you making fun of me?"

"I'm complimenting you."

Which made her uncomfortable because she found it hard to really believe him. Men usually complimented her on her brains not on her looks or on the fact that her breasts would win a wet T-shirt contest.

Feeling awkward, she tried to change the subject to something less personal. "So what do you think about the waterfall? I'm sure you've seen bigger and more impressive ones, right?"

"Are we just talking about the falls now? This isn't some code for your breasts, is it? That I've seen bigger and more impressive ones?"

"No, it's not code and forget I asked." So much for finding a less personal topic of conversation.

"The falls have made quite an impression on me."

"They have?"

Jake nodded. "The entire area has. You've gotta love a place with names like Goblers Knob."

"And Gobsmacked Knob."

"You made that up."

She laughed. "No really, it's just south of Rock Creek and about a thousand feet up. But then you've seen the most famous mountains in the world, right?"

"Right."

"Which are your favorites?"

"Well, I've got a log cabin up in Stanley, Idaho, with a rippin' view of the Sawtooth Mountains. Stanley—now there's a small town. The year-round population is only about a hundred people."

"That makes Rock Creek sound like a big place."

"Last time I visited Stanley, there was no Thai restaurant."

"The last time I visited Rock Creek, there was no Thai restaurant here either. But I'm glad it's here now. I think I'm getting addicted to their spring rolls."

"Another addiction to go along with your Dr Pepper and Cheetos, huh?"

"I don't eat junk food all the time. I'll have you know that I eat a healthy breakfast of yogurt, almonds, and fresh fruit most days."

"So the Cheetos are your walk on the wild side?" he mocked her.

"I've also been known to eat M&Ms accompanied by a nice Merlot," she confessed.

"I'm seeing an entirely new side of you tonight."

"I'm sure you are." She tried to tug the T-shirt further down around her thighs. "You were watching me when you shouldn't have. A gentleman would have looked away."

"I never claimed to be gentleman so you shouldn't have been surprised."

Emma saw the conversation heading onto dangerous ground and knew it was time to change the subject. She was stuck in the storm with him, which made it the perfect time . . . to have sex with him.

Whoa! That was hardly a change of subject. Had she

lost control of her own thoughts? Had her rational self left the building entirely? Had the champagne turned her into mush?

No, she refused to believe that. She could be rational. And her rational self said this was the perfect time for Jake to tell her more about himself. Maybe that would prevent him from seducing her.

"What do extreme sports guys actually do?" she said.

"Besides make out with hot babes in Jeeps?"

"Yes, besides that."

"I tend the bar at Nick's Tavern."

"I mean before you came to Rock Creek."

"You were there. You heard what Lulu said in the comic-book store. That I'm an extreme sports guy who's lost my nerve."

"I find that hard to believe. But if you don't want to talk about your work, that's fine."

"It's not work. It's more like . . . I don't know. What I was born to do. Like a calling. Or an addiction."

"Sounds like it could be a dangerous addiction."

"If you don't know what you're doing, maybe. But I do know what I'm doing, and I've been doing it most of my life. I started out on a snowboard when I was four and my parents were still alive. Snowboarding is where I first made a name for myself when I was older. Then I did some mountain biking and became a crossover athlete in all kinds of mountain adventures—everything from climbing to hang gliding to heli-skiing."

"Is that where you helicopter into a pristine area and then ski?"

"That's right. What can I say? I'm a sucker for pristine areas." He trailed his finger around the neckline of her, formerly *his*, T-shirt.

She tugged his hand away before she became too tempted to let him continue his seductive teasing.

"Why is it so hard for you to be serious?" she said in exasperation.

"If you don't think I'm serious, I must be doing something wrong," he drawled in that darkly hot way of his.

"You're not doing anything wrong—" Emma snapped her mouth shut.

"That's always good to hear." She couldn't see his smile in the dark, but she could hear it.

"Right. Like you don't already know what a hottie you are." Damn, there was another mistake she was going to blame on the champagne.

"A hottie, huh?"

"Puh-lease. Don't act surprised. You already know you're sexy."

"So you think I'm sexy?"

"*Everyone* thinks you're sexy."

"I'm only interested in you."

"At this second maybe. But how long would that last?"

"Would what last?"

"You being interested in me."

"Why do you find that so hard to believe?"

"Because you're you and I'm me."

"And?"

"And you like traveling at warp speed and I prefer a slower pace."

"Warp speed? You make me sound like some kind of *Star Wars* geek."

"Hey, a lot of the guys I know are *Star Wars* geeks."

"Then it's definitely time to move outside your comfort zone and try something different."

"I'm not into different."

"How about trying something better?" He started nibbling on her neck, working his way to her parted lips. They were only parted because she was about to tell him off.

Instead she kissed him back, which showed a lack of

self-discipline on her part that she was sure to find appalling by morning. But for now she allowed herself to enjoy the feel of his mouth covering hers, of his hands covering her breasts . . . hold on a second. How had he gotten his hands under her T-shirt so fast?

She pushed him away. "You are *not* seducing me tonight."

"Okay. How about tomorrow night?"

"No."

"How about *you* seduce *me* tonight?"

His suggestion took her breath away.

"Hah." He pointed at her. "You're interested in that, I can tell. Go ahead." He shoved his seat back so it was horizontal. "Seduce me."

"Forget it." There was no forgetting that the pile of his clothing was precariously perched on his privates.

"Come on. You know you want to."

"You are still naked."

"Which makes it easier for you to seduce me, right?"

"No, it's harder—"

"Yeah, it is," he interrupted her. "Can't get much harder without doing some damage."

"I wasn't talking about that."

"I'm not big on talking either. Actions speak louder than words." He grabbed her hand and placed it on his bare chest. "Go right ahead, take action and check things out."

"I am not checking your things out!"

His laughter dislodged her hand before she snatched it back.

"And don't even think about checking out anything of mine either," Emma warned him.

"You already know I don't obey orders well."

"How about polite requests?"

"I'm not real great about those either. But if you insist . . ."

"I do."

"I don't take women against their will," he said quietly.

"That's reassuring."

"Are you going to freak out because of your mugging?"

"What? No." She wasn't sure whether to be insulted or consoled by his concern.

"Close your eyes."

"Why?"

"Because I'm going to crawl into the backseat and get some clothes on."

"Oh. Okay." She squeezed her eyes shut but couldn't resist one teeny peek. "This is silly. I saw you when you stripped to go skinny-dipping."

"I've got a sleeping bag back here. You might as well get some sleep while we're waiting."

"Waiting for what? Maybe we should call for help." She dug into her purse for her cell phone. No signal. "What about yours?"

"What about my what?"

"Your phone? Do you have a signal?"

He reached for the console between the front seats and checked his iPhone. "No. Nada."

She heard the sound of him tugging on his jeans. *Zzzzippp.* "Okay, then." She'd never heard a zipper sound so loud. "So what's the plan? You must have a plan."

"We wait until daylight and then see if we can somehow get around the tree. The Jeep has four-wheel drive. Until then I'll stay in the front seat and you can have the back all to yourself."

"You don't have to treat me like I've got cooties just because I didn't want to have sex with you."

"Oh, you *wanted* to. You were just afraid to do what you wanted."

The fact that he was right was very aggravating. "You're impossible, do you know that?"

"Yeah, I've been told that before."

"Forgive me if I don't want to be just another babe in the back of your Jeep," she said tartly.

"You're not just another babe."

"You probably tell them all that."

"Now who's being impossible?"

"You. Always you. Fine. I'll take the back, you take the front." She abandoned her dress and crawled between her upright seat and his horizontal one, bumping into Jake as he was about to move to the front. Their bodies were sandwiched together so tightly a piece of paper wouldn't have fit between them.

Jake groaned. "Don't move."

Emma stopped wiggling and froze. "Are you hurt?"

"Hell, yes."

"Is it from your climbing accident?"

"No, it's from you."

"Me? What did I do . . . oh." She felt his arousal through the placket of his pants. "Oh."

"Yeah, oh."

"What can I do to help?"

His laugh was a little tortured. "Do you really want me to answer that question?"

"We seem to be stuck going in opposite directions."

"Tell me something I don't know."

"Maybe if I backed up . . ."

Instead of answering, he grabbed hold of her hips and pulled her into the back with him. They tumbled together, Emma ending up on top of him, their legs sprawled together. At least they were now facing in the same direction, her breasts pressed against his bare chest.

"Sorry." She propped herself up, but that just arched her back so that her pelvis was pressed against his.

He tugged her back down and kissed her. His mouth consumed hers until she was lost in the intimacies of his tongue dallying with hers. He slid his hand to the back of her head to hold her in place, intensifying the joining of his lips with hers and making her moan with pleasure. He molded her against his body, shifting his free hand from her back down to the hem of her T-shirt. Jake rolled until she was beneath him.

Suddenly it was all too much for Emma. "Wait!"

A bolt of lightning was instantly followed by a clap of thunder so loud her ears rang. The storm wasn't over yet. Maybe it was just getting started.

Jake set her free, moving away from her.

"I can't do this right now," she said unsteadily.

"Yeah, you're right." He handed her an unzipped sleeping bag with a soft fleece interior. "You might as well try and get some rest."

Emma was sure the storm would keep her awake, not to mention the fact that Jake was mere feet away from her, but exhaustion caught up with her and she dozed off.

Jake watched her sleep. He was no stranger to tussles with Mother Nature. This wasn't his first storm by any stretch of the imagination. But Emma wasn't a pro at this sort of thing—at weathering storms or at making out in the back of a Jeep. He knew that, yet he couldn't seem to resist her. He'd set her free the minute she'd asked him to. He hadn't lied when he'd told her that he didn't take women against their will. He'd had more than his fair share of hot hookups with women who'd been more than happy to have sex with him.

But Emma was different. He reached out to gently pull the sleeping bag over her shoulder. She had her back turned to him.

The rain continued. At first Jake thought the sound of it pounding on the Jeep's roof was causing Emma's restless movements. Then he heard her muttering, "No, no." He immediately realized that she was having a nightmare. He'd had enough of them himself to recognize the signs.

He didn't know whether to wake her or not. She jerked awake on her own.

"It's okay." He kept his voice calm. "You were just having a nightmare."

"It was the mugging," she said, her voice husky with sleep. "I was back in Boston and I knew he was waiting for me, coming for me, but I couldn't seem to move. I was just frozen."

"You're okay now. You're safe."

"Am I?"

"What do you mean? You don't think I'm going to hurt you, do you?"

"I just meant that it's hard to feel safe when the fear won't go away. I want to be bold and fearless."

"You are. Lightning strikes mere feet away from you and do you burst into tears? No way. Instead you recite lightning trivia for me."

"I didn't think you heard me."

"I always hear you." *Sometimes even when you're not talking*, he wanted to add but thought it too sappy to say aloud.

Emma loved the way his voice rolled over her like a warm hug. Which would seem to indicate a nonsexual thing, but that wasn't the truth at all. He made her feel safe and sexy at the same time. Even his silence had a powerful effect on her.

"Kiss me," she whispered, pulling him down to her.

This time she didn't panic when his mouth and body covered hers. Instead she urged him on, responding with the boldness she'd hoped for earlier. She didn't resist when he shifted his hand to her bare thighs.

The rain continued relentlessly as he slipped his fingers

between her legs, stealing beneath the edge of her silky panties and enticingly searching out the folds of her sex. He explored her body with exquisite care and skill until she was slick with desire. Only then did he ease one finger inside her damp core. His erotic strokes set her afire with a passion that stunned her. She'd never felt this way before.

Jake built her pleasure, taking his time, focusing on what movements brought her the most intense surges of delight. He brushed his thumb against her clitoris until her entire being pulsated. When he added a combination move, the silken friction had her gripping his shoulders and arching her back as powerful wave after wave of bliss signaled her climax.

He muffled her shout of release with his mouth, his tongue mimicking the thrust motion of his fingers.

Emma was stunned and awed by what had just taken place. She was even more awed when Jake repeated the erotic seduction again with his fingers and later with his tongue. Bold and fearless had never felt so good.

• • •

Once again Jake watched Emma sleep. There was nothing like a good seduction to keep the nightmares at bay. But since she was the only one who'd been seduced, he wasn't immune to the nightmares that prowled through his restless nights with stubborn insistence.

Not that Emma had been selfish. She'd wanted to give him the same kind of pleasure he'd given her. But somehow that smacked of taking advantage of her. He had his own sense of honor, and it called for him to make tonight all about her and not him.

This was a first for him. And he had the feeling that this was a first for her. Her body had been so responsive to his touch while her movements had indicated her delighted surprise at reaching her orgasm each time. It had just about killed him not to make love to her, but she deserved better than a roll in the back of his Jeep. She deserved the fancy stuff—scented candles, rose petals strewn across the bed. Which would be another first for him. He'd never gone in for that romantic stuff. Never had to. He didn't have to now. But he wanted to. He wanted it to be special for her because she was special to him.

That didn't mean letting down his guard enough to fall asleep with her curled beside him. Instead he sat here, fighting off sleep and the guilt-driven demons that resided there. He didn't want her seeing him gasping for air, torn apart by grief for Andy, broken by the regret of what had taken place on that mountain. He wasn't that bold or that fearless after all.

So Jake let Emma sleep while he found a flashlight and an ax in his gear. Quietly leaving the Jeep, he set to work on getting her back to safety. By the time he'd cleared enough of the fallen tree to get past it, the sky was brightening with the pearly gray light of impending dawn.

He returned to the Jeep to find Emma sitting up, her hair tangled around her face, her eyes still drowsy with interrupted sleep. "Time to get out of here," he said.

He got her home in record time, whisking her upstairs to her apartment before anyone could see her state of undress and leaving immediately before he could give into the temptation to finish what they'd started.

• • •

A loud knock on her door later that Sunday morning woke Emma up. It was Jake. She just knew it was. He'd left hours earlier without saying a word, taking off as if the hounds of hell were at his feet. How could he give her such supreme bliss and then just run off like that? She yanked the door open, prepared to see Jake. Instead a skinny beanpole of a guy stood there wearing a *Star Trek* T-shirt, plaid Bermuda shorts, and white athletic socks with sandals.

She blinked. "Oliver!"

"You don't look very good. What happened to you?" Oliver Howser asked.

What was the younger brother of her former boyfriend Ted doing on her doorstep?

"What happened to you?" Oliver repeated.

Emma moaned and pressed her fist to her forehead. She had a needs-more-sleep headache. "I went to my sister's wedding and almost got hit by lightning."

"Really? Because each year the odds of a person in the U.S. being struck by lightning is three hundred thousand to one."

"I'm telling you, lightning hit the tree right behind us and almost set it on fire. It split the tree completely in half."

"Impressive. Did you know that a bolt of lightning is only an inch in diameter and is fifty thousand degrees Fahrenheit, three times as hot as the sun?"

"No, and I don't need to hear any more of your science trivia right now, thank you very much. What are you doing here?"

"Visiting you. For a week or two."

Emma tried not to groan aloud. Instead she did it silently. "This isn't a real good time, Oliver. I have another sister getting married in two weeks."

"Two weeks? Then we've got plenty of time to hang out together until then."

"How did you know where I was?"

"You left a forwarding address at your apartment. My, this is a small space. What, eight hundred square feet?"

"I have no idea."

"Not that I need much space. Just a place on your floor to roll out my sleeping bag."

Sleeping bags reminded her of Jake in the back of his Jeep last night. The wedding and the storm were mere preludes to the really big event—him seducing her. Who knew that such pleasure could be had without even doing the deed?

"Earth to Emma." Oliver waved his hand in front of her face.

"Sorry. I didn't get much sleep last night."

"Did you know that the Japanese sleep less than anyone else on the planet?"

Emma belatedly reached for a robe. "Why have you come here?"

"To see you."

"Why now?"

"I missed you. And I've never been to Pennsylvania. I thought it might be fun."

She eyed him suspiciously. "Did your brother send you?"

"No. I didn't tell him I was coming."

"Why not?"

"We had a fight. About Comic-Con. He said he'd get tickets and didn't. I can't talk about it. It upsets me too much. Just let me crash here a night or two. If you want me to leave after that, I will. Come on, be a good friend."

"Okay." She was too tired to argue with him.

"Great." He dumped his sleeping bag and backpack by the door. "I can help you with your research."

"You're studying to be a quantum physicist."

"Yes, and I have an IQ higher than Einstein—not that I'm one to brag."

"How is that going to help my sociology study?"

"I'm sure I can come up with something. Show me what you've got so far."

"First let me take a quick shower and get some clothes on."

"Sure. I'll just check my e-mail." He sat at the table and opened his laptop.

Emma was back in ten minutes, wearing a scoop neck Penn T-shirt over black yoga pants. Oliver was eager to hear about her grant and her research project.

Talking with another academic, even one not in her own field, actually was invigorating. The conversation went beyond her work as they discussed everything from various research methodologies to comparisons between the old-world interactions of an Amish gemeinschaft-type community and the high-tech dealings of the industrialized world around them.

"Ferdinand Tönnies speculated that the gemeinschaft style of local villages was disappearing—" Emma's comment was interrupted by a knock on her door.

Jake stood there smiling at her—until he looked over her shoulder and saw Oliver and his sleeping bag. "Who the hell is he?"

Chapter Eleven

. . . .

.

"This is Oliver," Emma said.

"What's he doing in your apartment?" Jake demanded.

"Staying with me."

"Is he your boyfriend?"

Oliver laughed nervously. "No. My brother was her boyfriend, but they broke up a few months ago. Who are you?"

"Jake."

Oliver thought for a second before admitting, "I have no idea who you are."

Jake continued his interrogation. "Why are you staying with Emma? Is something going on between you two?"

"You sound a bit jealous of me," Oliver said in awe. "How cool is that?" His awe quickly turned to concern once he caught sight of the dangerous look on Jake's face. "Uh, he's not going hit me, is he, Em?" Oliver quickly stepped behind Emma, using her as a shield.

"What kind of man hides behind a woman?" Jake said.

"A smart man with a 5.0 GPA at MIT," Oliver said.

"Am I supposed to be impressed?" Jake said.

Oliver nodded. "Most people would be."

"I'm not most people," Jake said.

"Jake is an extreme sports competitor," Emma told Oliver.

"Oh yeah?" Oliver stepped from behind her to put his hands on his skinny hips. "Well, Emma here knows self-defense techniques so you don't want to mess with her."

"But she likes me to mess with her, right, Emma?" His voice was incredibly seductive.

She felt her face going red and her insides melting, which prevented her from speaking for a moment or two. "What . . ." She cleared her throat. "What are you doing here, Jake?"

The look he gave her was as sexy as his voice. "I came to check on you after our night together."

Oliver looked at Emma. "I thought you said you were at your sister's wedding last night."

"That's right," Emma said. "I was."

Oliver's expression clearly indicated that he was confused. "So you two met at the wedding?"

"I was her date to the wedding," Jake stated in the manner of a man staking claim to his territory.

Oliver frowned. "Where did you meet this guy, Em?"

Jake replied before she could. "At a bar. She floored me."

"With one of her self-defense moves?" Oliver asked.

Jake nodded. "Yeah, in a manner of speaking."

"She beat you up?"

"No." Now Jake was the one frowning. Glaring was really closer to the truth. "What's with all the questions?"

"Em is a close friend of mine and I care about her," Oliver said defensively.

"Yeah," Jake mocked him. "You care so much about her you hid behind her when you thought I was going to come after you."

"I did not!"

Jake gave him a narrowed eye stare that sent Oliver scurrying back behind Emma, saying, "Okay, so what if I did? That doesn't mean I don't care about her." Oliver awkwardly patted Emma's shoulder. "We're good buddies."

"Some buddy who doesn't defend her."

"Em doesn't need me to defend her, but I could if she needed me to. I could come up with some intellectual plan."

"Right," Jake scoffed. "Like that would work."

"As you can see, I'm fine, Jake," Emma said.

"What I see is a wimpy guy hiding behind you for protection."

"Because you're deliberately trying to intimidate him. Why is that?" she demanded.

Yeah, Jake wondered to himself. *Why was that?* It's not like he should feel at all threatened by this nerdy guy. So he was her old boyfriend's brother. So what? No big deal. Why did he care if Emma had a male roommate?

Because he'd come over hoping to continue what they'd started last night in the back of his Jeep and finding Oliver here cramped his style. Yeah, that had to be it. Because Jake didn't get jealous. He'd never had reason to. Bodacious babes chased after him all the time. He hooked up with them with no strings attached. They provided sex. Whenever he had an itch, they scratched it.

But Emma was different. He cared about what she thought, what she felt, what she wanted, what she needed. Not that he'd been an uncaring lover in the past. But every experience with Emma was different—from their first kiss to the awed look on her face last night in the storm.

She awoke something deep within him. He didn't know

what it was and frankly didn't want to examine it too closely. Inner reflection had never been his thing. He just knew Emma took him to another level and that was enough for him to want more.

He knew she wanted more too. So why wasn't she booting Oliver out?

"So, Oliver, when are you leaving?"

"He just got here." Emma folded her arms across her chest, which lifted her breasts.

Jake was sure she wasn't trying to draw his attention to her breasts, but that was what happened. She wasn't wearing a bra beneath that T-shirt. He didn't like her going bra-less in front of Oliver.

Man, he *was* jealous. Damn. The realization threw Jake and didn't please him at all. "I've gotta go," he growled. "We'll talk later." He shot Oliver one last hands-off look before he left.

• • •

Emma spent the rest of Sunday trying to ignore the myriad emotions that Jake had aroused in her. Outwardly she tried to be a good hostess to Oliver, but inside she was confused by Jake's behavior. He'd acted as though he was jealous, which was ridiculous. He was probably just aggravated and frustrated that he couldn't seduce her now that she had a houseguest.

She was frustrated too. The memory of what they'd shared last night in the back of his Jeep left her wanting more. But Oliver's arrival gave her the chance to regroup and examine her situation logically instead of responding to the pure pleasure Jake had given her.

Emma didn't sleep well that night, and it wasn't because of the sound of Oliver's intermittent light snoring as he slept on her floor. Across the alley, Jake's apartment was dark. Did that mean he was sleeping or working at the tavern? Wasn't it closed by now? She squinted at her watch in the darkness. Three a.m. Surely the bar was shut now. So Jake was home and asleep?

She punched her pillow and turned around so her back was facing the window and the alley and Jake's apartment. She needed to think about her research and not orgasms. Orgasms had nothing to do with her research.

But orgasms had everything to do with her thoughts. She restlessly shifted her legs against the cool sheets. Jake had done things to her that she'd only read about. And her body had responded in a way that was totally surprising and absolutely satisfying.

Satisfying . . . yes. Yet here she was yearning for more, wanting it to happen again . . . and again . . . and again.

Sleep deprived for a second night, Emma stumbled over Oliver the next morning on her way to the shower. By the time she had her first mug of coffee and started her morning tai chi, Oliver was right there beside her. After chomping his way through two bowls of Cap'n Crunch cereal that he'd brought with him in his backpack, Oliver stated that he was going out to explore what Rock Creek had to offer.

Less than an hour later, Oliver burst into her apartment, almost falling over his own Converse-clad feet in his eagerness. "I need your help! You have to be my wingman. Right now!"

Immersed in her research, Emma barely looked up from her laptop. "Wingman? Is that some video game you're playing?"

"It's no game. It's my destiny. She's my destiny."

"Who is?"

"The girl downstairs."

"What's her name?"

"I don't know. I was too nervous to speak to her. That's why you have to come with me. To be my wingman. You know, my moral support."

"But I'm in the middle of something here."

"And I'm in the middle of a quarter-life crisis here!"

"What do you know about quarter-life crisis?"

"I can read a sociology book as well as the next guy. Probably better and faster. And it's all over the blogs on the Internet. You think geeks don't have quarter-life issues? We do. We need help. I need help." He tugged her to her feet. "Come on before she disappears." Oliver rushed Emma down the stairs and out to the sidewalk.

"Okay." Emma looked around. "Where is she?"

"Oh no." Oliver looked ready to cry. "She's gone!" He ran up and down the sidewalk before pausing in front of Cosmic Comics. Then he ran back to Emma. "She's in there."

"Why are you whispering?"

"Because I'm nervous."

"Come on." Emma took his arm.

He dragged his heels. "Where are we going?"

"Inside Cosmic Comics."

"Wait. We don't have a plan yet. We can't go in without a plan."

"I have a plan," she assured him.

"Then tell me what it is."

"We'll go in and you point out this girl to me." She tugged him into the store. A group of people were on one side of the store, gathered around a rack of graphic novels. "Which one is she?" Emma whispered.

"That one." Oliver pointed in the opposite direction. "The one wearing the GOT BRAINS? T-shirt." He looked down at his own GOT QUARKS? T-shirt and said, "It's fate. We were meant to be together."

"That's Lulu."

"You know this fair maiden? She isn't married, is she? I didn't see a wedding band."

"No, she's not married. Come on, I'll introduce you."

"No, wait. I have to have an opening line. A good one. Quick, give me a good opening line."

"I don't have any. Just be yourself."

"That's never worked with a girl in the past."

"Lulu isn't like any girl you've met before."

"That's why I have to do this right. I can't afford to make a mistake."

"Stop worrying."

"I'm not worrying, I'm panicking."

Emma hung onto Oliver's arm to prevent him from bolting. "Listen up, newbie."

"Newbie?"

"I'm sorry. I couldn't think of the right word. Should I have used *dude* instead?" she asked in concern. "I want to do this wingman thing right. I'm a newbie at this assignment so I used that term. I didn't mean for it to be a pejorative one."

Oliver thought a moment before replying. "No, I don't believe it's pejorative. Newbie works for me. Continue."

"I forgot what I was going to say," Emma muttered.

"What's a quark?" Lulu said from behind them.

Emma and Oliver both jumped.

Lulu smacked her gum and waited.

"Does he talk?" Lulu finally asked Emma

"Of course he does. Oliver talks. His name is Oliver."

Oliver gave Lulu the Vulcan greeting sign with his hand. "Live long—"

"And prosper." Lulu returned the Vulcan finger thing and grinned. "So you're a Trekker? Me too. Not that I wear costumes and stuff. At least not all the time."

Oliver nodded. "Same here. I don't wear pointed ears and stuff."

"So Oliver, I'm Lulu, and you still haven't told me what a quark is."

"A subatomic particle, one of the smallest units of matter, along with leptons."

"You lost me at subatomic particle," Lulu said.

"Quarks and leptons are the basic building blocks for everything in the universe."

"Seriously?"

Oliver nodded enthusiastically. "At least as far as we know at this point. There's always the chance that we could discover even smaller particles. I don't like to brag, but quantum chromodynamics is one of my strengths."

"Does he belong to you?" Lulu asked Emma.

"Oliver is just a friend," Emma said.

"Great." Lulu hooked her arm with his and pulled him away. "So Oliver, do you have a favorite graphic novel?"

"Neil Gaiman's *The Sandman*, the most successful adult graphic novel of all time."

"Yeah? Wicked awesome. Me too."

Emma watched them walk away. "So you've been dumped, huh?" Jake whispered in her ear.

She shivered at the erotic feel of his warm breath against her lobe. He intensified the moment by trailing his finger around the curvature of her ear, setting her silver dangle earring in motion.

"Were you following us?"

"Maybe. Maybe not."

"That's not really an answer."

"I'm better at action than answers." He gently blew into her ear and her knees almost buckled. "Don't you agree?"

"Huh?" *Focus, Em, focus. Don't let him melt you in public. Think. Be logical. Focus on symbolic interactionism and the misuse of statistics. Just because 99 percent of women melt when Jake blows in their ear, that doesn't mean you will too.* Or was that wrong? Did the imaginary statistic represent women or melting?

Why, oh why couldn't she think straight? Because he was nibbling on her earlobe and she'd somehow tilted her head to the side to allow him better access. When had that happened? Her insides were going all strangely wobbly as pleasure filled every last particle of her body. Every quark was electrified by his touch. Her very DNA was steeped in blissful sensation. The swirl of his tongue over the curve of her ear had her wanting to get naked with him ASAP.

That wasn't going to happen . . . at least not right here in the middle of Cosmic Comics.

Jake apparently reached the same conclusion because he slid his fingers down her arm to her hand and quickly tugged her outside and down the block to "their" alley. They were upstairs in his apartment before she could find the breath to make a protest. Not that she was sure she wanted to protest. She almost wanted to tell him to go even faster.

As soon as they were inside his place, Jake pivoted and pinned her against the door, kissing her deeply, desperately, as though there was no tomorrow. The truth was that Emma didn't want a tomorrow if it didn't include him, seducing her with his tongue. Her need for him trampled any words of logic, stomping them out of existence.

Instead of melting against him, she tugged him closer. His body hardened against hers, the male contours of his lower torso erotically communicating his need while moving against the feminine shape of her pelvis. His actions moved their embrace to a new, deeper level of intimacy and desire.

He was close, and then he was *too* close, plastering her against the door. She panicked. She couldn't breathe. Couldn't move. She was pinned in place.

"Woof."

"Damn dog," Jake growled. "Get off!"

Emma's panic lessened as she realized that Jake was sandwiched between her and Mutt, who had his front paws on Jake's back, shoving him against Emma.

"Sit!" Jake yelled.

Now that the blind terror had retreated, Emma was able to focus on his body pressed hard against her. Her breasts were flattened against his chest. Not that she was hefty in the bra-cup department. At 36B she had no bragging rights in her family. Amazing how a mammogram could squeeze her breasts and cause her so much discomfort, but when Jake did the same thing . . . well actually, *this* wasn't comfortable either.

"Mutt, sit down!" she gasped.

"Woof."

She heard the click of Mutt's doggy nails hitting the hardwood floor.

Jake immediately stepped away from her. He left his hands on her shoulders, his touch gentle. "Are you okay?"

"Can we just sit down a minute and talk?"

"Okay." His voice was definitely cautious as he led her to a plaid couch. "What do you want to talk about?"

"You."

"I'd rather talk about you."

She didn't back down. "I know you would."

"So what about me?"

"Why don't you like talking about yourself?"

"Because, like I told you, I prefer action to words." He gently tugged her back into his arms and kissed her. They'd just gotten horizontal when the alarm on her watch went off.

"Wait." She put her hand to his chest and in doing so realized she'd somehow tugged his T-shirt out of his jeans, baring his skin to her touch. "I, um, I have to leave now. I have an appointment." Her watch beeped again. She pushed the button to stop the noise.

"You've got an alarm on your watch?"

"Yeah, geeky I know." She self-consciously slid out from under him to stand on her own two feet. Only then did she realize that her sandals had fallen off. She slid them back on and headed for the door.

"Can't you reschedule your appointment?"

"No."

Jake's cell phone rang, vibrating on the coffee table in front of the couch. He flipped it open. "Yeah?" He paused for a moment before telling Emma, "It's Walt Whitman, the mayor of—"

"Serenity Falls, yes, I know. He's the one I have the appointment with. I've got to go—"

"Hold on. He wants me to go with you."

"What?"

"Here." He handed his phone to her. "He can tell you himself."

"Hello? This is Emma Riley."

"Oh good. I was just telling Jake that you need to bring him with you when you come for our interview today."

"Why?"

"Because I need to speak to him about an important matter."

"Why can't you make a separate appointment to talk to him? Jake doesn't have anything to do with the study I'm doing about Rock Creek."

"If he plans on building a resort in this area, then he has something to do with Rock Creek and Serenity Falls both."

"That has nothing to do with my research."

"Maybe not, but it has a lot to do with my vision. So bring him along today or the interview is off."

She'd already included the mayor's name in the proposal she'd submitted to the grant people so there was no kicking him out now.

"Jake might be busy . . ." she began.

"No, I'm not."

"Fine." Her voice was curt. "We'll be there shortly."

She handed the phone back to Jake. "Why do you want to spend time with Walt Whitman?"

"I don't." He tucked a strand of her hair behind her ear. "I want to spend time with you."

Emma didn't know how to react to that. "We better go or we'll be late. I'll meet you there . . ."

"You drive a Prius. You believe in conserving gasoline. We should drive together. In my Jeep."

"No way." She remembered all too vividly the last time she'd been in his Jeep and he'd given her an orgasm or two or three. "We'll go in my car."

"Okay. Give me the keys."

"Why would I want to do that?"

"So I can drive."

"You are not driving my car."

"Why not?"

"I don't let anyone drive my car."

"What about Oliver?"

"What about him?"

"Would you let him drive your car?"

She might.

"Aha. So why won't you let me?" Jake said.

"Because you're no Oliver."

"What's that supposed to mean? Don't you trust me?"

"You have a need for speed. That's not a real good recommendation to drive. I drive or we go in separate cars. And we leave now or we'll be late."

Emma had to stop at her apartment to grab her laptop and notes before running back downstairs where Jake was waiting. His body was a little cramped in her Prius, but he didn't complain during the short drive to Serenity Falls Town Hall. He just shot her occasional dirty looks—not the sexy kind of dirty looks, the aggravated kind.

Walt greeted them at the door of his office. "Can I get you anything? Something to drink perhaps? No? Well then, let's sit down and get comfortable."

Emma's derriere had barely hit the seat of the plastic chair in the mayor's office when Walt said, "Jake, have you given any further consideration to my suggestion about building your resort here in Serenity Falls instead of Rock Creek?"

"I never said I was here to build a resort," Jake replied.

"I didn't mean you'd actually build it. Not by yourself. Would you?"

"Hell no."

"I didn't think so. You have people for that. Contractors, that sort of thing."

"Mr. Whitman, you're supposed to be participating in an interview with me," Emma reminded him. "Not arm-twisting Jake."

"I'm not arm-twisting. Jake knows that. He's an astute businessman."

"He is?" Emma turned to look at Jake in surprise.

"I am?" He lifted a dark eyebrow.

"Come now, don't be modest." When Jake made no comment, Walt turned to Emma. "Don't you look at the Internet? Jake's business savvy is there to see. The way he turned the early money he made from sponsors into even bigger bucks."

"Those days are over," Jake said flatly.

"Of course they are. You don't need people to invest in you anymore. Now you invest in other things. Like a resort. Here in Serenity Falls. We're much better than Rock Creek."

Emma couldn't let that insult to her hometown go unanswered. "Rock Creek has the Tivoli Theater. It is a town filled with new excitement."

"Your mayor is a clown."

"A retired clown," Emma said.

"Retired or not, the guy is a clown."

"Why do you feel the need to be so competitive with Rock Creek? Why not create opportunities where both towns can work together for the betterment of each one?"

"We're already better. We're one of the best small towns in America for three years in a row." He pointed to the elaborately framed large certificates on his office wall. "We've got the scenic waterfall." He pointed to a poster of the falls. "We've got a quaint town square with a lovely gazebo." He pointed out the window. "We've even got an historic Revolutionary war cannon."

"We've got a World War II tank."

"We have Maguire's sweet potato fries."

"We have the Thai Place spring rolls. And the Antiques Mall and the Time for Tea Shop, not to mention the Arts and Crafts Drive with fifty talented artisans," she said triumphantly.

"I hate to interrupt this civic pissing contest," Jake said, "but I have a suggestion."

"Great. I can't wait to hear it," Walt said.

"As mayor you want to be regarded as someone who can be trusted, right?" Jake said.

Walt nodded. "Absolutely."

"And you did agree to an interview with Emma during this time, correct?"

Walt squirmed in his chair. "Well, yes, but—"

"Then I suggest you honor your agreement and do that interview."

"Fine." Walt's wide chest fell in a sigh of resignation. "I suppose you and I can talk later, Jake. I just wanted to make sure you considered Serenity Falls before you commit elsewhere."

"I'm not gonna commit," Jake assured him.

"I'm glad to hear that," Walt said with jovial relief.

Emma wasn't thrilled to hear that. She wasn't surprised either. She'd already guessed that Jake was no fan of commitment to anything outside of extreme sports and the adrenaline rush they gave him.

"So go ahead, Emma, what's your first question?" Walt said.

Her first question would be what the hell she was doing hanging out with a risk taker like Jake. But that wasn't relevant to her research so she gathered her notes and began her interview with Walt. All the while, she was only too aware of Jake sitting nearby. His jean-covered leg was only a few inches from hers. She recognized the washed-out blue gray three-button thermal knit shirt and the beat-up black boots he wore. He'd worn them before.

Did he recognize her blue polo shirt as the same one she'd had on when she'd first walked into that bar and met him?

Irrelevant, Em. Focus. No, not on Jake, on Walt. Focus on your questions for Walt. Emma did manage to finish her interview without making a fool of herself despite the fact that Jake was invading her space.

As a sociologist, she knew all about the four different "distance zones" North Americans had—intimate distance, personal distance, social distance, and public distance—all measured in a varying number of feet.

She'd now experienced a new zone—"Jake distance." Forget about measuring in feet, Jake and his bad boy attitude merely had to be in the same *room* with her and she reacted with all the telltale physical signs of attraction.

Those signs of attraction built throughout their drive home. She lowered the driver-side window to allow the fresh air to cool her hot cheeks. They didn't talk much. She seemed incapable of forming complete sentences.

"I'll see you to your door," Jake said once they arrived back in town.

"You don't have to."

"Yeah, I do."

When she had trouble getting her key into the door lock, he reached around her to steady her hand. His body was warm against her back. "Jake distance" was at work again. Doing yummy stuff to her insides.

He was all about taking chances. She was all about playing it safe. How was that supposed to work?

His kiss told her that at least on a physical level it worked very well.

Chapter Twelve

· · · · · · · · · · ·

"Talk to me," she murmured against his lips.

"Mmm," he murmured back. "You taste good."

Once inside her apartment, their kisses continued. Jake kissing her. Emma kissing him.

"This could get complicated," she whispered.

"So what? If it's easy, it's not worthwhile."

It took a moment or two but then Jake's words hit her. The *wrong* way. Here she was, melting in his arms yet again as she had every time he'd touched her. She couldn't get much easier than that, unless she'd hopped into bed with him the second she'd met him. No doubt he'd had plenty of women do just that. At least she wasn't one of them. Which meant she wasn't a slut, she was just easy.

Somehow that conclusion did not reassure her. Which is what she meant by *complicated*. Emma was thrown by the way she automatically and unequivocally melted every time she got near him. Jake seemed to have all the power, leaving her subject to these bouts of unrestrained passion that weren't like her at all.

They'd never talked about what had happened in the back of his Jeep the other night. Had she been easy then?

She hadn't even known the guy for two weeks and yet that night she'd granted him intimacies she'd never shared with any other man in her entire life.

Panicked, Emma stepped on the emotional brakes and freed herself from his embrace. "Wait a second."

He reached for her, but she'd stepped away. "What's wrong?"

"You just said it all."

"What?"

"That if it's easy, it's not worthwhile. Does that apply to women too?"

He gave her a wicked grin. "I've got nothing against easy women."

His confidence totally aggravated her. "Well, I do." She grabbed hold of the doorknob and yanked the door open. She couldn't think straight when he was around. "I'd like you to leave now."

"See, this is why I don't like to talk. Because you females all take things the wrong way."

"Which makes me just another female, huh? Just another easy female who isn't worthwhile to you."

Jake grit his teeth and looked as though he wanted to kiss some sense into her.

Emma's glare dared him to try, which probably wasn't a good idea since the man had a track record of responding to dares.

Their standoff was interrupted by Oliver's exuberant arrival. "I did it! I did it!" He was practically bouncing on his Converse soles. "I haven't been this excited since I read the news about quantum fluids."

"What are you talking about?" Emma asked.

"Quantum fluids—"

"No, I meant you. You said, 'I did it.' Did what?"

"Asked Lulu on a date. Well, she sort of asked me and I agreed it would be a good idea. That makes it a mutual collaboration in the decision-making process regarding a date."

Emma looked over her shoulder to discover that Jake had left, which should have pleased her or satisfied her or something. Instead she felt even more mixed up inside.

Meanwhile, Oliver was doing a happy Snoopy dance across the floor toward the kitchenette.

"What's going on here?" Leena said from the doorway. "I nearly get run over by one sexy guy racing down the stairs from your apartment, and now I find another guy doing some strange dance in your living room." She came closer. "Who's the geeky guy waving his skinny arms around?"

"That's Oliver. He's celebrating."

"Celebrating what?" Leena asked suspiciously.

"That he's got a date."

"With you?"

"No, with Lulu."

"Hmm. An interesting couple. Hey, Oliver," Leena called out over Emma's head. "I'm Emma's sister Leena."

Oliver stopped dancing and turned around to face them. "I didn't know we had company."

"We?" Leena raised an eyebrow.

Oliver nodded. "Emma and I are roommates."

"Just for a short time," Emma said.

"Is that why Jake lit out of here as if his feet were on fire?" Leena asked.

"Of course not," Emma said. "Why should Jake care that Oliver is staying here?"

"He could be jealous of my superior brainpower," Oliver said.

"Yeah, right," Leena said. "Seriously, why was Jake in such a hurry?"

"I have no idea," Emma said. "Why did you stop by?"

"I was in the neighborhood."

Emma wasn't buying that excuse and her expression said so.

"Okay, I wanted to know more about what happened after you and Jake took off together at Sue Ellen's reception the other night," Leena admitted. "But I knew you wouldn't tell me much on the phone so I decided to drop by to twist your arm in person and invite you to lunch at the Thai Place. Just the two of us. For girl talk. Sorry, Oliver."

"No problemo. I've got to check up on my e-mail and blogs." He patted his laptop.

Leena had Emma downstairs, sitting at a table in the restaurant, in no time. "Okay, spill the beans. There's a rumor going around town that you were seen coming home in the wee hours of the morning, as in daybreak, in Jake's Jeep. Is that true?"

"We got held up in that terrible storm."

"Define *held up*," Leena said.

"You know, I used to think that Sue Ellen was the bossiest one in the family, but now I'm not so sure."

"Mom is the bossiest."

"I still can't believe that you think I'm her favorite."

"Because you are, that's why. And don't change the subject. Tell me what happened when you and Jake were"—Leena inserted finger quotes—"held up."

"We stopped by to see the Serenity Falls waterfall and got caught in the storm."

"Why did you go up there? It closes at nightfall."

"I'd forgotten that."

"So you hijacked Jake up to the waterfall after hours to make out? Way to go, little sis!"

"I did no such thing."

Leena frowned. "He hijacked you?"

"No, of course not."

"So you didn't make out?"

"I am not answering that question."

"You just did."

Emma shoved a menu at Leena. "What are you going to order?"

"Spring rolls and pad thai. Oh look, there's Jake. Shall we invite him to join us?"

Emma grabbed Leena's hand before she could rap on the plate-glass front window to get Jake's attention. "He's probably on his way to work."

Sure enough, Jake crossed Barwell Street and headed into Nick's Tavern.

"It's a shame that he has to spend such a beautiful June day in such a dark hole. I wonder why he does it. Haven't you been curious?"

"Yes." But Emma wanted Jake to tell her about himself, rather than her having to research him on the Internet. She wanted him to trust her enough to confide in her. Which was a pipe dream, no doubt. Although he had told her about snowboarding as a kid and a little about his life in extreme sports, it hadn't been much. Just tantalizing tidbits here and there.

"And?" Leena prompted.

"And nothing."

"He hasn't told you anything about his reasons for being in Rock Creek?"

"No."

"Have you asked him?"

"He's a very private person."

"Which means he blew off your questions. Did he at least complete your questionairre?"

"Yes. Which reminds me, I have a few questions to ask

you about the website and blog you created with your business partner."

The rest of their lunch was spent talking about Leena's business and the importance she placed on helping women with self-esteem and body-image issues. The subject then turned to women entrepreneurs and the requirements for successfully launching a new venture.

Only as they were walking out did Leena hug Emma and say, "Don't think I didn't notice how you avoided talking about Jake."

"You have a wedding to prepare for. You really should be concentrating on that and enjoying the momentary lull in hysteria while Sue Ellen is on her honeymoon."

"Hey, I can do hysteria as well as, if not better than, the next girl."

"You got that ability from Mom." Grinning widely, Emma quickly sidestepped Leena's attempt to sock her arm and made her escape.

Still in a good mood, Emma returned to her apartment to find Oliver engrossed in his e-mail.

"I brought you some spring rolls," she said.

"Thanks. I got an e-mail you might be interested in. A friend of mine is an assistant editor at a small press that's looking for nonfiction projects. Remember how you used to go on and on about writing a book someday? This might be the day."

"I can't write a book in a day."

"I meant this might be the most auspicious time to submit a book proposal. She's accepting e-mail submissions if someone has been recommended, which you have been. By me."

"What did you tell her I was writing?"

"Something great. I didn't go into any more detail than that. Just sit down and start with stream of consciousness and see what you come up with, what areas interest you. You've got this small-town regeneration research going."

"Yes, but I'm planning to submit that to a professional journal."

"Well, just try brainstorming other subjects within your field that interest you."

Jake interested her. What made someone take the risks he had? What made someone an adrenaline junkie? An hour later she'd written several pages of notes, filled with more questions than answers.

• • •

Across the street in Nick's Tavern, Jake had more questions than answers too. Why did women freak out when you least expect it? Why had Emma practically tossed him out of her apartment? It wasn't because she hadn't enjoyed their kisses. So what was the problem?

He really didn't need a distraction like her right now. He should be thinking about finding his birth mother. She held the answers to who he was. Or so he hoped. No, *hope* wasn't in his vocabulary. He just wanted the facts. Why had she given him away? Who was his father?

Jake's near-death experience on the mountain in Peru made him question everything, including who he was. Some answers were beyond his reach—like why Andy died in that avalanche and not him. But this, finding his birth mother, this was an answer he could pin down.

Jake was much more accustomed to wondering about the external things in his life. Was this snowboard faster than the previous one? Was this mountain route tougher than another? Was this trick more difficult than the last, this endeavor more challenging?

Jake looked up from the glass he was wiping clean to see Emma's mom climbing onto a bar stool. "Hello, Jake."

Had Emma sent her mom after him? No, she'd never

do that. Emma probably didn't even know her mom was here.

Maxie said, "I'd like a Diet Coke—"

"With a slice of lime, right?"

She beamed at him. "Right. How nice of you to remember." She looked around. "The tavern isn't busy this time of day."

"It's early yet." The place was empty aside from Old Mo. Every weekday the grumpy old geezer sat in the far corner working the newspaper crossword puzzle while nursing a glass of beer for two or three hours.

"This gives us a chance to talk," Maxie said. "I didn't get to speak to you at my daughter's reception. I know that you and Emma left before the conga line started."

"I'm not much of a dancer."

"I find that hard to believe, a muscular athlete like you. You do know that Emmitt Smith, the football player, became a championship dancer on *Dancing with the Stars*, right?"

"I must have missed that."

"They even called him Twinkletoes."

Jake, aka Slayter the Slayer, had no intention of being called Twinkletoes in this lifetime or any other.

"You do know that before we moved down to Florida, I was a hairdresser here in town, right?"

Did he know that? Had Emma mentioned it? He wasn't sure so he just agreed with Maxie. "Right."

"Well, in small towns like this your hairdresser knows everything. Granted, most of my customers were collecting Social Security, but I still picked things up. Information. I've told my daughter that I could help her with her study about Rock Creek, but she turned me down. I was thinking that maybe you could talk to her."

Hairdressers. Knew everything. Emma might not need

Maxie's help, but Jake could sure use it. "So did you know Zoe, Lulu's mom?"

"Zoe hasn't been back in Rock Creek for a long time."

"Right." He knew the year she'd left. The investigator had been able to get that much info on her. She'd gone to Cleveland, Chicago, and they'd lost track of her in Toronto. But he was more interested in Zoe's life *before* she left Rock Creek. Like thirty years ago—the year he was born and the year she'd first left town.

"I can remember the day she left as if it were yesterday," Maxie said. "They say your memory gets worse the older you get, but not mine. Zoe's not a natural blond. She uses Miss Clairol. Or she used to in those days. She was quite the rowdy one. Her dad couldn't keep her under control."

"Do you know why she left?"

"She never said, never warned anyone she was leaving. She didn't even leave a note for her dad. She was just another runaway. I believe she was barely sixteen at the time."

"Is that when she had Lulu?"

"Heavens no. Lulu is only twenty. Zoe had been gone ten years by the time Lulu was born. Lulu was just a toddler when Zoe came back and moved in with her father. But it wasn't long before she took off again, leaving Lulu behind. Lulu's grandfather raised her. He did a good job, but Lulu's got her mother's wild blood in her."

Jake wondered if he had the same wild blood in him.

"Maxie, what are you doing gossiping in my bar in the middle of the day?" Nic demanded as she blew into the tavern.

"Nice haircut," Maxie said. "Where did you get it done?"

"At a new place over in Serenity Falls. I just came to

pick up some paperwork from the office and to enjoy some eye candy." Her eyes wandered over Jake. "Are you here to enjoy the view too, Maxie?"

"Jake is dating my youngest daughter Emma."

"The smart one?"

"Yes."

"That's too bad." Nic sashayed toward the tiny office in the back. Two minutes later, she was out the door, cursing under her breath about accountants and paperwork.

"It's probably a good thing Nic never had kids," Maxie said.

"How do you know she hasn't?"

"She had an infertility problem. She never wanted kids anyway so it wasn't a big deal to her. Not that she ever talks about it."

Which meant his boss wasn't his birth mother. Thank God.

"This bar is her baby," Maxie continued, "and she doesn't take good care of it. She doesn't like change. That must be it. That must be why she hasn't updated the place. I know Sue Ellen got a degree in interior decorating online and could help Nic out here, adding some splashes of color. But no, Nic turned her down."

"Does everyone in town know she owns this bar?"

"Not everyone, no. In fact, she likes to keep it pretty much under wraps. Nic . . . well, she's a real character. Rock Creek has a lot of those. Take Nancy Crumpler, for example. Her sister is a nun yet she's been married four times and divorced three. Rumor has it that at one point Nancy was a dancer in one of those places in the Poconos. From there she went on to be a dancer at a casino in Las Vegas."

"She was a Vegas showgirl? When was that?"

"Oh, that would be thirty years ago now. She left Rock

Creek for the Poconos, then went to Las Vegas maybe a year after that."

Which meant she was still in the running.

"She got married in Vegas, divorced, married again, divorced again. She came back to Rock Creek after that. Married a local businessman pretty quickly. Divorced him. Married Al Crumpler, who eventually died and left her the auto parts store."

"What about children?"

"She and Al didn't have any together, but she had two by a previous husband. Her kids are in their twenties now and live in Nevada. But there were rumors . . ." Maxie's voice trailed off.

"What rumors?"

"That when she was dancing in the Poconos that she might have been"—Maxie looked around before whispering—"pregnant."

With him? This felt so weird.

Maxie was right. Hairdresssers knew everything. She'd given him more info than the private investigator had. Granted it was all based on gossip and rumor, but it was better than nothing.

"Enough with the old history," Maxie said. "Let's get back to my daughter Emma. Did you two enjoy your time together?"

Jake nodded. He wasn't accustomed to being grilled by a girl's mom. Females had been chasing him since he was a teenager. He'd never had to go after a woman before. He never had to watch what he said to a woman's mom because he'd never met her mom.

"I'm so glad. Emma never tells me anything."

Jake stayed silent. If Emma never told her mom anything, he sure wasn't about to.

"You know, Leena's wedding is coming up next. I hope you'll be Emma's guest at that as well."

Considering the fact that Emma had just tossed him out of her apartment, he wasn't sure what the status was on the next wedding gig. He'd filled out her questionnaire so she'd gotten what she wanted

Or had she? She'd seemed to want him big time when they'd made out in the back of his Jeep. And when he'd kissed her earlier today in his apartment.

So again Jake stayed quiet and let Maxie do all the talking. Finally she finished her drink and left.

• • •

"Mom just walked out of Nick's Tavern," Leena told Emma over the phone.

"What?" Up in her apartment, Emma swiveled her head from her laptop to the large window facing Barwell Street.

"I just saw her walk out of the tavern. Uh-oh, she saw me. She's coming."

A minute later Maxie took the phone. "Hi, Emma. I was just talking to Jake."

"About what?" Emma said.

"About all kinds of things," Maxie said coyly.

"Did he tell you that Emma's living with a guy?" Leena said in the background.

"Emma, have you moved in with Jake?"

"No, of course not."

"Then who are you living with?"

"I have a friend staying with me for a few days, that's all."

"A male friend?"

"Yes."

"But where will he sleep? You only have a studio apartment. A tiny hovel."

"He has a sleeping bag. He'll sleep on the floor."

"Who is this man?" Maxie demanded.

"He's more a geeky guy than a man," Leena said in the background.

"His name is Oliver," Emma said, "and he's a friend from Boston."

"Why is he in town?"

"He's visiting."

"No one used to visit Rock Creek, but I guess things are different now that we have that crafty art loop and everything. Where is this Oliver? I'd like to meet him."

"He's here in my apartment."

"Good. I"ll come right up."

Emma heard Maxie handing the phone back to Leena, who then said, "I've already had the pleasure of meeting Oliver, so you two go ahead without me. I've got tons to do yet on my wedding list for today."

Emma didn't have much of a choice. She could see her mom out the window heading straight for Emma's building.

"My mother's coming," she warned Oliver. She wanted to add "Run for cover," but there was no place to hide in the small apartment.

Emma met Maxie at the door.

"I don't understand why you'd want to live in this rundown building when you could stay in your old bedroom at the trailer."

"This building is not rundown. They've just recently done renovations on it."

"Hmm." Maxie wasn't impressed. "And you must be Oliver."

"Yes, ma'am." He wiped his damp palms on his pants before awkwardly shaking her hand. "Oliver Howser."

"Are you her boyfriend from Boston?"

"Her boyfriend was my brother. *Is* my brother. Well, he's still my brother, but he's no longer her boyfriend. They broke up." Oliver gulped for air. "Okay, I'll shut up now."

"Who cuts your hair, Oliver?" Maxie asked.

"Uh, my mom."

"Is she a beautician?"

"No."

"I didn't think so." She ran her hand through his shaggy hair. "I can do a much better job. How do you feel about adding some blond highlights to your brown hair?"

"Mother!"

Maxie turned to face her. "What?"

Emma didn't know where to begin.

So Maxie turned back to Oliver. "She only calls me Mother when she's peeved with me. So Oliver, about those highlights—"

"Can't you just accept him the way he is? Why do you always have to pick on someone's appearance? Why do you always think you know best?"

Maxie did her customary eye roll and head shake combo, meant to indicate that the answer should be evident. "Because I'm a mother, that's why."

"Oliver has a mother, and she thinks his hair looks fine the way it is."

"What would Lulu think?" Oliver asked.

"Lulu?" Maxie repeated. "You mean Lulu who works at the comic-book store here?"

"Yes, that's her," Oliver hurriedly agreed. "What would she think of me getting blond highlights?"

"Are you kidding?" Maxie said. "She'd love it."

Emma wasn't ready to wave the white flag just yet. "Oliver, it doesn't matter what Lulu or my mom thinks. What matters is you."

"When can you do the procedure?" Oliver asked Maxie.

"Heavens, it's not brain surgery. It's not a procedure, it's a grooming treatment. Why don't you come on with me now over to our place and I'll get you all set up."

"Okay."

Oliver might be getting his degree from MIT but that didn't in any way prepare him for nor protect him from Maxie's clutches. Emma felt she had to do something. She just didn't know what.

"We have extra room at our trailer," Maxie told Oliver. "You're more than welcome to stay with us while you're in Rock Creek."

"You're getting ready for Leena's wedding," Emma reminded her mother. "Oliver stays here."

Maxie did another eye roll minus the head shake this time. "Okay, okay. Don't get your panties in a knot, Emma. Come on, Oliver." She hooked her arm through his. "Let's leave Emma alone to calm down on her own."

After they left, Emma sank onto the futon and wondered when was the last time she felt calm. No amount of tai chi could settle her nerves at this point. She was too far gone on far too many fronts.

Chapter Thirteen

. . . .

Emma didn't see Jake for two days and she missed him. She got a lot of work done but not as much as she wanted. Because she wanted Jake and that kept her thinking about him instead of her research.

Oliver was thinking about Lulu and their upcoming date. "She likes the highlights," he told Emma.

"Yeah, so you've told me." About three million times.

"Are you menstruating?"

Emma almost choked. *"Whaat?"*

"You just seem very, uh, irritable today."

"I'm not used to living with someone in such close quarters." Even growing up in the trailer and sharing a bedroom with Leena, she hadn't felt this cramped.

"Yes, well . . . I wanted to talk to you about that. I've got another place to stay."

"Not with my parents?"

"No, of course not."

Emma was thankful for that.

"I'm going to stay with Jake."

"Whaat?!" Emma was even more incredulous than when Oliver had asked her about menstruating.

"Don't look so surprised."

"I'm stunned. When did you talk to Jake?"

"At the bar where he works."

"And he invited you to move in with him?"

"He pointed out how small your place was and mentioned that his apartment has two bedrooms. So does Lulu's apartment. Did you know she lives over the Tivoli Theater? Not that I'd move in with her before we've even had our first date. Jake has been giving me great tips. You know, guy sort of stuff. Advice about women, that sort of thing."

"I'm not sure Jake is the best person to be giving you advice about women," Emma said.

"Why not? He's known lots of them. I don't have the exact mathematical number, but I'm sure it's very high, in the hund—"

Emma interrupted him. "I don't want to hear how many women Jake has had."

"Right. Of course you don't. That makes sense. I have to say that a lot of this male-female relationship stuff isn't very logical."

"I'll tell you something that's logical. A study done by sociologists in 1992 found that couples who think of each other as their best friend and who like each other as a person are the most successful at having a happy relationship. I'll bet that's not what Jake told you."

Oliver was confused. "I was only four years old in 1992."

Emma was aggravated. "You're missing the point."

"I think of you as a friend and like you as a person," Oliver pointed out with his customary logic. "That doesn't mean I view you as a potential girlfriend, and I told Jake that."

"Told him what?"

"That you and I are not a romantic couple. There are no pheromones here. The very idea . . . Ick." He scrunched his face as though he'd detected an offensive odor. "Plus you're a lot older."

"Stop." Emma held up her hand. "Enough already. Go move in with Jake."

"If you're afraid that I'm going to cramp your style by staying with Jake, don't worry. Just put a sock on the front door and I'll know you two are seeking sexual release with one another and therefore want to be alone. I can go to the library or to Cosmic Comics and hang out with Lulu."

Emma looked at him as if he'd just stepped off the Starship *Enterprise*. "Where do you get these ideas?"

"I read about the sock thing from a blog on the Internet." Oliver gathered up his large backpack and sleeping bag. "I can e-mail you the link if you'd like."

"Don't bother. If Jake sticks a sock on his front door, it's not because of me."

"Of course." Oliver opened the door to leave. "You and Jake can both seek your sexual release here in your place."

"Now that sounds like an interesting possibility," Jake said from the threshold.

"I was just assuring Emma that I wouldn't cramp your style," Oliver said.

"Nice of you." Jake sent a wicked grin Emma's way. "Wasn't that nice of him?"

Emma just gritted her teeth. She'd been a mess for the past two days and here was Jake, looking as sexy as ever, acting as if nothing had changed between them. Acting as if she hadn't panicked at her powerful response to him and kicked him out of her apartment the other day.

"So how long have you two been talking about this subject?" Jake asked. "And who brought it up first?"

"I did." Oliver raised his hand as if he were in class. "I was trying to be helpful, but Emma doesn't appear to have welcomed my comments."

"She's just shy. She's definitely not easy."

Emma's face burned. So did the heated glare she shot at Jake.

"In fact, Emma is one of the most complicated women I've ever run into," Jake said.

"Really?" Oliver was skeptical. "She doesn't seem that complicated to me. Lulu is more complicated."

"That's because you're attracted to Lulu," Jake said.

"So if a guy is attracted to a girl, he thinks she's complicated?"

"Only if she really is complicated. And worthwhile."

"Right." Oliver tried to sound confident, but he still looked confused.

"You two can leave now," Emma said.

"Not until I do this." Jake tugged her into his arms and kissed her. She was too surprised to protest. Then she was enjoying herself too much to protest. Then she remembered that made her easy.

Did she really care at this point? Could she be complicated and easy? Did Jake think so? When had she turned into the kind of woman who bowed to what a man thought of her? What happened to the smart woman who stood on her own two feet? She was right here, getting kissed senseless.

She had to regain control before she lost herself entirely. Emma pulled away.

"Definitely not easy," Jake murmured.

She didn't know what to say. She felt such a mixed-up mess of conflicting emotions—ranging from desire to doubt.

She watched Jake and Oliver leave and wondered when her life had started spinning so out far out of her control.

• • •

Jake wondered how he'd ended up with a dog and a room-mate. A male roommate. A geek.

Jake had shared apartments with guys before. There were plenty of times that a group of them had all crashed at someone's place, camping on the floor in wall-to-wall sleeping bags and staying until the beer and the snow ran out.

But they'd all been snowboarders, not a quantum physi-cist wannabe. Big difference.

So how exactly had he ended up here with a dorky Mutt and a dorky Oliver? Neither had anything to do with his reason for being in Rock Creek in the first place—to find his birth mother. He was getting closer to that goal, but he kept getting distracted. Mostly by Emma. She was the rea-son he was stuck with Mutt and Oliver. This was all her fault.

But the thought of another man, even a geeky scientific one, sleeping within feet of Emma had driven Jake crazy. He'd had to get Oliver out of Emma's apartment so he'd moved the geek in with him. Kind of a spur-of-the-moment thing. No surprise there. Most of his adult life was spur of the moment, living in the moment, and sometimes messing up the moment.

So here he was, four hours into his latest gig as Oliver's host and his advisor about all things female. The guy might be going to MIT but he sure was clueless about the ladies.

Oliver's date with Lulu was tonight. He was more ner-vous than a rookie in his first race.

"Which T-shirt should I wear?" Oliver held up a GEEK IS CHIC and then an EINSTEIN ROCKS tee.

"How should I know?"

"What about the pants? Are these okay?"

"Again, how should I know?" Oliver's crestfallen expression gave Jake a twinge of guilt so he added, "You look okay."

"Lulu said she liked my blond highlights," Oliver said proudly.

"Good for you." It was only now occurring to Jake that if Zoe was his birth mother, then Lulu would be his half sister.

Okay, maybe it had occurred to him before, but he'd wiped it from his mind because it felt weird. All of this was weird. That must be why he suddenly felt the urge to deliver some kind of protective big-brother speech warning Oliver not to take advantage of Lulu.

It was more likely that Lulu would take advantage of Oliver. The guy didn't stand a chance. Lulu could take care of herself. Oliver couldn't.

"Listen, just be cool, dude," Jake said.

"Right." Oliver pulled on the EINSTEIN ROCKS T-shirt, messing up his highlighted hair and making him look as though he'd just stuck his finger in an electric outlet.

Lulu was coming to pick up Oliver at Jake's place before Jake headed off to work the late shift at the tavern. Which meant she'd be here any minute now.

When Lulu knocked on the door, Oliver went berserk. "She's here! She's here!"

"Dude." Jake shook his head.

"Right." Oliver stood still. "Be cool. No problemo. I am totally cool. Cooler than liquid hydrogen, which is negative 252.87 degrees Celsius."

Lulu banged on the door.

Oliver nervously looked to Jake for his cue.

"Open the freaking door," Jake growled.

"Right. Of course." Oliver ran so fast he almost tripped over his own feet.

"Live long and—"

"Prosper. Yeah, whatever. Hi, Mutt." Ignoring Oliver, Lulu bent down to hug the dog.

Jake immediately knew something was up. Oliver remained clueless. "So how's it going?" Jake asked Lulu.

"Life sucks," she said.

"Yeah, sometimes it does."

"Zoe is still in town. I don't know why she doesn't just leave me alone."

"Because she's your mother."

"In name only."

"So I'm guessing you're still avoiding her?" Jake asked.

Lulu nodded. "All week long." She straightened and glared at Oliver, who had remained silent. "I've got my period and I'm in a rotten mood. Are you sure you still want to go out with me?"

The poor sap just beamed at her. "Definitely."

"Have fun, you two." Jake ushered them out the door.

Alone at last.

"Woof."

Not quite.

"What do you want?" Jake said.

"Woof."

"Don't even try to pretend that you understand what I'm saying. I'm not talking to you. I'm talking to myself. You just happen to be in the room."

"Woof."

"One thing's for damn sure. You're never going to see me acting so whacked out over a woman. Never gonna happen, my friend. I'm just here biding my time to get some answers about my birth mother and then I'm gone. Hitting the road. You know what my buddy Andy would tell me, don't you? He had this saying—'Handle every situation like a dog. If you can't eat it or hump it, just piss on it and walk away.'"

"Woof."

"I'm good at walking away. From women, from commitments, even from killer avalanches. Yeah, I'm a damn Olympic gold medalist at walking away." Jake paused to look at Mutt. "Don't give me that hang-dog look."

Mutt sat his bony ass down on Jake's bare foot.

"You're not gonna keep me here when it's time for me to go. No kick-ass sociologist with incredible legs and a complicated brain is gonna keep me here either. Got that?"

Mutt wagged his tail at him.

"I said got that?"

"Woof."

"Good. As long as we're clear. Now get off my foot before you break it."

"Woof."

• • •

"Did you see that? The guy in that rusty pickup just gave you the finger," Oliver told Emma as they walked toward her Prius on Sunday. "He's doing it again!"

Emma looked across the street to see Roy slowing his truck to stick his arm out the open window in order to give her the obscene gesture.

"Do you know him?" Oliver asked.

"You could say that." Even from this distance she could see the anger emanating from Roy.

"Is he a friend of yours?"

"Do you think a friend of mine would greet me like that?"

"Of course not. You're right. I wasn't thinking straight. It's just that everyone has been so nice here. I wasn't expecting to see something like that."

Roy had slowed his dilapidated truck to a crawl, making Emma very nervous.

"Come on." She grabbed hold of Oliver's arm. "Let's stop here." She tugged him into the tea shop. The owner, Steve Daniels, was a former pro wrestler who'd married an English nanny. She doubted Roy would come in and confront a man twice his size. She was right. Roy took off.

"Can I help you?" Steve asked.

"Do you have any organic green tea?" Oliver asked.

"Loose or in tea bags?"

"Loose."

"Right here."

She waited while Steve and Oliver talked about the health benefits of green tea. "Nice move." The compliment came from behind her, and she turned to see Nathan, the town sheriff, holding a box of tea bags in his hand.

"What?"

"Coming in here when you felt threatened by Roy. That was a smart move. I was just on my way out there to give him a ticket for holding up traffic, but there wasn't any other traffic. Has Roy made any other contact with you? Tried to intimidate or threaten you in any way?"

"No."

"Good. You'll be sure to tell me if he does, right?"

She nodded.

"You may have noticed that he has a drinking problem, and that makes him do stupid things. Not that he is all that smart to begin with."

"I heard that he isn't happy about the recent changes here in Rock Creek."

"If you're thinking that he was giving the finger to Steve here at the tea shop, then I have to tell you that I find that an unlikely scenario. I know he's got a grudge against you. I heard about the incident in Nick's Tavern a few weeks back."

"I'm sorry about that," she said guiltily.

"No need for you to be sorry. Just be careful."

"I try to be."

"Yeah, my wife Skye told me you seemed to be the careful sort. But then, compared to her, a daredevil would be considered careful. She made me come in here to get her some kind of weird tea. Algee's girl made him come in here too. We're not really tea guys."

The owner of Cosmic Comics gave her a self-conscious wave from the back corner of the shop where he was trying to be inconspicuous, no easy feat for a guy built like a Sherman tank.

Nathan continued speaking. "I hear your friend Oliver has moved in with Jake and is dating Lulu." Seeing her surprised look, he added, "There's not much going on in this town that I don't know about."

Which left Emma wondering if Nathan knew about Jake and her making out on her fire escape. Roy had been a witness to that. Which is why Emma hadn't gone back out on that fire escape since then.

"Do you know why Jake is here in Rock Creek?" The words were out before she could stop them.

"No. Have you tried asking him that question?"

"He doesn't really respond well to questions."

Nathan nodded. "Yeah, I noticed that about him."

Emma checked her watch. "Well, we'd better be going. We're heading for a family barbeque at the trailer park, and my mom will have a fit if we're late."

"Remember what I said. If Roy tries anything, contact me immediately."

She nodded. "I will."

"Who was that?" Oliver asked as he rejoined her.

"The town sheriff."

"Is he going to arrest the miscreant who gave you the finger?"

"No."

"Why not?"

"Because he didn't break the law."

"What about the law of civilized society?"

"Roy isn't real civilized."

"So I gathered."

Emma put her hand on Oliver's arm. "Don't tell Jake about what happened."

"Why not?"

"Because I don't want him going after Roy or anything like that."

Oliver reluctantly agreed to keep quiet.

Quiet was nowhere to be found at the Riley residence in the Regency Mobile Home Community. The party was already in full swing and looked more like a block party than a little family get-together. The blacktopped street in front of the trailer was filled with aluminum folding lawn chairs and white resin chairs populated with adults and kids alike. Several tables were set up, covered with cheerful paper tablecloths and loaded with all kinds of food, from Mrs. Schmidt's famous pink potato salad to Maxie's infamously spicy fiesta dip. A group of grills were sending up smoke signals on the far side of the cement patio, where Emma's dad appeared to be in charge. He even wore a barbeque apron that said IN CHARGE.

A large metal tub was filled with ice and a selection of soda and beer. Several plastic American flags all along the drive fluttered in the wind even though the Fourth of July was still over a week away.

"Your parents sure know how to throw a party," Oliver noted in appreciation. "I must go speak with the lovely Lulu." He was gone an instant later.

"You're late," Maxie told Emma before hugging her. "I wish you'd worn a more colorful outfit, hon. You should have left your hair loose. And those shoes." Maxie shook her head, nearly dislodging the bright yellow silk orchid she had tucked behind one ear.

"They're Doc Martens and very comfortable."

"I should hope so since they look so bad."

That did it. Emma had already dealt with Roy today, she didn't have the patience for any more hassle. Her mom's comment was the straw that broke the proverbial camel's back. Emma had finally had enough. "Do not insult my shoes!" Emma's voice was firm and emphatic.

Her mom blinked in surprise. "What did you say?"

"You heard me. Don't insult my shoes or anything else about me. I'm tired of it."

"I'm just trying to help—"

Emma held up her hand. "Don't."

"But—"

"Enough already," Emma interrupted her. "I love you and I know you love me, but these negative comments you aim at me have to stop."

"Aim? You make it sound like I've got a gun aimed at you or something."

"Words can be powerful weapons."

Maxie looked distressed. "I'm not trying to hurt you."

"Then don't. It stops here." Emma wasn't naïve enough to think she could instantly transform her mom's behavior after all these years. But Emma could change her own response. She had that power, she'd just never exercised it until now. Instead of continuing to allow her mom to get away with the barbs, however well meaning they might be, Emma was hereby putting her mom on notice. "I'm not going to take it anymore. If you insult me, I'm going to call you on it."

To Emma's utter astonishment, Maxie was silent a moment or two as she digested Emma's comments. Then she nodded and said, "Fair enough."

Emma narrowed her eyes at her. "I mean it, Mom."

"I know you do, hon. I can't promise something might

not slip out from time to time, but I really will try to do a lot better, I promise," she solemnly vowed. "Okay?"

Emma nodded. "Okay." She was so thankful Maxie didn't have a meltdown, Emma couldn't say another word.

Instead of going ballistic, Maxie focused her attention over Emma's shoulder. "Oh look! Leena and Cole are here." Maxie left to go greet them.

Needing a moment to reflect on what had just taken place, Emma headed for an empty chair as far away as she could get without leaving the festivities entirely. She probably should have stood up for herself a long time ago, but she hadn't actually spent that much time with her family since she'd left to go to college. As the designated family peacekeeper, she tended to avoid confrontations . . . but enough was enough. She wished she'd spoken up sooner, but she was sure glad she'd done it now.

Emma was still mentally patting herself on the back when Leena found her and joined her.

"Where's Cole?" Emma asked.

"Helping Dad grill."

"Thank God Dad is grilling and Mom isn't cooking," Emma said.

"Mom doesn't cook. She defrosts. If it doesn't come out of the freezer or a can, she can't deal with it."

"And everything tastes better with mixed frozen veggies."

"We single-handedly kept the Green Giant off the unemployment lines."

"Do you remember the time Mom put mixed frozen veggies in the Chef Boyardee ravioli and called it dinner?"

"Yeah. I also remember that you and I never finished our conversation about Jake," Leena said. "I hear via the grapevine that he had Oliver move in with him. What's up with that?"

"Did people grill you about Cole when you first came to town?"

"Yes."

"Did you like it?"

"No. But this is different," Leena said.

"No, it's not." Emma waved her hand. "Change of subject. I just put Mom on notice that I'm not going to put up with any more insults, however well-meaning they might be."

"Hah! Good luck with that."

"Mom was actually surprisingly accommodating about it."

Leena's perfectly made-up eyes widened. "I find that hard to believe."

"Anyway I wanted to let you know that the same goes for you and Sue Ellen too. No more insults."

"We're your sisters. It's our job to insult you."

"I'm serious. No more trying to make me over in your image." Emma wiggled her Doc Martens at her, comparing them to Leena's dainty floral sandals. "Agreed? If Mom can restrain herself, so can you."

"Fine, spoilsport."

"What are you two girls doing hiding out over here?" their dad walked over and demanded. "Come get some food. Bratwurst with sauerkraut, hot dogs, or hamburgers?"

Leena looked a little green so Emma said, "We'll be there in a minute."

"I haven't had the morning sickness that Sue Ellen has," Leena said quietly after their dad left. "But every so often I'll smell some food and it just sets me off. Don't worry, I'm not going to hurl in your lap."

"I'm relieved to hear that."

"Although you hurled in my lap."

"I was only six at the time and I got sick on the Ferris wheel."

"Who gets sick on a Ferris wheel? On a roller coaster maybe." Leena shook her head. "See that's why I'm worried about you being with Jake."

"Because I threw up on an amusement park ride?"

"Because you're not comfortable taking chances and being wild."

"I'm not six years old anymore."

"I know that but—"

"But nothing. You don't have to worry about me. I'm fine."

"Jake—"

Emma interrupted her. "Jake is fine too."

"He sure is. And he's walking this way."

"What?" Emma swiveled in her seat. Sure enough, he was strolling toward them with that walk of his, full of confidence and sex appeal. He was wearing his usual black jeans and black T-shirt. His brown hair curled over his ears and fell across his forehead. "What are you doing here?" She really had to stop asking him that.

"I invited him," Maxie said cheerfully as she strolled up beside him. "You haven't lived until you've had my spicy fiesta dip, Jake. The secret ingredient is—"

"Frozen mixed vegetables," Emma and Leena said in unison.

"Leena, Mrs. Schmidt wants to talk with you." Maxie tugged her out of her seat. "Come along."

"I'm sorry if my mom has been hassling you," Emma told Jake. "I saw her go into the bar the other day. I hope she didn't ask you a bunch of embarrassing questions."

Jake took the seat Leena had just vacated. As he did so, the sun shone a little brighter, the robins chirped a little more cheerfully, the Dr Pepper soda he brought her tasted a little better.

"Here." He handed her a small bag of Cheetos. "I thought you might need these."

She grabbed the bag and ripped it open. "You're a saint."

"You're the first person who's ever called me that." He leaned closer. "You've got Cheeto dust on your lip." He brushed her mouth with the ball of his thumb. Looking down, he added, "You've got some on your fingers too." He lifted her hand to his mouth and licked her fingers, one by one, until she was ready to jump him right there and then. Luckily she was prevented from doing so by the piercing sound of an air horn activated by her dad.

"Now that I've got everyone's attention, I want to propose a toast," her dad said. He raised his bottle of nonalcoholic beer. "To family and friends."

A minute later, Mrs. Schmidt piped up to say, "Okay, Bob and Maxie, how are you two ridgerunners handling retirement living down there in flatlander Florida? It's no PA. I mean this state has the QVC headquarters. And if that's not enough, there's Frank Lloyd Wright's Fallingwater house. How about Independence Hall and the Liberty Bell, huh? Or Indiana, PA, the birthplace of Jimmy Stewart with a museum dedicated to him."

"I loved him in *It's a Wonderful Life*," Maxie said.

"And then there's Hershey PA. Chocolate, chocolate, chocolate. What does Florida have?" Mrs. Schmidt asked.

"Great weather," Maxie said.

"Hurricanes," the other woman retorted.

"No snow," Maxie instantly shot back.

"She's got you there," someone called out with a laugh.

Emma turned to Jake and grinned at him. "I'm surprised no one mentioned the Crayola Factory over in Easton."

His grin turned wicked. "Or Gobsmacked Knob."

"I'll have to take you up there sometime," she murmured.

"I look forward to it."

. . .

The next evening Emma was looking forward to seeing Jake again. He'd had to leave the party early to go to work, and she was tracking him down there tonight because she missed him so much. She'd been dutifully working on her research project all day, entering data from the stack of completed questionnaires she'd received in the mail, and she deserved a reward. Seeing him would be the best kind.

She hadn't actually returned to Nick's Tavern since that first day when Roy had grabbed her. The memory was still unsettling, but she refused to let him prevent her from going where she wanted.

Emma walked in, her confidence pinned firmly in place. Unlike her first visit, there was quite a crowd there tonight. They blocked her view of the bar and Jake. Then, like the Red Sea, they parted and Emma saw the man she'd been dreaming about, the man who'd given her multiple orgasms even if they hadn't made love yet. The man who had his hand on a woman's bare breast as she laughed up at him adoringly.

The other woman was everything Emma wasn't—bold, beautiful, and sexually confident. This was the kind of woman that Jake was accustomed to dealing with. Not an academic bookworm like her. Who was she kidding?

"Enjoying the view?" Roy asked from beside her. "I saw you and pretty boy Jake playing grab ass on your fire escape, and here he is playing grab tits with another babe." His sleazy laugh made her stomach turn. "How clever are you now, smart girl?"

Emma was smart enough to turn around and walk out of the tavern before she started to cry. If she happened to step on Roy's foot on her way out, so much the better.

Chapter Fourteen

. . . .

The phone was ringing when Emma entered her apartment. She would have ignored it but caller ID told her it was her coworker Nadine from Boston and Emma was afraid something might have gone wrong with her job or her apartment.

"Hey, Emma," Nadine said. "I'm sorry to bother you, but I needed to tell you what Liam did."

Emma really wasn't in the mood to hear some proud-parent story. The tears she'd held at bay in public were now on the verge of falling in private.

Nadine continued before Emma could protest. "Liam loved that autograph you got for him and was so proud of having it. Apparently he went online and posted on a blog site that was talking about Jake Slayter. They were saying how he'd disappeared and I guess were even doing some kind of contest or game like Where's Waldo. Anyway, my kid didn't think, he just posted that Jake was in Rock Creek. I hope that doesn't create any trouble for you or Jake."

Trouble? Hell yes. Now every groupie under the sun and on the Internet would find him. "I've got to go. We'll talk later."

A minute later Emma was online. It was about time she found out who Jake Slayter really was.

An hour later she had her answer. He had his own website stating that he was the owner and CEO of a high-tech, high-quality snowboard factory in Austria. He had half a dozen fan sites and an official fan club on Facebook.com. Many of the posts over the past two months speculated about Jake's future.

Lulu was right. Some of the posts claimed Jake had lost his edge after the climbing accident eighteen months ago. Since then, most of his sponsors had backed out after his injuries kept him from competing. Meanwhile, the media was hot to track him down and get the real story about the death of his best friend Andy Kent on that mountain in Peru.

She pulled up several media reports around the time of his accident and discovered that the press had accused him of cutting the rope to save himself. The third climber, a British friend of Andy's who was there, was quoted as saying, "It looked like the rope was severed, but that could have been done by a piece of ice in the avalanche. Jake said he didn't do that, so I guess I believe him."

Not exactly a ringing endorsement and the press had pounced on that and attacked Jake even more intensely.

No wonder he'd been angry when he'd accused her of being a reporter wanting an interview with him.

Despite those insinuations and accusations by the media, many of his fans were still loyal followers of Slayter the Slayer. A majority of those fans were female, drooling over Jake's looks or his body. They wondered if the speed freak on the mountains was equally fast in bed.

Some women even claimed to have hooked up with him at various events. They posted photos of themselves with him kissing or hugging them. They were all as beautiful as the woman in Nick's Tavern.

Emma's research only reinforced what she'd known when she'd seen Jake fondling that woman's breast in the bar tonight. She'd been an idiot not to have checked him out online before. But like a romantic fool, she'd wanted him to confide in her on his own.

Yeah, right. Like that was going to happen.

She'd given Jake plenty of opportunity to talk to her. Instead he'd told her very little, claiming he preferred action to words. Obviously. That was clear by the photos posted online with busty snow bunnies fawning over him like girls in a harem. He was caressing them, not conversing with them.

Emma compared herself to the other women and knew there was no contest. *Not even close*, her dulled brain told her. The same thought kept repeating itself over and over again: *How could you be so stupid?*

The snow bunnies would be coming out of the woodwork now that Liam had posted Jake's location online.

She shouldn't care, but she did. Emma had never been the kind to turn her feelings off and on at will. But then she'd also never been the kind to fall for a guy so fast and so damn hard.

The sociologist in her clinically continued the research, searching for answers. A link from one of the sites took her from Jake's sex life to more information about his sport activities, where one tiny miscalculation or one bad turn of the dice could snuff out a life. *The need for adventure is hard-wired into some people.* She knew that. She just didn't know why.

Which led her to more research and notes on risk

takers. None of which reassured her about Jake or stopped the pain she felt inside, but at least her inner academic diva was distracted by the information she was gathering.

Maybe her encounter with Jake was fate's way of pushing her to write the book proposal after all. Her heart wasn't in it, but her head battled on, making her polish her notes long into the night and finally push the Send button to the assistant editor's e-mail address.

The screen returned to a website with a photo of a grinning Jake looking sexy as he stood with a trophy and a babe beside him.

A knock on her door made her jump a foot.

"It's me," Jake said through the door.

"Go away!"

"I saw your light was still on so I know you're not sleeping. I just got off work."

She wondered if he'd just gotten off the half-naked snow bunny.

"Come on, open up," he coaxed her, his voice a powerful influence on her even through a few inches of door. "We need to talk. Someone said they saw you rush out of the bar."

Emma yanked open the door. "Did Roy tell you?"

"Roy?" Jake stepped inside and carefully closed the door behind him. "No. Was he there?"

"I can see how you wouldn't notice that, seeing that you were distracted by a bare-breasted woman hanging all over you."

"Is that why you left?" Jake said.

"I left because you're a man who goes for girls like her." Was her voice quivering? How sappy was that? She cleared her throat and tried again. "You're not the kind to go for a woman like me."

"Wrong." Jake pulled her close so she could feel how much he wanted her.

She wasn't that easily impressed. She stepped away from him. "Then you're the kind of man to go for any woman."

"I don't want any woman. I want you."

"And that's why you were fondling her breast?"

"She wanted me to autograph it."

"You told me you don't do autographs. Apparently you only do them if a woman offers her bare breast to you."

"That's not true. She walked into the bar. I don't know how she found me. She hangs around all the greatest shows on snow and hooks up with the winners. I told her tonight that I wasn't interested."

"So you know her." It wasn't a question since she already suspected the answer. "You hooked up with her in the past, didn't you?"

"That was before my accident, before I came here, before I met you."

"I spent the past hour researching you on the Internet."

"Don't believe everything you read."

"Even if I only believe half of it, that's enough."

"Enough to what?"

"Enough to know we've got nothing in common."

"That's not true." He took her in his arms, her body pressed tightly against his. "You want me. I want you."

"You're not the kind to want me once you've had me." Her voice was steady even if her emotions weren't.

"Wrong again. Let me prove it. Let me prove you wrong."

"Why?" She wiggled out of his embrace. "So you can prove that you're a winner? Risk takers like you always have to come out winners, right? That's why you want to have sex with me. So you can win."

"I don't give a rat's rectum about winning tonight," he growled.

"That's a lie and you know it. I'm not some mountain you can conquer."

"I know that. I also know that you're the first thing to make me feel alive in a very long time." There was no faking the vulnerability in his brooding eyes.

She looked away.

"Emma." He whispered her name as if it held all the treasures in the world.

She didn't realize until that moment how much she desperately wanted to believe him. "I'm not one of your groupie snow bunnies."

"No, you're not. You're a kick-ass sociologist with the power to bring me to my knees." He lowered his mouth to hers. "Let me show you," he murmured against her lips.

She wasn't easily convinced, but in the end Jake had some very persuasive arguments. His hungry kiss was very convincing. She boldly greeted the velvety insistence of his tongue with her own. His fingers trembled as he reached under her favorite polo shirt to undo the fastening of her bra.

The possibility that she could make a bad boy like him lose control was incredibly sexy. She had to investigate further.

Leaning into him, she tugged his black T-shirt from his dark jeans and trailed her fingertips across the bare strip of skin she'd revealed. The tiny caress had him growling his approval.

Jake back-stepped her toward her futon, which was open in preparation for her going to bed. When she fell onto it, he followed her down, twisting so that she was on top of him. She knew he did that so she wouldn't feel confined and panic because of the mugging. That knowledge made her want him even more. She pulled off her shirt and bra and shimmied out of her jeans.

Jake tugged her closer, so that her bare breast hovered right above his mouth. He teased the tip of her nipple with his tongue until she shivered with delight. When his mouth surrounded her she arched against him.

After that, things escalated quickly. His clothes came off and a condom went on. She pulled him down to her, silently telling him that she was ready for him. He positioned her so that she sat astride him. Running a hand up her thigh, he slipped his skillful fingers over and into her moist feminine core, propelling her closer and closer to climax.

Only when he was sure she was ready did he slowly ease into her until he was buried deep within her. She lifted her hips and slid down again, creating a friction that drove her wild. He set the pace and she matched him surge for surge.

He encouraged her to experiment with angles and movements to maximize her pleasure. This was all new sexual territory for Emma, and she explored it with joyful enthusiasm. She could feel the erotic tension building deep within her until she was propelled into a climax so blissfully powerful it was almost beyond belief.

Jake gave one final thrust before he came too.

Ten minutes later Emma was still speechless.

Jake wasn't. "Are you hungry?"

She eyed his bare body warily. "Don't you need some recovery time?"

"I was talking about food, but if you want something else . . ." He nuzzled her neck until she giggled. "Are you laughing at me?" he demanded.

"With you. I was laughing *with* you."

"You're the one giggling, not me."

"I can fix that." She reached out to tickle him. He stoically remained unmoved until her hand accidentally on purpose brushed his arousal. "Oops."

He had her flat on her back an instant later. She tried to be helpful by assisting him with a new condom, but all she did was make him groan with need. "You're killing me," he growled.

"*Le petite morte.* A little death. French for"—she gasped with delight as he entered her with one powerful thrust—"orgasm." She could barely speak.

This time he made love to her with a wild abandon that left her vibrating with bliss until she quickly came. He followed soon after.

Later, as she lay curled up with him, she tried to keep her eyes open, but it was a hopeless battle.

She wasn't sure how much later it was when a creak in the floor woke her up. She saw Jake preparing to leave.

"Go back to sleep," he said.

"You can stay the night."

"No, I can't." His voice was curt. "I've got to go. You understand, right?"

"Sure." *Not sure. Totally unsure.* "I understand." *No, I don't. I don't have a clue. Does this mean you regret having sex with me? That it was a mistake?*

Jake returned to sit on the futon beside her. He threaded his fingers tenderly through her loose hair. "I can read your mind."

"No, you can't." Could he? She sure hoped not.

"I can make a pretty good guess what you're thinking. Guy makes love to you and then takes off. What a rat bastard, right?" He sighed. "Look, I get nightmares."

"So?"

"So I don't want you seeing me that way."

"What way?"

Guilty, vulnerable, torn up inside. He feared the nightmares would come as soon as he fell asleep, and he couldn't risk that. But Jake couldn't admit that so he kissed her instead. One thing led to anther and soon he'd used his last condom and was embedded deep within her.

Dawn was stealing across the sky when Jake finally let himself out of her apartment, leaving a sleeping Emma behind and taking his nightmares with him.

• • •

Emma woke around noon to find the bed beside her empty and no sign of Jake. She was immediately struck by a surprising sense of loneliness at his absence. She reassured herself with the X-rated memories of the night they'd shared. After a quick shower and her usual breakfast she started feeling more in control and less of a hussy.

She told herself she wasn't waiting for Jake to call her, but that was a lie. She looked across the alley, but there was no sign of him in his apartment. Instead she saw Oliver waving at her. Five minutes later, he was at her front door.

"Jake didn't come home last night," Oliver said before putting his hand to his mouth. "Uh-oh. Maybe I shouldn't have said anything. I just assumed he was with you."

"He was."

"That's a relief. I never seem to say the right thing. If I knew as much about relationships as I do nanotechnology, I'd be in great shape."

"How are things going with you and Lulu?"

"Not as good as with you and Jake."

That was just it. Emma wasn't sure how good things were between her and Jake. Oh, the sex had been incredible. At least she'd thought so. But maybe it was nothing special as far as Jake was concerned.

He'd said he wasn't interested in other women, only in

her. But what if he was only saying what she wanted to hear? He wouldn't be the first man to do that.

He'd told her that he had nightmares and that's why he couldn't stay. Had that just been an excuse?

"Did I say something wrong?" Oliver asked her. "I didn't mean to."

"No, it's not you: it's me."

"I hear that's what a girl says to you right before she dumps you. That or they text you saying you're a loser. Not that either of those two things has ever happened to me. You don't think Lulu would dump me with a text message, do you?"

"She seems the direct sort. If she wanted to dump you, she'd tell you to your face, I think."

Oliver nodded. "You're right."

"Why are you afraid she'd dump you?"

"It's more that I'm afraid in general about relationships, you know?"

"Yeah, I know." *Only too well.* Emma didn't realize how much fear had taken over her life. It was as if the mugging had triggered a closet full of anxieties—had she picked the right job, the right research project, the right man?

Her inner pop quiz was interrupted by the sound of someone knocking on her door. It was Jake and Mutt.

"I was just leaving," Oliver quickly assured Jake.

"Take Mutt back with you."

The dog bounced over to Emma and sat at her feet adoringly. She rubbed his ear. "He likes me."

"He's not the only one." Jake sent her a heated look that just about sizzled her.

"Come on, Mutt," Oliver said. "We're not wanted here."

He'd barely closed the door before Jake had Emma in his arms again. He was peeling her T-shirt off while kissing her with fiery urgency. "I got more condoms," he told her.

"Good." She removed his T-shirt and undid his jeans. "I hope you brought more than one."

He held out a handful. Her eyes widened as she started counting. "One, two, three, four, five, six, seven—"

"Anyone ever tell you that you talk too much?" a naked and fully aroused Jake demanded before scooping her in his arms and depositing her on the still unmade futon.

The only talking she did after that was to shout his name each time he brought her to the heights of an orgasm.

• • •

"I call this meeting to order." Bart Chumley banged his gavel to indicate he meant business.

Bart had invited Emma to attend tonight's community meeting because he wanted to address the concerns some of Rock Creek's citizens had stated. She recognized many of the faces in the meeting room, including Roy. She sat as far away from him as possible.

Emma was still finding it a little difficult to concentrate after her marathon sex with Jake, a fact that Oliver had noticed when he and Lulu accompanied her to the meeting. Tonight Lulu was wearing her ALLERGIC TO STUPID PEOPLE T-shirt.

Emma hoped that Oliver wouldn't make any comments about Jake not coming home last night. She really didn't want her private life being dissected by Lulu or anyone else.

"As you know, some people have expressed certain concerns regarding the revitalization of Rock Creek," Bart said. "I'm here this evening to assure you that these changes are all positive ones."

"It's not positive when a man can't even walk into his local bar without out-of-towners getting all pissy on you," Roy said. "There was nothing wrong with this town before."

"Except that a majority of the buildings along Barwell Street were empty."

"As long as the bar stays open, I don't care."

"You should care," Bart said. "This is your hometown, and if we don't take action, then it's going to die. The young people will keep leaving and pretty soon the place will be a ghost town."

"We don't need people like her"—Roy stood and pointed directly at Emma—"coming in and stirring up trouble."

"Emma, would you care to say a few words?" Bart invited.

No, I'd rather eat bugs. She reluctantly stood.

"Do you want to come up here to the podium?"

No, I want to leave the building. Instead Emma made her way to the front of the room, pretending she was just speaking to another freshman class of students, albeit a hostile class. "I'm really only here to observe and not interfere."

"Yeah, right," Roy scoffed. "If you believe that, then I've got some Enron stock to sell you."

"You should all be proud of the way that Rock Creek has continued to evolve," Emma said.

"She's one of those evolutionists," Roy told the others. "They invade God-fearing towns with their liberal ideas and beliefs."

"Yeah, and then we snatch your body and ship it to outer space," Lulu said.

Roy's face flushed as several people laughed at Lulu's mocking comment.

"Nothing you did would surprise me," Roy said.

Sister Mary stood to speak. The crowd quieted. "Most of the small businesses are entrepreneur driven, and I believe the concern some have is that those kinds of businesses don't create a lot of jobs."

"Right," Roy said. "We need something big like the lunch-pail factory."

"Those jobs are gone," Bart returned to the podium to say. "And they aren't coming back." He held up his hand to quell the crowd's grumbling. "But I agree that we do need larger-scale businesses and companies that are able to offer more jobs, and that's something we need to investigate further."

Bart gestured for Emma to add a few words. "You know it's natural for people to be afraid of change," Emma began when Roy interrupted her.

"I'm not afraid of anything!"

"No? I heard she beat you up her first day in town," someone in the back row yelled out.

Emma refused to let things get out of hand. She'd once had to deal with a food fight in the middle of one of her classes. She could certainly deal with this. "Violence never solves anything," she firmly stated.

"Then why did you beat Roy up?"

"That's not what happened. Regardless, that incident was a mistake and I'm sorry. Now if we could return to the matter of Rock Creek. I think we all share the same love for our hometown, and we all want what's best for it to continue."

"Not if it means turning the place into some haven for weirdos," Roy said.

The meeting deteriorated after that, with the attendees leaping to their feet and shouting their differing opinions.

"And that concludes our meeting tonight," Bart said with the calmness of a circus ringmaster. "Thanks for coming out this evening, folks, and drive home safe."

• • •

Wednesday morning, 10 a.m. Jake stood outside of Crumpler's Auto Parts for fifteen minutes trying to screw up his courage to go inside. He studied the sign in the window—WE HAVE THE BEST PARTS AROUND—as if it held the answers to all the questions he had. Stupid. Finally he just walked inside.

"Hi, there," Nancy greeted him. "Do you need a part for your Jeep, or have you come to get those NASCAR lessons I offered you?"

"Neither." Jake paused, uncharacteristically nervous. Speeding down mountains was what he did best. This interpersonal stuff was not his strength. He'd been trying for days to come up with a good way to approach the subject and he had nada. "Look, I know this sort of comes out of left field, but bear with me here. I, uh . . . hell, I'm just going to flat out ask you." But he didn't know how to do that without sounding like an idiot. "I was adopted as a baby. I'm, uh, doing a kind of personal search."

"And you need my help in your search for your birth mother?"

"You could say that."

"Well, hell yes, I'll help any way I can." She patted his hand reassuringly. "What do you want to know?"

"Is it you?"

Nancy frowned in confusion. "Is what me?"

"Did you have a baby and give it up for adoption?"

"Are you going around town asking all the women this question?"

"Of course not."

"Then what makes you ask me?"

"You're the right age. I don't have much to go on," he admitted. "Just that the birth mother is from Rock Creek and her age. The investigator I hired narrowed it down to three candidates."

"And I'm one of those candidates? Because of my age?"

"And other factors."

"Well, before you get your hopes up, I can't be your birth mother since I never had a baby that I gave up for adoption."

He believed her.

"Who are the other candidates?" she asked.

"I'd rather not say."

"Am I the first one you asked?"

"Directly asked, yes."

"Is that why you're here in Rock Creek, to find your birth mother?"

"Yeah, and I'd appreciate it if you kept that piece of information to yourself."

"No problem. I can do that. I'm good at doing that."

"Yeah?" he wasn't really paying attention because it was starting to sink in that Zoe was winning the possible-birth-mother race by default. Odds were she was his birth mother, unless he'd messed up and none of them were.

"Yeah," Nancy said. "What about the resort rumor? Was that just a story to cover your real reasons for being here?"

"I didn't start that rumor. People just made assumptions."

"Yeah, people tend to do that. Does Emma know?"

Jake shook his head.

"I don't usually give advice . . . well, okay, I do. But

only to people I think deserve my help. But I think you should tell Emma."

"She's busy with her sister's wedding plans."

"Well, right after the wedding then."

"I'm not the kind of guy who talks about my private life."

"Not even with the woman in your life?"

Jake shrugged.

"So you haven't told Emma much about your life?"

Another shrug.

"You don't think she's going to find out when you discover who your birth mother is? And you don't think she's going to be hurt that you didn't confide in her? Didn't trust her?"

"It's not a matter of trust."

"Isn't it?"

"Okay, so maybe it is. So what?"

"So who else knows the real reason you're here?"

"Just you."

"And you only told me out of desperation."

"I wouldn't put it that way. I was running out of options so I decided to just come out and ask you."

"If it's not me, do you know who it might be?"

"Yeah, I have an idea."

She waited for him to say more. He kept quiet. She sighed. "Okay, I can tell you're not going to give me any more information. Just know that if you need any moral support, I'm here. My sister is a nun. Some of that empathy has rubbed off on me. Not a hell of a lot, but some."

"Thanks but—"

"You're a loner used to doing things on your own. I got that. But I still think you need to tell Emma . . . soon. Especially if the two of you are getting close."

Jake made no comment. Emma had gotten close to him in ways he hadn't expected and didn't quite know how to deal with. So he preferred not to think about it. The sex had been great. He knew it was more than sex, knew she made him feel and think things he never had before. And that freaked him out more than he liked.

Chapter Fifteen
· · · · · · · · · · ·

"**Oh** no!" Emma consulted her Blackberry and the detailed wedding "Master Schedule" Leena had painstakingly entered into a Microsoft Outlook spreadsheet program.

> 7:45 a.m.—Hair for bride and bridal party
> 9 a.m.—Makeup for bride and bridal party
> 11 a.m.—Videographer arrives
> Noon—Limo arrives for bride and bridal party
> 12:20 p.m.—Groom arrives at church
> 12:25 p.m.—Groom meets photographer at St. Francis
>   church parking lot for groom and groomsmen photos

Emma stopped checking her Blackberry and glanced at her watch: 7:55 a.m. Damn, she was already late. Leena was going to kill her.

Reaching into her parked Prius, Emma grabbed the garment bag holding her cornflower blue bridesmaid's dress, her backpack, and a tote bag filled with miscellaneous stuff and took off toward the groom's house behind the Rock Creek Animal Clinic. Leena had taken over the large house and temporarily given her groom-to-be the boot during the preparations.

"Sorry I'm late," Emma was breathless from running . . . and from the memory of making love with Jake until the wee hours of the morning.

"I was a little late too." Mindy, Leena's friend from high school and a fellow bridesmaid, gave Emma a reassuring smile.

Leena was not equally welcoming. "I told everyone to be here earlier than the schedule said."

"I know, I know." Emma hung her head.

Sue Ellen sidled up to her and whispered, "Bad hormone alert."

Emma looked at her.

"Not me," Sue Ellen said. "Leena."

"Just a reminder, I'm not doing the bouquet-throwing thing," Leena stated. "I'm not lining up my single friends and humiliating them."

"Because they feel bad enough as it is. Isn't that right, Emma?" Sue Ellen said.

Emma got defensive as all eyes turned to her. "Why ask me?"

"Because you're single."

"And likely to remain that way for the rest of my life, right?"

"Uh, maybe." Sue Ellen blinked, clearly surprised by Emma's attitude. "You told Mom you didn't want to get married."

"Maybe I lied."

"You don't usually lie, do you?"

Emma squirmed guiltily before regaining control. "Why are we even having this discussion now? Leena is supposed to be getting ready for her wedding. Aren't we supposed to be getting our hair done now?"

"Right." Leena clapped her hands to get their attention. "Everyone, this is Cherry. She's the best hair person in the state. She's here with Kelly, who is our makeup artist. They've both worked on high fashion shoots so they know what they're doing."

"Speaking of high fashion photo shoots, what did you decide about trashing your wedding dress?" Sue Ellen asked Leena.

Seeing Emma's startled expression, Leena explained. "The top wedding photographers in the country are taking cutting-edge photos of brides rolling in the sand with their grooms, or splashing through the surf, or standing in the water of a large fountain. They create photos that are unique and creative, not stiffly posed. Some brides even buy less-expensive wedding dresses specifically so they can get them dirty."

"So are you trashing your dress?" Emma asked.

"It's a Vera Wang," Leena said reverently. "I decided I just couldn't do it."

"Besides, we're miles from the ocean," Sue Ellen said. "But there is a large fountain on the church grounds."

"Right. We're taking photos there before and after the wedding ceremony," Leena said. "Check your schedules and you'll see what I mean. The section is marked 'Groom sweeps bride off her feet by fountain.' The photos will be creative."

"Just not dirty," Sue Ellen said.

Emma looked at her sisters and almost snorted the orange juice she was drinking from the bottle.

A split second later they were in the midst of another Riley sister estrogen-driven gigglefest.

Mindy looked on in concern. "Are you all getting hysterical?"

"I'm—" Leena hiccupped. "I'm fine."

"Where is Mom?" Emma asked, wiping the tears of laughter from her eyes.

"I had a limo take her to a top-notch spa for a luxury treatment this morning," Leena said. "She'll be done by eleven to get dressed."

Three hours later, Emma looked in the full-length mirror Leena had set out and couldn't believe her transformation. The strapless tea-length bridesmaid's dress had a sweetheart neckline that suited her to perfection. The cornflower blue color complimented her ivory complexion, which Kelly had highlighted with smoky eyes and a rosy pink lipstick. Cherry had coaxed Emma's hair into a cascade of loose curls that tumbled to her shoulders in a style that was sweet and sexy. "I look *really* good."

Leena laughed. "Yeah, you do. Not as good as me naturally." She grinned. "*I am* the bride after all."

"You look gorgeous," Emma said, turning to face her.

"I always wanted to wear the wedding dress at a fashion show, but that never happened. Until today."

"Everyone's eyes will be on you."

"Except for Jake's. I suspect his eyes are only going to be on you, Em. Think you can handle that?" Leena looked concerned.

"Absolutely. Bring it on."

That confidence stayed with Emma through the short limo trip to St. Francis Church. The Gothic Revival style church had always been one of her favorite buildings in Rock Creek. As a little kid, she'd thought the steeple was tall enough to scrape the sky.

The church grounds were ample, filled with mature maple and oak trees as well as that fountain Leena had talked about.

The reception was being held in a huge tent behind the

building, complete with dance floor and seating for one hundred. Skye's friend Pam Denton from Bloomers in Serenity Falls was in charge of the floral arrangements.

When they all walked by on their way to the church's back entrance, Emma couldn't resist pausing to take a peek inside the tent. The tables were draped with crisp white cloths. In the center of each one was a violet-and-blue colored centerpiece matching Emma's nosegay bouquet of blue delphinium and hydrangea with purple lisianthus. The place already looked magical.

The weather was cooperating with blue skies and no threat of rain in the forecast. Thinking of rain reminded Emma of the last wedding and making out with Jake in the back of his Jeep.

Making love with him was even better and was the reason she'd been late this morning. She was just glad her sisters couldn't tell, that her face didn't give her away. This thing she had with Jake was too new to share yet. She hugged it to herself the way she had hugged a Kermit the Frog stuffed toy she'd had as a little kid. Not that Jake and Kermit had anything in common. She had to laugh at the idea.

"What's so funny?" Leena asked.

"Nothing."

"Let's stay focused, people. The videographer is taking video of the beautiful landscape and side rose garden area as we speak. We're going to meet him now and get some shots of me with my bridesmaids. Phil the photographer will be there too."

During the ensuing photo shoot Leena checked both men's work, adding her own critique as she looked at the photographer's digital camera display. "Sue Ellen, you're posing too much. You need to face the camera more."

Sue Ellen pouted. "That makes me look fat."

Emma and Leena shared a look. Sue Ellen was starting to show and wouldn't be able to hide the truth of that baby bump of hers much longer.

"Everybody here knows you're pregnant," Leena said.

"Do they know you're pregnant too?" Sue Ellen retorted.

Leena glared at her. "They do now. Thanks for being discreet."

"You started it."

"Smile ladies," Phil the photographer cheerfully requested.

Leena and Sue Ellen instantly turned to the camera and put on a happy face. Emma was sure she and Mindy had more of a deer-caught-in-the-headlights expression.

Cole joined them shortly afterward along with his three groomsmen—his brother, and his friends Nathan and Algee. The guys all looked great in their formal attire. More group shots were taken before they moved to the fountain with St. Francis in the center. The statue of the saint had a bird perched on one hand and was petting a deer with the other. The artist had given St. Francis an expression of calm that Emma envied at that moment. She was tired of all this picture taking.

"Look, Mommy, it's Bambi!" Skye's daughter Toni exclaimed as she ran out to join them.

Nathan scooped his stepdaughter up in his arms. "Aren't you the beautiful princess."

"You look pretty too." Toni patted his cheek.

Sue Ellen dabbed at her eyes. "Just think, in another few months I'll have a little one of my own."

"You're going to have your own Bambi?" Toni was impressed. "I want one too."

"Come on you." Skye took her from Nathan. "Let's go before you con your way into getting more pets."

"It seems fitting that a veterinarian is getting married in

a church named after the patron saint of animals," Nathan noted with an elbow jab at Cole. "Unless you're wishing you eloped like Skye and I did?"

"No way." Cole didn't appear the least bit nervous. "I'm exactly where I want to be."

"No you're not!" Maxie exclaimed as she hurried to join them. "You're not supposed to see the bride before the wedding."

"That's an old wives' tale," Leena said. "I wanted our photos taken while we look good."

"Why wasn't I consulted about this?" Maxie demanded.

"Because it's *my* wedding," Leena said.

"I need the parents of the happy couple to join them for photos," the ever-cheerful Phil said.

Cole's parents were very sweet. They played well with others, as the T-shirt saying went.

Despite the early sparks between Maxie and Leena, the wedding went off without a hitch. Nathan escorted Emma down the aisle of the beautiful church to the musical accompaniment of Pachelbel's Canon. The stained glass windows created splashes of color on the marble floor around the alter, lending a mystical feel to the setting.

Bart Chumley sat near the front of the church, not because he was the mayor but because he was a good friend and mentor to Leena.

Emma found herself getting emotional several times during the ceremony as her thoughts flashed back through the many childhood memories she shared with Leena—walking around in their mom's high-heel shoes, arguing over which New Kids on the Block member was the cutest, lamenting over the length of time between Johnny Depp movies. Emma and Leena had shared a bedroom for the first nine years of Emma's life, until Sue Ellen had moved out at eighteen and Leena had moved into her bedroom. Emma had had a hard time sleeping that first night because she'd missed the sound of her sister in the same room.

And now here Leena was, moving on again into a new chapter in her life. And once again Emma was having a bit of a hard time. Of course, she was thrilled for her sister, who was marrying a great guy. Emma had always liked Cole. She kept telling herself that she wasn't losing a sister, she was gaining a brother-in-law.

And it really was inspiring to see the love on both their faces as Leena and Cole repeated their vows. Sentimental tears threatened again, but she was saved from making a fool of herself by catching sight of Jake in the third pew. He was seated directly in her line of vision, and he was grinning at her as if he knew what she was thinking.

Jake was wearing the same black shirt and pants that he'd worn to Sue Ellen's reception. Naturally that reminded her of him peeling off his clothing before skinny-dipping at Serenity Falls at midnight. The look he gave her heated up as if he, too, was remembering that night.

Then there was last night . . . Emma's face flushed as images of how he'd used the burgundy tie he was wearing to tie her hands to the bedpost of his bed and have his totally wicked way with her, much to her delight. Hours earlier he'd made a point of putting a sock on the apartment doorknob, giving them the freedom to move around his apartment without worrying about Oliver showing up.

Emma hadn't felt guilty about giving Oliver the boot for the night since he'd spent the time at Lulu's apartment.

Love or lust, call it what you would, it was definitely in the air in Rock Creek these days . . . and nights.

Emma was so engrossed in her thoughts that she didn't even realize the ceremony was over until Sue Ellen nudged her. Leena and Cole were already kissing before turning and walking out of the church.

"Get a move on," Sue Ellen hissed. "I have to pee really bad!"

. . .

Jake couldn't get over how great Emma looked. He'd watched her throughout the ceremony, unable to take his eyes off her. She'd left his bed early that morning, her face flushed from their night of awesome sex, her lips still rosy from his kisses. And now here she was, at the reception, her hair curling with a silky abandon that made him long to reach out and wrap a strand around his finger. She wore more makeup than usual, making her eyes stand out. The pink shimmer of her lip gloss tempted him to kiss it all off.

"How are you holding up?" Nancy Crumpler's question interrupted his thoughts.

"Fine." Jake still felt like an ass for confronting her the way he had.

"I'm assuming you haven't had that talk with Emma yet?"

"What talk?" Emma said from behind them.

Nancy shot him an I'm-sorry look before turning to Emma. "You look so lovely in that dress," she told her. "Don't you agree, Jake?"

"Yeah." And to think he used to be a smooth talker. Apparently those days were gone, along with the rest of his racing career.

"The dress is a big improvement over my last bridesmaid's dress," Emma said with a laugh.

The sound made Jake hot. Since when did a woman's laugh turn him on? Especially since Emma snorted when she laughed really hard. He knew that because he'd tickled her until she'd snorted and then he'd laughed *with* her, not at her.

She was really smart about a lot of things and really innocent about others—like sex. He got such a thrill out of teaching the sociology professor the pleasures to be had in that arena. She might have the advanced degrees but he had the experience to tutor her in the darkly erotic arts and sciences.

"What talk was Jake supposed to have with me?" Emma looked a little nervous at the possibilities that came to mind.

"Nothing important," Jake reassured her. Standing behind her, he slid his arms around her waist and kissed the top of her head. "Nothing for you to worry about."

"Are you sure?"

He squeezed her fingers. "I'm positive."

"Everyone, it's time to cut the cake!" Sue Ellen called out.

Nancy moved to join the gathering crowd.

The multitiered wedding cake was wheeled onto the dance floor where the bride and groom stood ready. Jake eyed the cake with a frown.

"What's that on top of it?"

"A Kate Spade bag. Not a real one of course, one made out of icing and sculpted to look exactly like the designer's purse."

"Why?"

"Because Leena is into bag love versus shoe love. The way she tells it, shoe love fades as your feet get bigger and your shoes pinch you. But bag love remains and lasts forever. Cole is a keeper, he's bag love. That's why the bag is on their wedding cake."

Jake didn't know what to say to that so he remained silent. He tilted his head so he could see Emma's face.

"You'd probably have a mini snowboard on top of your wedding cake," Emma said before clapping her hand over her mouth. "Not that I'm thinking about your wedding cake. Or your wedding. I wasn't trying to drop a hint or anything.

Jeez . . ." She scrunched her face and shook her head. "Just shoot me now."

"I'd rather kiss you and strip you naked," he whispered in her ear.

"Mmm, sounds good," she murmured, leaning back.

He just about came undone when she rubbed her sexy bottom against him. "What are you trying to do to me?" he growled.

"Remind you what a fast learner I am." She tossed him a sexy look over her shoulder that instantly made him get even harder.

"Trust me, I'm not likely to forget."

"I'm glad to hear that."

"So, Jake, have you had a chance to go try Adele's sweet potato fries at Maguire's yet?" The intrusive question came from Walt Whitman, the mayor of Serenity Falls, who'd barged right into their private moment with his usual disregard for others.

Jake's curt "No" should have been enough to send the guy on his way.

But it didn't. "Maybe Julia can convince you." He grabbed the arm of a woman walking by. "Julia, come over here and convince Jake to come to Maguire's. This is Julia Maguire. She's married to Luke, one of the owners of Maguire's."

"You're the librarian," Emma said.

Julia smiled. "That's right. And you're the sociologist."

"The kick-ass sociologist," Jake added.

"And Julia is the kick-ass librarian," a dark-haired guy said as he joined them. He stuck his hand out to Jake. "Luke Maguire."

Jake recognized a fellow rebel.

After giving him a narrow-eyed stare, Luke seemed to reach the same conclusion. "I've heard a lot about you."

Walt puffed out his chest. "Jake here is considering building a sports resort in this area, and I've been telling him how wonderful Serenity Falls is."

"The place sucks," Luke said.

Jake cracked up.

Walt sputtered and turned purple.

"The fries are good, though," Luke added.

"They're part of the wedding dinner here," Julia said.

"You've gone and ruined it," Walt said.

"The dinner? No, it should be great," Julia said.

Her answer seemed to make Walt even angrier. "I don't mean the dinner and you know it. Ignore them," he told Jake. "They're troublemakers."

"My kind of people," Jake said before he and Luke exchanged high fives.

"I've got to return to the head table for the toasts," Emma said.

Jake watched her leave.

"Man, you've got it bad," Luke quietly noted.

Luke's words stayed with Jake for the rest of the evening. He couldn't take his eyes off Emma, and his thoughts were equally stuck on her. He watched her talk to her mother and immediately knew that Maxie said something to drive Emma nuts.

"Are you okay?" Jake asked Emma a short time later.

"Yes." Emma sighed. "It's just that sometimes family issues are complicated."

Jake looked at Nancy across the dance floor. "Yeah, tell me about it."

• • •

Jake held out until Monday afternoon before making his way to the Broken Creek Trailer Park. Like Nick's Tavern, the place had seen better days. He parked his Jeep in front of a trailer that was neater than most of the others.

This time he wasn't going to sit there waiting like he had in front of Crumpler's Auto Parts. This time he was going right in. No thinking about it. He'd done enough thinking to last him a lifetime. Seeing Emma with her family at her sister's wedding had hit home the fact that he needed some answers about his own family.

He opened the screen door and rapped on the Harley logo pasted on the front door.

Zoe came to the door. "Yes? Can I help you?"

"I know this comes out of left field, but I'm just going to come out and ask you—did you have a kid and give it up for adoption thirty years ago?"

Zoe's face paled. "How did you know?"

"Because . . . I'm that kid."

Chapter Sixteen

. . . .

Jake had had no idea how Zoe would react so perhaps he shouldn't have been surprised when she shut the door in his face . . . but he was.

"Well, that went well," he sarcastically muttered to himself. Once again he felt like an ass. What had he expected? That she'd greet him with open arms?

As he turned to leave, the door opened again. "I'm sorry," Zoe said, tears slowly streaming down her face. "I just wasn't expecting this. Come in, please. We need to talk."

He cautiously entered the trailer. It was nothing special—living room with kitchen to the right and a hall presumably leading to bedrooms to the left.

"Would you like something to drink?" Zoe asked.

Hell, he'd like a bottle of freaking vodka, but getting ripped wouldn't solve anything. He'd been there, done that. "No thanks."

She motioned for him to sit on the overstuffed brown

couch. She was no longer crying, which was a relief to Jake. "Did the adoption agency tell you where to find me?"

"No. A fire burned most of their records. The only lead I had was that my birth mother came from Rock Creek, PA, and her age. The other possibilities were ruled out until you were the only one left."

Zoe wiped away her tears with the heel of her hand. "Does Lulu know?"

"No one knows except for you and me."

She nodded as if relieved.

"Look, I'm not looking for any maternal affection or anything here. I just want some facts, that's all. Any medical problems I should be aware of?"

Zoe blinked. "Huh?"

"Medical problems that might be inherited. Cancer, that kind of stuff."

"No."

"What about my father?"

"What about him?

"Any health problems there I should know about?"

"He died in a motorcycle accident before you were born. He liked going fast."

"So do I."

She kept her gaze fixed on him as if he were Bigfoot and had just stepped out of the woods. "I can't believe you're real."

He shifted, uncomfortable with the awe he detected in her voice. He wanted to keep things as impersonal as possible. He hadn't come here for hugs and kisses.

Zoe started talking very fast but not very coherently. "I had to hit rock bottom. It took me twenty years to do that. I'm married now to a great guy. He's a therapist. Helps troubled kids. He helped me. He said I had to come back here and face my fears or I couldn't move on. I've got two stepsons, aged eight and ten, and I've been a good step-mom to them. I need to make peace with my past."

"Meaning Lulu?"

Zoe nodded.

"You never wondered what happened to the kid you gave away?"

"I knew you were adopted by a wonderful couple, and I heard they moved to California with you. I couldn't keep you. I was a sixteen-year-old runaway."

"Did you do drugs when you were pregnant?"

"What?! No!"

"Who are you to be asking my daughter questions like that?" growled a big bear of a man from the doorway. He entered the trailer, glaring menacingly at Jake. He looked like a card-carrying member of the Hell's Angels, every inch of his arms covered in tattoos.

"Who am I?" Jake repeated. "I'm the bastard baby she gave away."

Old Biker Dude turned his attention to Zoe. "Is that true?"

She nodded.

He looked back at Jake. "You want some lasagna?"

"I, uh . . ." Jake didn't know what to say to that.

"It's homemade. Everything looks better after you've had lasagna."

"This is my dad, Jerry Malick," Zoe said. "He's a good cook."

"You're that extreme sports guy, right?" Jerry said.

Jake nodded. "Did you know your daughter had a baby when she was sixteen?"

"I had my suspicions, but we never really talked about it."

"You never wondered what happened to your grand-child?"

"Of course I did, but I wasn't even sure there was a grandchild. She disappeared. Ran away. I didn't have any contact with her for years."

"Yeah," Jake said. "I gathered she's not good at staying in touch."

"So how about that lasagna?"

Old Biker Dude was certainly one laid-back guy. "I'll pass on that for now. I'd rather have some answers."

Zoe reached for her purse. She pulled out a wallet and riffled through the back compartment until she pulled out a tattered color photo. "This is your father."

"My birth father," Jake corrected her. "My father is the man who raised me until I was twelve."

"What happened when you were twelve?"

"My parents both died in a car accident."

Zoe's face went pale and another round of tears slid down her face. "I didn't know," she whispered.

"Hey, I didn't come here to lay any kind of guilt trip on you. Like I said, I just wanted some information." Jake belatedly looked at the tattered photo he held in his hand and felt like he'd been sucker punched. The guy looked an awful lot like him. Same dark hair, same cocky tilt of his head.

"His name was Brady," Zoe said. "He was seventeen. A rebel. His grandma raised him. She died shortly after he did. She was his only relative."

Jake didn't know what to say. He clutched the old photograph so hard he got a cramp in his hand. But still he didn't let go or look away. He couldn't.

He heard Zoe ask him, "What happened to you after your parents . . . died?"

He couldn't answer her. He was consumed with an avalanche of unexpected emotions. Was this what he'd been looking for? Had he finally found the answers he'd been seeking? A teenage runaway mom, a rebel teenage dad—not a new story by any means. But it was part of *his* story.

"You know, I love Lulu to death, but I did kind of wonder what it would be like to have a grandson," Jerry said. "I just wasn't expecting to get a full-grown one out of the blue."

"Lulu doesn't know," Zoe said.

"Lulu doesn't know what?" Lulu stood on the threshold of the trailer, outside the screen door. "Jake, what are you doing here? If you're trying to get me and her"—she jerked her thumb in Zoe's direction—"together, you can just forget it."

"Come on in, Lulu." Jerry held the screen door open for her. "This discussion involves you."

"You set me up," she accused her grandfather. "Told me you made lasagna and had leftovers."

"That's true."

"You didn't tell me she'd be here."

"Because I knew you wouldn't come if I did."

"Damn right." She turned to leave, but Jerry caught her hand and brought her to a halt.

"I've been pretty damn patient with all this emotional junk going on between you and your mother, but the time has come to get over it."

"How can you say that?"

"Because I'm older than you and I've learned that life is too short to hang onto hate and grudges. That crap just eats you up inside."

"Did she tell you why she came back here? And what does any of this have to do with Jake?" Lulu demanded.

"It seems we're related," Jake said.

Her pierced eyebrow rose. "What are you talking about? Are you doing your family tree or something?"

"He's your half brother," Zoe said.

"No way!" She looked at Jake for confirmation that such a claim was a lie.

"Way," he said with a nod.

Lulu sank into a nearby pine dining chair. "How did that happen?"

"Zoe had a baby when she was sixteen. Me. Gave me up for adoption."

"So you're another kid she dumped? Lucky you."

Lulu's voice was bitterly sarcastic, but Jake was close enough to see the pain and confusion in her eyes as she looked at him. "Why didn't you tell me? Is this why you came to Rock Creek?"

"I didn't know Zoe was my birth mother until a few minutes ago," Jake said.

"She told you?"

"No, I tracked her down," he admitted.

"Why would you do that?"

"Because I had questions."

"And you thought she'd have the answers?" Lulu shook her head. "She doesn't give answers, only excuses."

"That's not fair—" Jerry began when Zoe interrupted him.

"No, she's right. I messed up badly with you, Lulu. I know that. I wasn't a good mother."

"You were no mother at all."

"Because I was barely able to take care of myself let alone a five-year-old daughter."

"More excuses."

Jake figured he didn't need to be present for this. "I'll leave you to work things out."

"No way." Lulu grabbed hold of his arm. "Like it or not, you're part of this family now."

"Please stay," Zoe said. "I'm not even sure where to begin. I've screwed up so much of my life, and that's no one's fault but my own. I'm so sorry for so many things."

"Sorry you even had kids, right?" Lulu said.

"No! I wanted the best for you both. That's why I gave the baby up for adoption and that's why I left you, Lulu, with your grandfather. I knew he'd take good care of you when I couldn't."

"Why come back now, that's what I want to know," Lulu said. "After all this time . . . what were you hoping to accomplish?"

"I wanted to try to explain . . . I couldn't find the words before. I still don't have the right words to express my regret at hurting you. I'm married now to a great guy, a therapist who's helped me deal with a lot of stuff."

Jake couldn't help seeing the shock flash across Lulu's face at this news. Clearly she hadn't expected Zoe to be married. A moment later Lulu had her angry expression back. Jake could relate to his half sister . . . Wow, he had a half sister. And it turned out she was a lot like him. Not that he could feel her pain or sappy stuff like that, but . . . okay, he *could* feel her pain. There was a hell of a lot of it hidden inside her and he could relate to that.

"He's taught me how to be a better person."

"I suppose you've got kids with him now."

"I've got two stepsons. I'm a good stepmom . . ."

"Do you really think I want to hear about how you're great with your stepkids but couldn't be bothered with me? How do you think that makes me feel? Do you even care? Obviously not. This is all about you, not me. You came here to make yourself feel better." Lulu shook her head, as if denying everything around her. Jake saw the tears well up in her eyes before she turned on her heels and ran out.

"I'm, uh, gonna take a rain check on that lasagna," Jake told Jerry and Zoe.

"Tell her that I love her," Zoe pleaded with him.

Jake met Lulu outside. "I'm not crying," she said

fiercely, angrily scrubbing away the few tears that escaped. "I'm not a crier. Ask anyone."

"I don't have to ask. I can tell you're not a crier."

Half an hour later Jake and Lulu were seated in Angelo's Pizza place eating a loaded pizza. "I suppose I should look on the bright side," she said around a mouthful of pizza.

"Which is?"

"That I got a kick-ass half brother out of the deal."

"And I got a kick-ass half sister."

"Yeah, right. Like that was on the top of your holiday list last year."

Actually it was. He'd wanted to track down his roots to find out who he was because he'd started to question everything after that deadly day on the mountain. But he didn't know how to convey that to Lulu.

"That's okay." She patted his hand. "You don't have to lie."

"You remember that day I came into Cosmic Comics to ask you to walk Mutt?"

"Yeah."

"I really came to check you out. I had a short list of three possible birth mothers."

"Really? Who were the other two?"

"I'm not saying. It's not relevant. Anyway, I wanted to meet you in case you were related to me, in case Zoe was my birth mother after all."

"Aren't you angry with her for giving you up?"

"No, I'm actually grateful. My parents were awesome people."

"But you ended up in foster care after they died."

"Shit happens."

"I know. I've got the T-shirt *and* the bumper sticker on that one."

"Your grandfather was right, you know."

"About what?"

"About hanging onto hate and grudges. That crap does eat you up inside. Your grandfather seems like a guy who knows what he's talking about."

"He's your grandfather too. And he does know what he's talking about usually. He also makes great lasagna."

"So I've heard. Maybe you should consider his advice about letting go of the past and starting new. Will you at least think about it?"

She snatched the last piece of pizza before reluctantly saying, "Okay, I'll think about it. No promises, though."

"Good enough." Jake snatched the pizza right out of her hand before she could take a bite.

"Nice move."

He grinned. "I thought so."

She snatched the remaining piece back and stuck it right in her mouth.

Jake cracked up. "Oh yeah, you and I are *definitely* related."

• • •

Emma was pumping gas at Gas4Less, trying to remember the last time she'd had to fill up her hybrid car. Today was Monday . . .

"Are you the one doing that survey about Rock Creek?" a woman approached her to ask.

"Yes." Emma couldn't place the woman but then there were a lot of participants in her study and she didn't remember them all by sight. Unless she was someone from the town meeting? "Did you have a question about it?"

"Yes, I have a question. How do you sleep at night?"

Emma belatedly noticed the woman's belligerent stance.

"I'm not sure what you mean."

"I mean you have some nerve coming back here after all these years and telling us how to live."

"I'm not doing that at all."

"Telling us we should be happy with all the changes. Well, we're not happy. I know what happens in these situations. Outsiders come into a place and the next thing you know the property values go up and then the property taxes go up and the local people can't afford to live here anymore."

"You don't agree that Rock Creek was in trouble before?"

"Sure, but we've been in trouble before and come through."

"All I'm doing is trying to document what's going on here—"

"Then you need to include the fact that not everyone is happy about the changes."

"Are you participating in my study?"

"Hell no!"

"Why not?"

"I don't want any part of it. I believe a person's life is private and no one has any business nosing around in it."

"I'm not nosing around in people's private lives. I'm just asking about their relationship to this town—how long they've lived here, what kind of work they do—"

"That's all personal stuff," the other woman said. "So just butt out and stop looking for trouble or you'll get more than you bargained for." With that ominous note, she hopped into her Camaro and zoomed out of the gas station.

"What were you and Rhonda talking about?" Nancy Crumpler asked as she walked out of the Gas4Less Mini-Mart with a bag of chips and an extra-large cup of coffee.

"She never told me her name."

"That's Rhonda. She's Roy's sister. You remember Roy, right?"

Emma nodded. How could she forget?

"What did she want?" Nancy asked.

"She isn't happy about the study I'm doing regarding Rock Creek."

"She's not happy about much in her life. Her husband recently took off with a younger woman and left her in a trailer with two kids and no child support."

"I wish I'd known. There are organizations that can help her get the child support owed to her," Emma said.

"E-mail me the information and I'll make sure she gets it."

"Okay. She said she was worried about property taxes going up."

"Tough economic times make you worry about a lot of things. Things are going better here in Rock Creek than they have in the past, but it's a rough world out there for all of us. A lot of uncertainty."

"I realize that." Her life was filled with uncertainty too. Would she still have a job in a year? Would her research study turn out to be a bust? Was she an idiot to get involved with a risk taker like Jake?

• • •

For some reason Emma had felt nervous about Tuesday night's family dinner all day. Leena and Cole were still on their honeymoon in Bermuda. Which left Sue Ellen and Donny along with Emma and her parents all gathered around two tables pushed together at the Thai Place.

Maxie had her hair piled up and held in place with two hair sticks to give herself some Asian flair. Sue Ellen was wearing a loose smock top with a vivid paisley design that reminded Emma of the wallpaper at the Ritzee Day Spa. No one had said a word about Emma's new haircut, which she'd only gotten done that morning.

She'd been impressed by Cherry, the designated hair

stylist at Leena's wedding and had sought her out. Cherry had added light honey-colored highlights to Emma's brown hair. Her haircut, while not drastic, had a sassy swing to it. Emma was pleased with the results, but she was no beauty expert. To accompany her new look, she'd chosen one of her favorite dresses, the floral one that she'd worn to the bridal shower. But she might as well have worn her good luck running shorts and Penn T-shirt for all the attention her family paid to her. At least they were obeying her "no insults" rule.

Emma couldn't miss the challenging looks that Sue Ellen and Maxie were tossing each other across the table. Emma glanced at Donny to see if her brother-in-law had a clue what was going on. He looked as nervous as she felt. Something was definitely up.

"So how do you feel about being a grandfather?" Sue Ellen asked their dad out of the blue. "What?" Sue Ellen's question was addressed to Maxie, who'd just gasped. "You already know I'm pregnant so don't try to act surprised."

"I'm surprised you would make such an important announcement in a public place like this," Maxie said in an undertone.

"I'm no fool," Sue Ellen said. "I figured there was less chance of Dad going ballistic if we're out in public than back at the trailer."

"What the hell are they talking about?" Bob addressed his question to Emma, which infuriated Sue Ellen.

"Don't ask her, ask me!"

"Fine." Bob shifted his eagle-eyed glare to Sue Ellen. "What the hell are you talking about? I don't go ballistic."

Sue Ellen's eye roll was so intense that Maxie said, "Don't do that or your eyes will get stuck that way and you'll scare your baby."

Bob looked at Maxie. "You knew she was pregnant and didn't tell me?"

"Have some tea, sweetheart."

"I don't want tea, I want answers. Am I the last person to know you're pregnant?" he bellowed.

"There are probably people down the block who didn't hear you," Sue Ellen retorted angrily.

"Is that why you got married? Because you got knocked up?"

"I love your daughter and I'm not going to sit hear while you talk to her that way," Donny said in a quiet but I-mean-business voice. "Come on, Sue Ellen. We're leaving."

Two minutes later Emma was alone at the table with her parents. Accustomed to being a peacemaker, she tried to think of some words of wisdom to make things better but couldn't come up with a thing.

"What do you have to say for yourself?" her dad demanded, clearly still itching for a fight.

Emma just shook her head. "I've got nothing."

"I suppose you think I was too hard on your sister."

"Affirmative."

"You could have given me some warning so I'd know what to expect."

Emma wasn't sure if the reprimand was aimed at her or her mom or both of them. "Sue Ellen wanted to tell you herself, but she was nervous about your reaction," Emma said. "With good reason as it turns out."

"I just hoped that my first-born daughter had gotten it right for a change."

Emma stuck up for her. "She did. She and Donny are thrilled about the baby. They planned on getting married before this happened. They genuinely are in love with each other."

"Any idiot could see that," Maxie sniffed.

"So now you're calling me an idiot, are you?" Bob growled.

Maxie shrugged. "If the shoe fits."

Great, now her parents were fighting. "Come on, guys, let's all calm down and order something to eat."

"Calm down? You're always calm." Maxie made it sound like an accusation, a deep character flaw of some kind.

"Hey, it's a tough job, but somebody's got to do it," Emma said. She waved a server over and told her, "I need an order of spring rolls really badly right now. Please."

"Sure thing. On the house." The server patted Emma's hand reassuringly. "Do you need some Dr Pepper too?"

Emma blinked in surprise. "How did you know?"

"Jake told me. He eats here a lot or gets takeout."

"Right." Emma nodded. "Jake."

"Speaking of Jake, how serious are you two getting?" Maxie asked. "Should we start planning another wedding?"

Emma's dad groaned. "I sure hope not."

"What do you have against Jake?" Maxie demanded.

"She can do better than a bartender."

"He's an extreme sports hero," Maxie said.

"She can still do better," he insisted stubbornly. Then he narrowed his eyes suspiciously and looked very Marine-like as he glared at Emma. "You're not pregnant too, are you?"

"Shh." Maxie looked around nervously. "Everyone is staring."

"This dinner was obviously a mistake." Emma's throat was so tight she could barely get the words out.

"You still haven't answered my question," her dad said.

"And I don't intend to. I'm an adult. My private life is my business. Could I have these spring rolls to go?" she asked as the server placed them on the table.

"Certainly. I'll just be a second."

"What do you mean your private life is your business?" her dad said. "I'm your father."

"I realize that. But that doesn't give you the right to interrogate me as if I were a private and you're the drill sergeant."

"That's not what I was doing. If I were, then I'd be yelling an inch from your face. That's the problem with you young people today. You're spoiled. You demand instant gratification. You don't know how to work for something."

Emma put her hands on the table and angrily leaned forward. "I know damn well how to work for something. I've worked my butt off to get my degrees."

"And a very nice butt it is too," Jake noted from behind her. "And before you ask me what I'm doing here, I heard there was an altercation and I figured you had to be involved."

"Meaning Sue Ellen and Donny went to Nick's Tavern and told you," Emma said with a toss of her head.

"Nice haircut," Jake noted approvingly.

"I'm glad you showed up," her dad told him. "It gives me the chance to ask you what your intentions are regarding my daughter."

"Dad!"

"What? I'm your father. I have a right to know."

"Don't answer him," Emma told Jake.

"Maybe I should pull up a chair," he said.

"No. You have to get back to work."

"I quit," Jake said, taking the empty seat beside her.

"What? When?"

"Last night."

"Why didn't you tell me?"

"How are you going to make a living?" her dad demanded.

"He's the CEO of a snowboarding company," Emma said.

"Did it go belly-up?" her dad asked.

"No, it's doing well," Jake said.

"Jake's private financial affairs are none of our business," Emma said.

"They are if he's involved with you." Her dad returned his attention to Jake. "Why work as a bartender if you're some CEO?"

"Dad!"

"What?"

"I need to speak to you. In private. Outside." She stood. "Right now."

"I'll wait here with Jake," Maxie said.

"Ignore all her questions," Emma told Jake.

"She never used to be this bossy." Maxie shook her head and rolled her eyes almost clear up to her penciled eyebrows.

"What do you think you're doing?" Emma demanded the moment they were outside the restaurant.

"What? I'm just looking out for you."

"Well don't!"

Her anger turned to panic as Emma saw Roy's rusty blue pickup jump the curb and head straight for them. An instant later her dad shoved her out of the way. Emma screamed as she heard the sickening *thud* of her dad bouncing off the truck's right front fender before he was thrown to the cement sidewalk.

Chapter Seventeen

. . . .

Emma vaguely heard shouts and screams from onlookers as Roy's truck plowed into a lamppost and finally came to a stop. But her concentration was on her dad. He was on his back and he was bleeding heavily from a jagged cut to his leg. His eyes were open, but his face was deathly pale and he wasn't moving.

"Call 911!" Emma cried, hurrying to her dad's side.

"Already done," Jake said

The next thing she knew, Jake had yanked the leather belt from his jeans and was applying a tourniquet to her dad's leg. He did so with a calm confidence and speed that told her he knew what he was doing.

Their server from the Thai Place had come out to try to calm an hysterical Maxie. The ambulance arrived shortly thereafter, as did Nathan.

Roy was getting out of his smashed truck and weaving drunkenly. "My sister," he shouted. "My sister is hurt!"

"It's nothing. I hurt my arm, that's all," Rhonda called out.

The fire department was now also on the scene, focusing on getting her out of the damaged vehicle. One of the paramedics checked her status while the other two focused on Emma's dad.

Jake moved aside to let them work on him. "Are you okay?" he asked Emma, putting a protective arm around her as she stood. "Did your head hit the pavement? Did you black out?"

"No."

"Your knees are scraped and bleeding."

"I'm fine." Her voice was shaking. "Is my dad going to be okay?" she asked one of the paramedics.

When he didn't answer she panicked. "Is he going to be okay?"

Again the paramedic ignored her as he and his partner worked quickly to put Emma's dad on a backboard and then a gurney, and finally into the ambulance. Maxie climbed in and they were off, sirens blaring.

Emma grabbed hold of Jake. "I have to go to the hospital."

"I'll take you. My Jeep isn't far away."

Jake tenderly helped her into his vehicle. The trip to the county hospital seemed to take forever. When they arrived at the ER Emma hurried to the information desk. "My dad was hurt in an accident. The ambulance from Rock Creek brought him in."

"His name?"

"Bob Riley. Robert Riley."

The assistant checked her computer. "He's with the medical staff now."

"Is he okay?"

"As soon as they have any information they'll let you

know. Your mom is back there with him so you'll have to wait here in the waiting area."

"Emma was injured in the accident too." Jake pointed to her bleeding knees.

"It's nothing," Emma said.

"Let's let the medical staff determine that," the assistant said. Ten minutes later Emma was being examined. Her injuries were cleaned up and bandaged. "What about my dad?" she kept asking.

"He's being taken care of."

"Yes, but is he going to be okay?"

The last nurse she'd asked had squeezed her hand reassuringly and said, "I'll see what I can find out for you."

"Thank you." Emma felt tears threatening.

Jake, who'd remained at her side throughout, took her hand in his. "It'll be okay," he said gruffly. "Your dad is a tough dude. Former Marines aren't wimps."

"He was bleeding so badly."

"Yeah, but we put a tourniquet on his leg."

"Not we, *you*. How did you know what to do?"

Jake shrugged. "What can I say? Extreme sports can get messy sometimes and it pays to know basic first aid."

"That was more than basic first aid."

"I'm no doctor, although I'd be more than happy to play doctor with you anytime." He lifted their clasped hands to nibble on her fingers.

Yes, Jake distracted her but not enough to stop her from worrying about her dad.

The nurse finally returned. "Your father is upstairs getting prepped for orthopedic surgery for his broken leg. There don't appear to be any internal injuries. If you'd like, you can wait with your mom in the surgical waiting room on the second floor. I'll have an orderly show you the way after you sign your paperwork."

Emma didn't think they'd need assistance finding the surgical waiting room, but the hospital was a maze of dissecting corridors and conflicting elevators. She heard Maxie's voice down the hallway and followed it.

"Where have you been?" Maxie demanded.

The accusatory tone of her mother's voice hit Emma hard and had her taking a step back.

Then Maxie's tone changed to one of maternal concern. "What happened to your knee? Why are you all bandaged up like that? Baby, are you okay?" Maxie engulfed her in a hug. "Speak to me. Did you hit your head? Is that why you can't talk? Do you know who I am?" Maxie leaned back to look at Emma. "I'm . . . your . . . mother." She turned to Jake. "Does she have amnesia?"

"No, I don't have amnesia," Emma said.

"Thank heavens." Maxie released her. "Sue Ellen wanted to come, but I told her to wait at home and that I'd call as soon as we had more news. Too much stress wouldn't be good for her baby."

"Right." Emma nodded. "That was smart."

"Come sit down," Maxie said.

"Do you want me to find some Dr Pepper and Cheetos?" Jake asked Emma.

"No thanks." She sat in a surprisingly comfortable chair. Every bone in her body was starting to hurt from the fall she'd taken when her dad had pushed her to safety.

"How about some tea?" He pointed to a machine on a table in the corner that offered a variety of hot beverages.

"That would be lovely," Maxie said. "I'll have some Earl Grey. How about you, Emma?"

"How about me what?" Emma felt as though she were having an out-of-body experience. All of a sudden she couldn't seem to fully comprehend everything going on around her. She knew she was at the hospital, but it didn't seem real. Except for the smell of disinfectant. That seemed real and it was making her queasy.

"Here." Jake held a paper cup of warm tea up to her lips. "Take a sip."

She did. The tea was very sweet, as if he'd dumped an entire bowl of sugar into it. A second later she took the cup from him. "Thanks. I can do it myself."

Two hours later, Emma tried not to obsess over the clock on the wall. Operations took time. That didn't mean anything was wrong.

"They need a better variety of reading material here." Maxie tossed an out-of-date copy of *Parenting* magazine onto an end table.

"The Library of Congress has over five hundred miles of shelves." Emma bit her lip at her mom's blank look. "What? You know I list trivia when I'm under stress."

"I always thought you just made that stuff up," Maxie confessed. "You mean there *really* are that many miles of shelves at the Library of Congress? I wonder who's job it is to measure all that and how much they get paid?"

Emma didn't have to answer because a doctor walked into the waiting room. "Are you Bob Riley's family?"

Emma nodded. So did her mom. Jake grimaced as Emma clutched his hand and squeezed hard while she waited for the doctor to continue.

"He came through the surgery just fine."

"Thank heavens." Maxie practically sagged with relief. "Can I see him?"

"He's still groggy, but yes, you can see him. It's best if we wait until tomorrow for anyone else to visit."

Emma nodded.

"You look like you could use some rest," the doctor said with a kind look at her and her bandaged knees. "Go on home. The worst is over."

Emma sure hoped so, but the guilt was starting to set in.

By the time Jake let her into her apartment, she couldn't keep silent any longer. "It's my fault. My dad being in the hospital is all my fault."

"How do you figure that?"

"If I hadn't had that fight with Roy in the bar that day, then he wouldn't have come after me and run over my dad."

"That's bullshit," he said bluntly.

"Roy aimed his truck at me. My dad pushed me out of the way and was hit instead." She scrubbed at the tears racing down her face. "You don't know how it feels—"

"Yes, I do," he interrupted her. "I know exactly how it feels. Not only to feel guilty about being responsible for someone else's injuries but for their *death*. To wonder why you're left standing when someone you care about dies."

"I'm sorry," she whispered. "I wasn't thinking. Your climbing accident . . ."

"You read the reports on the Internet. Not everyone believes it was an accident."

"That's why you were so angry when you thought I was a reporter that first day I walked into the bar, right? Because of what the media wrote about you."

"They were all looking for a story. 'How did it feel leaving your best friend under tons of ice, rock, and snow?' he mimicked a reporter's voice. "Hell, I'll tell you how it feels. It feels like shit. There aren't even words to say how bad it feels. So you don't say anything and the guilt just keeps building up inside you."

"Survivor's guilt."

"Yeah, you probably know all about it, studied it, but you never experienced it until now, have you?"

She shook her head. "It sucks."

"Yeah, big time," Jake said. "I keep thinking that if I'd only done something different, if we'd moved our descent earlier, or later, then we wouldn't have been in the avalanche's path." He clenched his hand into a fist as the memories washed over him like a tsunami. The huge wall of ice, rock, and snow roaring down the mountain without warning. Boulders, some the size of cars, shooting past him like toys. One second Andy was above him, and then he was gone.

"Andy and me . . . we made up our own rules, always pushing the envelope," Jake said. "What's life worth without the edge of danger?"

"It's worth a lot," Emma said.

"Yeah, it is. That's why I fought to stay alive. The avalanche separated us all. We were roped together. Something severed the climbing rope connecting me to Andy, but not until I'd been dragged several hundred feet." Jake paused. The memory of that excruciating pain ripping through him remained to this day.

"I didn't cut that rope." Jake's voice was hoarse with emotion.

"I know."

There was more to the story. Andy's British friend, Piers Russell, wasn't as experienced a climber. He'd panicked. Piers was the one who'd cut the rope tying him to Jake. Jake had been teetering on the jagged edge of unconscious at the time, but he remembered that.

He couldn't blame the guy. He hadn't thought Jake would live long enough with his injuries to make it down the rest of the mountain alive. But Jake had. And when Piers realized that, he'd helped get Jake back to so-called civilization—the nearest village. That belated assistance was the reason Jake hadn't said anything when Piers hid his own guilt by dropping subtle innuendoes about Andy's rope.

Jake had never talked about that part of the story and he never would. He'd already told Emma more than he had anyone else.

She didn't ask him questions, didn't press him for more details. Instead she held him in her arms. They held each other, lending each other silent support. They didn't have sex . . . yet it felt like the most intimate night of his life as they slept together, his arm around her to keep her close and safe.

Jake's nightmare returned at dawn. The mountain peaks, the awesome view from the summit in the Andes, then the horror as everything went so horribly wrong. He stood by helplessly as Andy disappeared. He felt the violent pull as the rope yanked him off his feet. But before he went down he saw Emma there. *No! Not her! Don't take her too!*

He woke in a cold sweat, still forming the silent but vehement *no* on his lips. He sat straight up as if to escape his demons.

"What's wrong?" Emma asked sleepily.

"Nothing." His voice was unsteady. "Go back to sleep. Everything's fine." Jake had told more than his fair share of lies in his life, but that might have been the biggest one of all. His silent anguish was a warning that he was in over his head with Emma and he was heading for disaster.

Which could only mean one thing. It was definitely time to think about getting the hell out of Dodge. Time to walk away while he still could.

Jake stared down at Emma, the curve of her cheek, the silkiness of her hair. Hell, maybe it was already too late.

• • •

That afternoon, Emma stood with the rest of her family in her dad's hospital room.

"If you didn't want to be a grandfather, you could've just said so instead of stepping in front of a speeding car," Sue Ellen said.

Their dad grinned at Sue Ellen. "It was a truck, not a car." He squeezed her hand. "You got your sense of humor from me."

Maxie wasn't similarly amused. "That truck hit your father. He didn't step in front of it. Which reminds me, the sheriff stopped by first thing this morning and said Roy has been arrested. Roy's sister Rhonda also stopped by and apologized for her brother's actions. She had her arm in a sling but said she was okay otherwise. She said Roy didn't want to kill anyone. He just wanted to scare Emma, but he lost control of his truck. It's not Rhonda's fault that Roy is the way he is so I don't blame her. But her brother is a different matter." She grabbed her husband's hand. "He could have killed you!"

"It takes more than a rusty pickup truck to do in this former Marine," he said with a stoic bark of laughter. "Semper fi!"

"It's not funny." Maxie shook her head so hard that one of the plastic cherries on her hairclips went flying and nearly hit Donny in the face. He ducked just in the nick of time.

They were all silent for a moment. Then Emma, Sue Ellen, and Maxie cracked up while Donny looked on in confusion.

"You'll get used to them in time," Emma's dad told Donny.

Ten minutes later, Emma was alone with her dad as the rest of her family went in search of a late lunch at the hospital cafeteria.

"You really scared us," Emma said.

"I didn't raise you to be afraid."

"How could I not be afraid with all the yelling and

screaming?" The words were out before she could stop them, and they surprised her as much as him.

"What yelling and screaming?"

"When you had too much to drink," she said quietly.

Her dad looked stunned. "That was a long, *long* time ago. You were too young to remember those times."

"I do remember them."

"I've been sober for over twenty years now."

"I know you have and I'm proud of you."

"You never said that before," her dad said.

"Well, I am."

"And I'm proud of you too, Sweet Pea." His voice was gruff as he took hold of her hand. "I know you, Sue Ellen, and Leena are all grown up and don't need your old dad anymore."

"That's not true. We'll always need you. *I'll* always need you."

She saw the sheen of unshed tears in her father's eyes before he pulled her to him for a fierce bear hug. "Holy crap!" He sniffed. "You nearly made your old man cry." He cleared his throat. "Don't tell your mother."

• • •

"Tell me again why I have to be here for this?" Jake asked Lulu as they stood in front of the trailer where she'd grown up.

She grabbed hold of his arm as if afraid he'd take off, which he was damn tempted to do. Emma was visiting her dad at the hospital. He hoped she was doing okay because he sure as hell wasn't. He was still rattled from his nightmare about her early this morning.

"You're here as moral support," Lulu told him.

"Yeah, well, the thing is I'm not real good at that. Oliver would be a much better guy for that job."

"Yes, Oliver is very supportive," Lulu agreed. "But this is a family matter. And like it or not, you're family."

"Not really—"

"Shut up and get used to it. You're family now."

Jerry opened the door. "What are you two shouting about out here? Well, don't just stand there. Get your butts in here before you let all the air-conditioning out."

Jake entered the trailer to find Zoe busily wiping the kitchen counter and sink. She dried her hands on a kitchen towel imprinted with the state map of South Dakota. "It's good to see you both."

"See, here's the thing," Lulu said, still hanging onto Jake's arm as if they were fellow prisoners chained together. "Things have changed."

"That's what I've been trying to tell you," Zoe said. "I've changed."

"You were almost killed. Yesterday. When Roy aimed his truck at Emma and her dad. I saw it all out the store window. That truck was going to hit you next. You were on the sidewalk. Then he veered and hit the lamppost. Anyway that got me to thinking."

"Yeah, near-death experiences tend to do that," Jake said.

Lulu shot him an aggravated look.

"What? I was just agreeing with you."

"I'm trying to be all emo and stuff here," Lulu said.

"Hey, go for it," Jake encouraged her.

Her eyes narrowed. "This isn't easy."

"Nothing worthwhile is." That comment reminded Jake of how Emma had flown off the handle when she'd thought he was calling her easy. He'd go see her as soon as he finished here.

"As I was saying, the accident got me to thinking," Lulu said. "And it hit me that I didn't want anything happening to you and that maybe we might have a second chance at not being so angry at each other."

"I'd love a second chance," Zoe said unsteadily. "With both of you."

"I'm just along for the ride. For moral support," Jake said.

"Yeah, right," Lulu scoffed. "He's the one who said I should come out here and talk to you, tell you how I felt."

"I said you should come out here," Jake reminded her. "Not me."

"And I told him I wasn't coming without him because he's family now."

Zoe nodded. "That's right."

Jake eyed them all suspiciously. "You're not going to do a group hug or something, are you?"

"Hell no." Jerry walked up to him and gave Jake a bear hug that just about cracked his ribs. "We're gonna hug you one at a time."

"Not necessary," Jake said.

Lulu's hug was almost as tough as Jerry's while Zoe's was tentative and hopeful.

"Okay, not that that's settled, how about some lasagna?" Jerry said. "I made a new batch last night."

Jake checked his watch. Emma would still be at the hospital for a while yet. "Lasagna sounds good," Jake said.

"Our first family dinner sounds even better," Zoe said.

• • •

Emma was on her cell phone when she opened the door for Jake. That didn't stop him from kissing her.

"Hello? Hello?" Emma heard the woman's voice in her ear, but Jake's tongue was in her mouth and that was where her focus was for the moment. "Are you there?"

Jake ended the kiss but kept his arms around her.

"Is this Emma Riley?"

"Yes."

"This is Cynthia Abrams from Academic Media Press. You e-mailed your book proposal on risk takers to me. I have good news. We'd like to buy it."

"What?" Emma stepped away from Jake, only then realizing he'd released her bra.

"We'd like to buy your book about risk takers," the editor repeated.

"You would? Really?"

"Yes, really."

Emma handed Jake a beer and then locked herself in the bathroom so she could concentrate on what the editor was saying. She emerged ten minutes later and did her own version of Oliver's happy Snoopy dance.

"What was that all about?" Jake asked.

"They want to buy my book!" She still couldn't believe it.

"What book?"

"About risk takers. I e-mailed a proposal, but I never thought they'd buy it."

"Risk takers? You mean like me?" His expression turned cold, as cold as the mountains that had almost killed him. "Is that all I was? Some sociology experiment for your book?"

"No, of course not!"

Emma saw the change come over him, saw him revert back to the dark and dangerous man he'd been when she'd first walked into the bar. A man ready to lash out at anyone who threatened the protective wall he'd built around himself. "What right do you have to pry into my private life?" A muscle jumped in his clenched jaw. "Too bad I found out before I spilled my guts to you for your tell-all book."

"That's not what this is. The publisher is a small press specializing in nonfiction."

"Like tell-all books. How long have you had this in the works? From the day you walked into the bar looking for me?"

"No! I e-mailed the proposal after I saw you and that bare-breasted woman in the bar."

"And this was your payback for that?"

"No. I'd honestly forgotten I'd even e-mailed it because I was so upset that night. You came over . . . and we made love for the first time."

"We had sex."

"It was more than just that. It was something special."

"It's always special."

"No, it's not."

"Maybe not for you . . ."

His insinuation was clear. Emma felt the cruel barb like a blade through her heart. She was nothing special. Words failed her for a moment.

"But you said . . ." Her voice was too unsteady to continue.

Jake shrugged. "If you're studying risk takers, then you should know we like to win and we'll say or do whatever it takes to do that. Chalk it up to male curiosity. I wondered what it would be like to nail a brainy girl."

Another direct hit. She wasn't sure how many more she could take. But she saw a flash of vulnerability beneath the anger in his golden brown eyes that kept her doggedly soldiering on. "You don't mean that. You're angry—"

"Damn right I'm angry. I'm not usually this gullible."

"I wasn't trying to fool you or to hurt you."

"It takes a hell of a lot more than this to hurt me." He headed for the door.

"Wait! Where are you going?"

"Far away from you."

Her final scrap of hope died with his words . . . and his departure.

Chapter Eighteen

. . . .

Emma sank to the floor and angrily wiped the tears away as fast as they fell. His words still echoed inside her head. *I wondered what it would be like to nail a brainy girl.*

Jake had certainly done that and more. He damn well may have broken her heart. The pain came in recurring waves of burning tears followed by periods of humiliation and numbness.

Okay, enough. She got up off the floor. She might have been knocked down, but she refused to stay there.

She should be celebrating her good news about the book deal. Instead she was a mess. She curled up in a fetal position on the futon before realizing the sheets smelled like him. Like Jake.

Just last night he'd held her so tenderly in his arms and made her feel as though she were the only woman in the world he cared about. Had he really cared about her, he would have listened to her explanation about the book.

Was that project worth losing him over?

You never really had him in the first place. He'd told her so himself.

Emma leapt up and yanked the sheets off the bed, replacing them with a new set. Then she opened her laptop and got to work. She had plenty to do now that she had a book deadline as well as her research project to complete.

And talk about research, she had tons of that to do about risk takers. One hard lesson she'd already learned thanks to Jake—risk takers were total heartbreakers.

Emma worked through most of the night, avoiding the futon even with its new sheets. She finally crashed around 4 a.m. But she didn't sleep well at all.

After a few hours of tossing and turning she got up and inserted a new tai chi DVD into her laptop. She needed to calm down and tai chi was her best bet for doing that.

It didn't work.

She kept at it. "Relax. Breathe easy," the tai chi instructor on the DVD said. "This movement is known as stroking. Gently stroke an invisible wall . . ." Yeah, a sexy, muscular wall like Jake's bare chest. No, wait, that wasn't the image she was supposed to have.

"Now we gently move into our next movement called stoking the fire . . ." Jake was an expert at stoking her fires, his devilishly skillful fingers knowing exactly where to touch her for her maximum pleasure.

Tai chi not helping.

She clicked off the DVD and collapsed on the futon. Her prone position gave her an unrestricted view of the ceiling but did nothing to help her discover the answers she'd hoped to find by returning to her hometown.

Where was she going? *Downhill fast* was her immediate answer.

Had she made the right choices? *Not where men were concerned, that's for sure.*

What about her future? She didn't have one with Jake. *Move on.*

What if she failed? Hell, she'd already messed up so many things that failure was no longer a fear but a fact.

Whoa. That last agenda item hit her. *Let's go over that one again.* Failure was no longer a fear but a fact.

Yeah, she liked it. Liked it a lot. She had finally given herself permission to screw up and it was surprisingly liberating.

She took a shower and ate a power breakfast, doubling the amount of fresh blueberries and toasted almonds on her organic yogurt. She was worth it.

The mantra *I am academic diva, hear me roar* worked hard at drowning out *I am dumped woman, hear me cry.* And it even succeeded to some degree until Lulu and Oliver showed up on Emma's doorstep.

"What's going on?" Lulu demanded.

"What do you mean?"

"I mean that Jake left town."

"Left town?" Emma repeated stupidly.

"Yes, as in he's vacated this location."

"His apartment?"

"The entire town."

He'd said he was getting away from her, but she hadn't expected him to leave so fast or so far. "But what about Mutt?"

"He gave the dog to me."

"You mean he asked you to take care of Mutt for him until he comes back."

"No, I meant what I said. Jake gave the dog to me along

with a big bag of kibbles and Mutt's bowls. The dog is back at my apartment now, probably gnawing on the woodwork with separation anxiety. Mutt really loves Jake. And so do I."

Emma looked at her in surprise. "I didn't realize you guys were that close."

"He's my brother. Well, my half brother."

Emma blinked. Maybe it was her lack of sleep last night, but she was having a hard time keeping up with Lulu. "What are you talking about?"

"He didn't tell you?"

"No. He angrily informed me I had no right prying into his private life."

"Then maybe I shouldn't say anything."

"Yes, you should," Oliver said. "Emma loves that guy."

"The feeling is not returned," Emma said, her throat tightening with suppressed emotion. "Jake doesn't love me."

"Yes, he does," Oliver said.

Emma shook her head. "Trust me, he doesn't."

"Jake isn't the emotional kind," Lulu said. "That runs in the family. He got it from me."

"Actually traits don't run that way," Oliver said. "They come from the two parent's genes. Besides, as the eldest sibling—"

"I wasn't speaking scientifically," Lulu said.

"Oh. Right. My mistake." He blushed. "I always speak scientifically."

Lulu kissed Oliver's cheek. "That's one of the things I love about you. But getting back to Jake . . . Why did you think he was here in Rock Creek?" she asked Emma.

"I don't know," Emma said. "I asked him but . . ." Now Emma was the one who blushed.

"He distracted you with sex," Lulu filled in. "Yeah, I do that with Oliver."

"You do not!"

She kissed him with a lot of tongue. "Yeah, I do."

"Can we get back to Jake?" Emma said.

"You have to swear you won't tell another soul."

"I swear."

"If you were Leena or Sue Ellen, I'd have you swear on some designer bag, but I don't know what to have a smart girl swear on."

"Swear on your laptop, Em," Oliver told her.

"Fine. I swear on my laptop."

"You didn't put your hand on it," Lulu pointed out.

Emma glared at her.

"Okay, okay. Jake came to Rock Creek to find his birth mother," Lulu said. "And he found her. Zoe."

"Your mother?"

"That's right. You can figure out on your own that since we share the same biological mother that makes us half siblings."

"Yes. I can figure that out." Emma could also figure out that Jake didn't trust her enough to confide in her about his real reasons for being in Rock Creek. Which clearly indicated that he felt no emotional connection with her. She was merely the brainy girl he'd nailed, nothing more. "I'm . . . happy for you both."

Then she burst into tears. Like her sisters, Emma was not a pretty crier. But she was a quiet one. Usually. Not now. Now the pain just came pouring out in big honking sobs that had Oliver looking panicked and Lulu looking confused.

"Why are you so upset that Jake is my brother?" she asked Emma.

Oliver thought a moment before snapping his fingers. "I've got it! She's crying because Jake didn't tell her any of this himself. Am I right, Em? Did I get it right?"

Emma nodded and reached for a handful of tissues to

mop up her face. She felt like an idiot. She'd shed enough tears over Jake.

"Yes!" Oliver punched his fist into the air and did a brief happy Snoopy dance. He stopped the instant he saw the look on Lulu's face.

"That dance may be appropriate when you master a song on *Guitar Hero III,*" Lulu said, "but not when your friend is clearly suffering."

"Right." Oliver nodded. "Inappropriate behavior. Got it."

"Actually, I'm not sure that dance is good in any situation, but who am I to judge?" Lulu shrugged. "Dancing is such an individual expression."

"I'm sorry about that." Emma had her self-control back and was determined to hang onto it no matter what new revelations came to light.

"Don't be sorry about my dancing," Oliver said.

"I was referring to my total meltdown," Emma said.

"Don't worry about it." Oliver awkwardly patted her shoulder. "I had the same reaction when my brother didn't get the Comic-Con tickets he promised me."

"So what happened with you and Jake to make him take off the way he did?" Lulu asked Emma.

"I told him a publisher wants to buy my book proposal about risk takers."

"Uh-oh." Lulu shook her head. "And Jake thought you were using him, right? You weren't, were you?"

"No, of course not. But he wouldn't listen to me."

"He's stubborn. Like me. But you can't give up on him."

"Sure I can," Emma said.

"No. You have to at least try and get him back. My granddad always tells me to follow my dreams, to shoot for the stars, and if you miss, you may land on the moon."

"Yes, but there's no oxygen on the moon," Oliver pointed out. "If you landed there without the right equipment, you'd die. And what about gravity or the lack thereof?"

Lulu gave him another look.

"Right. I was thinking scientifically again." Oliver hung his head. "Sorry about that."

"Don't be sorry, just help me convince Emma to go after Jake," Lulu said.

Oliver frowned. "How can she do that? We don't have any idea where he went."

"Right. Wait." Lulu snapped her fingers. "I have his cell phone number. You must have it too, Emma. You should call him."

"No way." Emma shook her head so hard her vision blurred. "Not in this lifetime! It's over. End of discussion."

Of course, it wasn't the end of the discussion since an hour after Lulu and Oliver left both her sisters showed up on her doorstep. Word traveled fast in a small town like Rock Creek.

"The rat bastard," Sue Ellen growled. "How dare Jake dump my baby sister and skip town! How about I have Donny dump septic sludge on his Jeep?"

"Or I could have Cole dump camel poop on his Jeep. I think I read someplace it smells really bad. I'm not sure where he'd get any around here, but I'm sure he could come up with something." Leena had just gotten back from her honeymoon and looked fit and tanned from her time in Bermuda.

"Jake and his Jeep have already left," Emma reminded her sisters.

"Right," Sue Ellen said. "The rat bastard."

"Don't call him that," Emma said.

"Why not?

"Because it reminds me of something he said."

Sue Ellen was infuriated. "He called you a rat bastard?"

"No, he said he didn't give a rat's rectum."

Sue Ellen's anger cranked up another ten notches. "He said he didn't give a rat's rectum about you? He's worse than a rat bastard! What's worse than a rat bastard? Come on, help me out here."

"You've got it all wrong," Emma said. "He said he didn't give a rat's rectum about winning."

"The bleeping buzzard. How does that sound? Worse than a rat bastard?" Sue Ellen asked.

"Are you listening to me?" Emma said.

"Of course I am. Wait, I think the baby just kicked. That or it's indigestion from the pepperoni and Cheerios I ate for breakfast." Sue Ellen burped like a trucker. "Yeah, it's indigestion. False alarm, folks."

"How can we help you, Emma?" Leena asked.

"Don't tell Mom. Or Dad."

"Well, Dad isn't a problem since he's still in the hospital. Cole and I visited him first thing this morning. Mom is something else again."

"Yes, she is."

"She's going to hear it from someone. She probably already has."

As if on cue, there was a knock on Emma's front door. "Emma, open up. It's your mother. You don't have your head in the oven, do you? Don't do anything stupid."

Emma opened the door before her mother said anything else to fuel the gossip fires.

Maxie rushed in and hugged Emma. "Oh, hon, I just heard that Jake dumped you. I brought some hair coloring so you could wash that man right out of your hair."

Seeing the desperation on Emma's face, Leena said, "Emma needs some time alone right now."

"But I just got here."

"And now you're leaving. With us. Come on, Mom. Let's go."

Maxie continued protesting even as Emma's sisters led her out. Emma closed the door after them and leaned against it.

"What doesn't destroy me strengthens me" was one of her favorite quotes by Nietzsche. Emma wondered if he'd ever been dumped . . . and then threatened with hair coloring. Probably not.

• • •

Jake drove as far as the state border with New Jersey before he realized that Newark Airport might not be the closest exit route. Maybe he should have driven to Philadelphia or Pittsburgh and caught a flight from there.

Today was the first of July. No snow in these parts but plenty down in the Andes. It was time for him to test his strength and get back on a snowboard again. Time to prove to himself that he still had what it takes, if not to race competitively then to face his fears.

Let Emma put that in her damn book. He'd e-mail her a picture of him back on the slopes with a couple of snow bunnies at his side.

Aw, hell. Who was he kidding here? He wasn't facing his fears, he was running from them. He was smart enough to know that it wasn't just the book deal that freaked him out. It was the fact that he'd somehow fallen for Emma. As in fallen in love. L-O-V-E. A freaking four-letter word to him. Because the few people he had loved ended up dead.

Just like Emma had almost ended up dead when that pickup had headed right for her. It might have taken a few days for it to sink in with him but eventually it had. And then there was the big family gathering with Lulu saying how the thought of losing Zoe made her feel closer to her mom. He was glad for them both.

But having Emma nearly killed didn't bring him closer to her. Instead it scared the shit out of him. Made him want to head for the hills. Hop on the nearest flight and not look back.

Her book deal had given him the perfect excuse to do just that.

She hadn't set him up. She didn't have a devious bone in her body. He, on the other hand, had plenty. He had devious down to an art form.

Not that he'd deliberately used the book thing as an excuse to dump her. He wasn't that much of a bastard. He'd honestly been stung by her news that she was doing a book on risk takers. And he had honestly wondered if she had used him.

But now that he had some time to think on it, he no longer believed that.

All this thinking made Jake hungry. He needed a burger. He pulled off the expressway at the next exit and got a Big Mac, large fries, and a soda. He saw the Dr Pepper logo on the dispenser and flashed back to Emma's face. "Aw, hell."

Go back, a voice inside his head told him.

Go to Peru, another voice said.

His inner argument escalated as he ate his Big Mac.

Go freaking back!

Go to freaking Peru!

What should he do? He should probably just eat his burger and stop all this conflicted thinking stuff. Easier said than done.

His choice should be clear, but it wasn't. Heading for the slopes with a snowboard had always been the answer for him in the past. Risk was addictive. He knew that. He'd lived it. And nearly died doing it. But the urge was still there. Part of him wanted to hit the slopes ASAP.

The other part of him wanted to return to Emma.

Emma, who could be both fragile and fierce. She might look like she needed protection but he knew that she could kick ass if she really needed to. She'd kick his ass big time if he went back.

He'd hurt her badly, and that was the thing he regretted the most. He'd lashed out at her in a blind panic, like an animal caught in a trap.

But it was a trap of his own making, not Emma's.

Maybe he should just hit the road and keep going. Maybe she was better off without him.

What did he have to offer her? She was a smart woman with a bunch of degrees. He'd never attended college. She came from a loving family. Strange maybe, but loving. He'd grown up in foster care learning to depend on no one but himself.

But Jake had a family now. That still felt weird to him. He had no experience with long-term relationships or with family stuff. What if he messed up?

Hell, he'd already messed up with Emma.

What if he didn't know how to make amends? What if she refused to have anything to do with him anymore? What if she kicked his sorry butt from PA to Peru? What then?

Only one way to find out.

• • •

Emma wanted to cancel the presentation she'd promised to give at the community center about her research, but then everyone would think she was a mess because Jake dumped her. That was unacceptable. So she showed up two hours early to make sure she got everything prepared. She had a room with a blackboard. The smell of chalk was reassuring to her, reminding her of her job back in Boston.

Her hand was steady as she wrote "Keys to Small Town

Successes" and then "1) Adopt a Can-Do Attitude" on the blackboard.

Yeah, right. That can-do attitude hadn't helped her avoid getting her heart battered by Jake. He'd not only walked out on her, but he'd also left town. He'd probably done her a favor, showing her what he was really like before she fell even more in love with him than she already was. She just needed to change her frame of reference here.

She tested the words, saying them out loud. "It's a good thing."

"What is?"

She pivoted to find Jake standing in the doorway.

"You dumping me." She was so proud of how steady her voice sounded even if her heart was racing a mile a second. "It was a good thing."

"No, it wasn't." He entered the meeting room, closing the door behind him. "It was the stupidest thing I've ever done, and trust me, I've done plenty of stupid things."

"I'm sure you have."

"I came back."

"I can see that." She turned her back on him and continued writing on the blackboard.

"Don't you want to know why?"

"Not really, no."

"I'll tell you anyway."

"Don't bother. I'm not interested."

"You want me to grovel. I get that. I really messed up. I hurt you."

"I'm over it."

"I'm not."

"Your problem, not mine."

"Can you put that chalk down a minute and talk to me?"

She kept writing.

"Please?"

She turned and threw an eraser at him. It hit him smack in the middle of his black T-shirt leaving a puff of white chalk powder before falling to the floor. "How dare you! How dare you come back here and try to act all charming like nothing happened."

"I'm so sorry. Forgive me."

"Forget it. You're not going to nail this brainy girl ever again."

"You scared me."

"Yeah, right," she angrily scoffed. "The man who's not afraid of anything. The extreme sports guy who only feels alive if he's courting death."

"I'm telling the truth."

"And I'm telling you I don't give a . . . a rat's rectum."

"Will you at least let me try and explain."

"No, I don't think I will. Aren't you afraid I'd print your explanation in my supposedly tell-all book about you?"

"No. I trust you."

"Well, I *don't* trust you. How could I after what you've done? And how can you say you trust me when you never told me your real reason for coming to Rock Creek? It wasn't to build a sports resort. It was to find your birth mother. Lulu told me. Don't worry. She swore me to silence about it."

"I only discovered Zoe was my birth mother a few days ago."

"That doesn't change the fact that you knew all along that you'd come here to find her but you never told me, never said a word. And that was before you knew about my book so you can't use that excuse. You didn't tell me because I didn't matter to you."

"Don't put words in my mouth."

"Somebody has to since you never talk about the things that are the most important to you. Except for extreme sports. Sometimes you'll talk about that." She reigned in her anger and fell back on her logic. "You do realize that the intense excitement or stress you experience while doing all those wild extreme sports things releases a flood of dopamine to your brain, creating a feeling of well-being, right?"

"So?"

"So taking risks is a way of keeping the dopamine flowing. The behavior becomes addictive."

"You like being logical."

"Yes."

"It excites you, being logical, right? So you're addicted to logic because it keeps your dopamine flowing. See? We're not that different after all."

"Yes, we are. We are totally different. You love taking risks. I avoid them."

"I love *you*. I didn't see it coming. I knew you were special and that I cared about you more than I ever had about a woman before, but I didn't know I was in love with you until I was. And by then it was too late."

"Too late for what?"

"To protect myself."

She saw the vulnerability in his golden brown eyes, but she was afraid to believe it. She had to protect *herself*. She couldn't risk getting hurt again. Could she?

"It hit me at McDonald's," he said. "I was headed for the closest airport, planning on going to an alpine resort in Peru and proving that I could get back on a snowboard. Then I saw the Dr Pepper logo and bam, that was it. Was I going to keep on running scared, or was I going to bare my soul to you and risk you stomping my heart to bits? Did I . . . did I really have the balls . . . the courage to do that?"

Her eyes shimmered with tears at his halting words. This was no smooth-talking charmer out to nail her. This was a man spilling his guts to her. A man who hated revealing his inner thoughts and emotions. "That was it?"

Jake nodded. "I knew I loved you. Knew I had to come back and fight for you."

"Seeing the Dr Pepper logo made you realize you love me?"

"Yeah. Sounds stupid, I know," he muttered.

It was the first time she'd ever seen him embarrassed. She doubted it would be the last. Her sisters and mom would see to that if she let him back into her life. Could she really do it? Could she take a chance on him?

"Okay, now I know you're telling the truth because no one could make up a story like that. But how long until you take off again?"

"Don't you get it? I'm more addicted to you than I am to extreme sports. You're scared. I get that. I'm scared too. All the people I care about die." Jake's voice was rough with pain. "That's why I lit out of here the way I did. Because when I saw that truck headed straight for you . . . Hell." He rubbed his hand over his face as if to erase that awful image. "That's really when I knew I loved you, but I didn't want to admit it even to myself."

"It took Dr Pepper to make you see the light, huh?"

"Yeah." For the first time since walking into the room, he looked hopeful.

For the first time she *felt* hopeful.

She might still be uncertain about a lot of things in her life, but she was sure that Jake was the man for her.

"Did you lock the door?" she asked.

"What?"

Emma walked over, locked it, and pulled down the shade on the door's window.

Jake eyed her warily. "Do you plan on beating me with an eraser?"

"Have you been a bad student?" she asked in a sultry voice.

He grinned. "Yes, I've been very, *very* bad, teacher."

She placed her hands on his muscular chest and back-stepped him up against the blackboard. "You're getting chalk on your T-shirt. Maybe we should take it off."

"Are you just after my body?" His tone of voice was teasing, but there was an underlying thread of uncertainty there.

"I'm after your heart."

"You already have it," he vowed.

She kissed him. How could she not after a confession like that? He returned her kiss with fervent hunger and a newfound tenderness that he hadn't expressed before. Off went his T-shirt. Off went her prim white blouse. Down went the zipper on his jeans. Up went her flowery summer skirt.

Emma reached into the back pocket of his jeans. "What are you looking for?" he murmured against her lips.

"A condom."

He shifted her hand to his black briefs. "Look here."

She moved her fingertips against his arousal. "How can you store a condom there?"

"I can't. I just couldn't go another second without you touching me."

"Touching you like this?"

He growled his approval then moaned as she shoved his briefs completely out of her way.

He removed her panties with haste before brushing his thumb through the crisp curls guarding her moist feminine core. Tenderly, skillfully, erotically he caressed her until her knees trembled and pulses of sexual joy shot through her.

"Now," she said. "I need you inside me now."

He fumbled for his wallet, where he'd stashed a few condoms the last time they'd made love. She was the one who confidently rolled it on him, adding a few feathery caresses along the way.

Shaking with need, Jake slipped his hands beneath her bare bottom and lifted her in his arms so she could wrap her legs around his waist. Seconds later he entered her with a glorious rush. She was eye to eye with him, staring into his glorious golden brown eyes, watching him watching her. The very first time she'd met him his brooding eyes made her think of orgasms.

And now here she was, merged with him in the most intimate of embraces. He moved deep within her, increasing her pleasure tenfold. Her hands clutched his bare shoulders. Her breasts were pressed against his bare chest.

He turned, pinning her between his body and the blackboard as he increased the rhythm of his powerful thrusts. Her orgasm slammed into her, the walls of her vagina clenching around him with fierce bliss.

Jake captured her scream with his mouth even as he captured her body with his. He arched against her as he reached his own climax.

When he finally lowered her to stand on her own she had to cling to him for a moment to regain her balance. Her skirt covered her naked lower torso, which still vibrated with the memories of sexual joy.

"I think we broke the blackboard," she noted unsteadily.

"You'll have to marry me now."

She blinked. "What did you say?"

"You heard me. Marry me. Please."

She stared at him in shock.

"What? You want me to go down on my knees to propose?"

She remained speechless.

"Okay. I'll have to adjust a few things first . . ." He rearranged his briefs and jeans and then knelt before her. He gazed up at her with love in his eyes and a wickedly sexy devil in his heart as he caressed her ankle with his fingertips. "Emma . . ."

He slid his fingers up to the back of her knee and caressed her there.

"Emma . . ."

His fingers climbed higher beneath her skirt to the softness of her bare thighs, to the cave of her sex.

"Emma, will you marry me?"

"Are you trying to distract me with sex?"

He blinked at her and removed his hand.

"No, don't stop." She brought his hand back to her most intimate place and moved against his fingers. "Tell me why I should marry you. Besides the incredible, mmmmm, awesome sex . . . yes, right there, mmmmm." She gripped his shoulder to stay upright and not collapse in a heap on the floor as she luxuriated in the undulating passion he was creating within her.

"Because . . . I love you and . . . you love me . . . and we were meant to be together. Because I love the way you snort when you laugh. Take a chance on me." He stopped caressing her. "Oh God, now I sound like an ABBA song."

Emma laughed and tugged him to his feet. "Yes, I'll marry you. That romantic proposal was too good to turn down. *You're* too good to turn down."

He put his arms around her. "I'm not letting you go."

"You don't have to." She brushed his hair back from his forehead and trailed her fingertips down his stubble-darkened cheek.

"You're sure? Your logical side won't talk you out of it?"

"Are you sure? Your risk-taking side won't talk you out of it?

"Never." He pulled her close. "I found what I've been looking for. Jeez, now I sound like U2."

"Then I guess we should stop talking."

"You are so smart."

"Yes, I am," she said with the confidence of a woman who is well loved. "And so are you."

Epilogue

· · · · · · · · · · · ·

One year later, Jake's custom-built log home outside Rock Creek

"Out of all the places you could have gotten married—Aspen, Peru, Boston, even Stanley, Idaho—you pick this." Maxie shook her head. "Who gets married on top of a mountain?"

"It's not a big mountain," Emma said.

"It's big enough." Maxie rolled her eyes. "I can't believe you're marrying Jake on top of Gobsmacked Knob."

Emma grinned. "Just be thankful we didn't go with the glacier in Alaska plan, with everyone being flown in to the site by helicopter."

"I must say, we've certainly had more than our fair share of weddings around here," Maxie said.

After her sisters' weddings, the marriage bug had taken hold in Rock Creek with winter weddings for Cosmic Comics store owner Algee and English high school teacher

Tameka, as well as for Skye's grandmother Violet and funeral home director Owen Dunback.

Nancy Crumpler eloping with mayor Bart Chumley had surprised everyone since no one even knew they were dating.

But it was her own wedding today that held Emma's attention. The sunlight glinted off her engagement ring—a princess-cut diamond solitaire. The ceremony was going to take place in a mountain meadow covered in wildflowers and surrounded by trees. Only family and close friends would be attending.

"I was glad to see Lulu back in town. I can't believe she's got a graphic novel coming out next year. She and Oliver seem happy in Boston. You don't miss teaching in Boston, do you?" Maxie asked.

Emma shook her head. "I enjoyed it while I did it, but it wasn't the right fit for me."

"And what you're doing now is?"

She nodded. "I really love the research and writing."

"And the traveling."

"And the traveling with Jake, yes." Emma couldn't believe how much her life had changed in a year. Her article about her hometown's rebirth had come out two months ago and created such a stir that her publisher wanted her to do more on the subject of small-town revitalization. Her book about risk takers, *Taking Chances*, had been published last month to great reviews and was already in its second printing. Her publisher also wanted her to write a sequel about the women who loved risk takers.

"I can't believe how many people came to the ground breaking for Jake's extreme sports resort last week," Maxie said.

"It was quite a crowd." A group of investors with deep pockets had gone in with Jake to create the environmentally friendly resort project, which would provide plenty of jobs for locals. The plans included a lodge, log cabins, a snowboard school, and snowboard runs from half-pipe to cross.

"Walt Whitman is still fuming that Jake is building it in the area near Rock Creek instead of Serenity Falls."

"He'll get over it."

"I wouldn't count on it," Sue Ellen said as she and Leena joined them. "He's a bit of a drama king."

Emma had to laugh at that commentary from her sister, the drama queen. But motherhood had softened her big sister's temperament. She and her husband adored baby Donny Jr., who was now eight months old. Sue Ellen jiggled him on her hip. "He has my eyes I've decided."

"And your mouth," Leena said as Donny Jr. let out a yodel. "My dainty girl would never yell like that, right sweetie?" Adorable little Annelise responded by spitting up on Leena. She then grinned at them all with a happy smile on her perfectly dainty bow-shaped lips.

Leena took it in stride. "Good thing we're not wearing our bridesmaids' dresses yet."

Two hours later, Emma took her father's arm as she prepared to walk down an "aisle" comprised of rose petals. "You look beautiful, Sweet Pea," he said gruffly.

Emma blinked back tears as she smoothed a hand down the Cinderella-style satin skirt of her wedding dress. She felt like a fairy-tale princess . . . with a sociology degree.

"Don't say anything to make me cry," her dad warned her.

Emma grinned at him. "Semper Fi!"

A harpist played the "Wedding March" as Emma walked down the aisle. Emma deliberately didn't look at Jake. If she did, she'd cry. Instead she focused her attention on the people in the audience who'd come to share her special day—Skye and Nathan with their little girl Toni, Julia and Luke with their toddler Jayne Ann. Angel and her life partner Tyler, Zoe and Jerry, Cole and Jake's dog Mutt.

Finally she risked a quick glance at Jake and almost tripped over the rose petals at the way he caressed her with his eyes. He was wearing a suit tailored to fit him to perfection. He wore the burgundy tie he'd used again last night to tie her to his bed's headboard. Their passion hadn't diminished in the past year. Instead they'd had the time to share so much more than physical intimacy. He never let her forget how grateful he was that she took a chance on a loner rebel like him.

Jake was a loner no more. His half sister Lulu proudly stood beside him as his best man and Oliver stood beside her as his second groomsmen.

Okay, so Jake was still a rebel and that was fine with her.

Because Emma was discovering that she had some rebel blood in her too. Jake was the one who brought out that side of her.

Jake reached out his hand to her.

She took it.

And began the rest of her life . . . with him.

Turn the page for a preview of the next romance
from Cathie Linz

Mad, Bad, and Blond

Coming soon from Berkley Sensation!

It was the perfect May for a wedding. Too bad the groom hadn't shown up.

Faith West fingered the rich white satin skirt of her wedding dress as she sat very still in the bridal anteroom of the historic Chicago Gold Coast Church, unable to believe this was really happening to her. Alan Anderson, the man she'd agreed to marry, was late for his own wedding.

There had to be a reasonable explanation for Alan's absence—car trouble, a dead cell phone, maybe even an accident, heaven forbid.

Faith caught sight of herself in the large mirror on the opposite wall. A few wisps of her brown hair had escaped the confines of her upswept hairstyle, and her blue eyes appeared haunted despite her perfect makeup. Did she look like the kind of woman a man would leave at the altar? Possibly. She was certainly no raving beauty. She was just a librarian. A librarian with a rich private investigator father.

Faith's family flitted around her like a skittish school of fish, coming and going—offering help, offering suggestions, offering vodka. She remained calm in the center of all the chaos, strangely distant from her surroundings. The reality was: she was probably going into shock and should accept the offer of alcohol purely for medicinal purposes.

The question was: What would Jane Austen do in this situation? Whenever Faith was in trouble, she looked to her favorite author for the solution. And Faith was armpit deep in trouble at the moment.

"I bet you scared the poor man away." Faith's pain-in-the-butt aunt Lorraine interrupted Faith's racing thoughts to declare. "A children's librarian whose father taught her how to shoot a gun. A big mistake."

Aunt Lorraine, also known as the Duchess of Grimness, was the bane of the West family's existence. With her demonlike black hair and Hellboy eyes, she was scarier than anything written by Stephen King. Not exactly the model wedding guest, but Faith's mom had insisted on inviting her.

For a wild second Faith wondered if Alan had stayed away because he was afraid of Aunt Lorraine, having met her for the first time at the rehearsal dinner the night before. Maybe *she* was the reason he hadn't shown up. Could Faith really blame him for wanting to avoid Aunt Lorraine's stinging barbs?

Hell yes, she could blame him! How could Alan leave her sitting here wondering what had happened to him? How could he be so cruel? How could anyone, aside from Aunt Lorraine, be that cruel?

Alan wasn't just anyone. He was her fiancé, a reliable and respectable investment banker she'd known for two years. They'd been engaged for the past eleven months. They were perfectly suited for each other, sharing the same interests, values, and aspirations. Neither one of them was blinded by passion or prone to wild behavior.

That's not to say that the sex between them hadn't been good; it had been. Not great but good. She loved him. He loved her. Or so he'd said last night before kissing her.

Faith looked around. Someone had led Aunt Lorraine away. She was replaced by Alan's shame-faced best man. "Alan just sent you a text message."

"Where is he? Is he okay?"

Instead of answering her anxious questions, the best man hightailed it out of the room, heading for the nearest exit and no doubt the nearest bar.

"Where's my BlackBerry?" Faith asked her maid of honor, her cousin Megan, who was like a sister to her. Faith and Megan were born two days apart, grew up within a few blocks of each other, and had been known to complete each other's sentences. Their dads were brothers. Faith had only wanted one bridal attendant, and of course, that was Megan.

"I'm sure Alan has a good reason for being late." Megan had always been the optimist in the family. "Maybe he was in an accident. Your dad is still checking the area emergency rooms."

Faith's über-workaholic father owned the most successful investigation firm in Chicago. If Alan wasn't in an emergency room, then her father would be tempted to put him in one.

"Where's my BlackBerry?" Faith heard the edge of hysteria in her voice but couldn't do anything to stop it.

"Here. It's right next to you." Megan handed it to her. Sure enough, there was a text message from Alan that had been sent two minutes ago.

> thought i wanted marriage. i don't. i need to find
> who i really am. i want adventure and excitement.
> don't want u. sorry.

Alan hadn't left her because she could shoot a gun. He'd left because he didn't think she was exciting enough. She'd scared him away by *boring* him to death.

"What did he say?" Megan demanded.

Her cousin was her best friend, but even so, Faith was too humiliated to show her what Alan had written. Instead she turned the BlackBerry off with trembling fingers. "I've been dumped via text message," she said unsteadily. "And not just dumped, but left at the altar."

"We never actually walked down the aisle."

"Close enough." Faith angrily wiped away the tears that were starting to stream down her face. "There are people waiting out there. Lots of them. And they're all expecting a wedding."

"They'll all be on your side."

That was cold comfort at this point. Faith welcomed the anger starting to surge through her. It kept the pain and humiliation at bay.

So much for her happy ending. Faith had continued to believe in her fairy-tale wedding even when Alan hadn't shown up for the preceremony photographs, even when his best man had refused to look her in the eye, even when the minister had approached her privately to ask if she wanted to delay the proceedings.

"He'll show up," Faith kept saying. "You'll see. He'll show up. And he'll have the lamest excuse for being late."

Her belief in Alan and her faith in a positive outcome had lasted longer than it should have and was now as tattered as the lace handkerchief she'd nervously shredded with her beautifully manicured fingers.

Last night he'd claimed he loved her, yet today he didn't want her. How did that work? Did Alan love her like he loved fine wine and the Cubs instead of the way you loved the person you were supposed to marry? Weren't Cub fans supposed to be the most loyal guys on the planet?

Faith was having a hard time thinking coherently, and she felt cold enough to get frostbite. The man she loved didn't want her. She couldn't think about that or she'd dissolve into a sobbing mess. But she could think of nothing else.

Her parents burst into the anteroom. "I finally tracked him down," Jeff West said. His usually smooth brown hair was mussed from him running impatient fingers through it. "The bastard took a flight to Bali an hour ago. One way."

Alan has gone to Bali searching for adventure and excitement because he couldn't find any with me. So much for love and commitment. I guess those things don't matter to him. I don't matter to him.

What had she done to make him change his mind about marrying her? He couldn't have thought she was boring when he'd proposed. So what had changed?

Would Alan have stayed if he'd known she was a crack shot with a gun? Her dad had taken her to the firing range and taught her himself when she was ten. Faith had never told Alan about her weapons training because she didn't like to brag about the marksmanship awards she'd won. Maybe she should have. Maybe then he'd have thought twice about dumping her. Maybe then he'd have thought she was more exciting. A children's librarian who had a gun and knew how to use it. Yeah, that ranked right up there on the excitement scale with . . . What?

What *was* Alan's definition of exciting? Baseball and the stock market? Sex in the middle of Wrigley Field? A blow job in Bali?

"You poor baby." Faith's mother Sara sat beside her and hugged her. "He seemed like such a nice investment banker."

"There was nothing in his background to indicate he'd bolt like this," her dad said. "I had him thoroughly checked out. He wasn't seeing another woman or another man, wasn't defrauding the bank or his clients."

"Maybe he just got a case of cold feet," Megan said. "He could still come back."

"And when he does, I'll beat the crap out of him," Jeff growled.

Faith would have thought that her fiancé would be smart enough to figure out that dumping her at this late date meant there was no place he could hide. Not even Bali. Her father would track him down and make him pay . . . big time.

Only one person was more imposing than Jeff West and that was Aunt Lorraine, who was now trying to push her way back into the room.

"Get rid of her," Faith begged her parents.

"Gladly," her dad said. "Do you think I haven't wanted to make her disappear for years now? But your mother would never let me."

"She's my much older sister," Sara said apologetically. "She practically raised me."

"And she scares you shitless," Jeff said. "Believe me, I get it."

"She implied it was my fault Alan left," Faith said. It turned out the Duchess of Grimness was right. According to Alan's brief text message, it was obvious that he blamed Faith for being too dull for him.

"Your fault? That does it." Sara glared at Lorraine who was still trying to get in the room but was being prevented by Megan. "She's gone too far this time." A curtain of fierce determination fell over Sara's face. "Don't worry, I'll handle her." She marched over and moved Lorraine out of the room.

Watching her mother's totally uncharacteristic behavior, Faith realized anything was possible. Anything but her wedding. There was no saving that now.

"What are we going to do?" Faith asked her dad. "All those people are out there waiting. We've got the wedding reception at the Ritz-Carlton. You paid so much for everything." Tears welled again, but she dashed them away. Alan had said there were only a handful of people he wanted to invite. His parents were dead, and he had no other close family. Since almost all of the guests were from her side of the family, Alan had been perfectly happy to have Jeff foot the bill, and her dad had done so with boatloads of paternal pride.

Again, what would Jane Austen do? She would take control.

"Tell the people in the church that due to circumstances beyond our control, the ceremony has been cancelled," Faith said. "Tell them the reception is still on. Don't cancel it. You might as well enjoy it."

"That's my girl," her dad said. "We'll get our money's worth as a celebration of friends and family. And it makes good business sense since a lot of West Investigation's top clients are also in the audience and will be at the reception."

"Are you nuts?" her mom said, having rejoined them in time to hear Faith's request.

"Probably," Faith muttered.

"I was talking to your father." She turned to face him. "Your daughter is suffering and all you can do is talk about business and money?"

"I could put out a hit on Alan," Jeff growled, "but I'm restraining myself."

"I know people who could do the job," Faith's paternal grandmother spoke up for the first time. Her blue eyes and high cheekbones proclaimed her Scandinavian heritage while her gelled spiky haircut revealed her rebel nature. "They're in the Swedish mob."

Jeff frowned. "I never heard of the Swedish mob."

"Of course not. They're very discreet. Not like the Finnish mob."

"I appreciate the offer, Gram, but it's not necessary," Faith said.

"Well, if you change your mind, the offer stands," Gram assured her.

"I'll keep that in mind."

"You do that." She patted Faith's hand. "I'm sorry things didn't work out."

"Thanks." She took a deep breath but felt the walls closing in on her. "Listen, you guys don't have to stay with me. Go on to the reception. Please give everyone my regrets, but I just can't . . ." She shook her head, unable to go on.

"You have nothing to be regretful about," her mom said.

"Except regret at ever hooking up with Alan the Asshole to begin with."

"Are you sure you want us to go?" her mom looked uncertain.

"Yes, I'm sure. Megan will stay with me, right?"

"Of course I will."

"See, I'll be fine."

"Of course you will . . . in time." Gram patted her hand again. "A year or two should do it."

When they finally left, Megan looked at her with concern. "Are you okay?"

"Not yet. But after a few mojitos I will be. Now please help me get me out of this damn dress!"

• • •

Faith woke with a hammering headache and the sound of intense roaring in her ears. Her eyelids didn't seem to want to open, but she was able to sneak a peek through a narrow slit. The limited view was not enough to tell her where she was.

"This is your captain speaking. We'll be landing in Naples in about an hour."

Her eyes flew open.

"The flight attendants will be going through the cabin . . ."

Faith didn't pay attention to the rest of the announcement as the events of the day and night before came rushing back. Left at the altar. Humiliated, broken-hearted, angry. She and Megan downing several mojitos at a neighborhood bar before heading to Faith's Streeterville condo only to trip over Faith's suitcases just inside the door. A matched set of luggage packed with carefully chosen outfits for her dream honeymoon to the Amalfi coast in Italy.

Alan wanted to spend their honeymoon riding elephants in India because his boss at the bank had done that and raved about it. Personally, Faith was not that fond of pachyderms. Had he left her because of that? Because she didn't want to boogie with the elephants?

It wasn't like her choice was dull or boring. Who didn't like sunny Italy? Faith had longed to go to the Amalfi coast ever since she'd seen the movie *Under the Tuscan Sun* and watched Diane Lane be swept off her feet in the beautiful town of Positano.

She distinctly remembered shouting at her living room wall last night. "Alan ruined my wedding, but he's not going to ruin this too! I refuse to allow him to mess up any more of my life! I'll show you exciting and adventurous! I'm going to Italy! Solo! Sole mio!"

Faith had spent the last two years trying to please Alan. This trip was one of the few times she'd stood her ground and refused to back down. Once he didn't get his way, Alan had completely lost interest and told her to handle all the arrangements. Gladly, she had, which was why she had possession of the nonrefundable tickets and the rest of the travel reservations.

Megan had been supportive as always. "Go for it! I'd come with you, but I can't get away from work right now."

Sitting on the plane, Faith felt as if she'd just woken up from a long, drugged sleep. Unlike Sleeping Beauty, she hadn't been brought back to life by a kiss from a handsome prince. Instead she'd been brought back to reality by the handsome prince screwing her over.

The ironic thing was that Faith was usually a worst-case-scenario specialist, always prepared in case things went wrong. One of her dad's favorite mottos was "Expect the worst, and if it doesn't happen, you'll be pleasantly surprised." Her relationship with Alan was the one time she'd allowed herself to believe . . . and look what happened.

She ended up on a flight to Italy. Alone. Her first solo trip ever. But it was better than moping in her condo crying her eyes out. She'd taken action. She'd left the mayhem behind in Chicago, calling her dad and telling him she was fleeing the country.

There was no time to reflect further on her actions as the flight attendants prepared for their landing. Her arrival in Naples went smoothly as she cleared customs with no problem. Two aspirins and a bottle of Pellegrino water took care of the headache. Her rental car was ready . . . and so was she.

She *was* ready, right? She wasn't going to let fear hold her back, right? She could do this. She *would* do this.

Faith put her iPod into the sound system and moments later music blared out of the sporty little red Italian convertible's speakers. She'd had to put her smaller suitcase in the passenger seat next to her since it didn't fit anywhere else.

The instant she hit the road, all the other drivers seemed determined to *hit* her. She refused to let them. She'd handled rush hour traffic in Vegas, not to mention on the Kennedy Expressway in Chicago during construction season. The crazy Italian drivers didn't scare her. Being alone on her honeymoon scared her if she thought about it. So she refused to think about it and instead stepped on the gas, cranked up the sound system and sang along with Bon Jovi.

• • •

Caine Hunter had his instructions. Keep an eye on Faith West, track her actions, and report back to Chicago. He knew a lot about her already: children's librarian, jilted bride, handy with a gun. Her team from the library in Las Vegas where she'd worked two years ago had come in second place in the city's Corporate Challenge, an event where organizations compete in various sporting events. She'd aced the shooting event.

Caine was only mildly impressed. She still seemed like a spoiled little rich girl to him, with her fancy wedding in one of the most prestigious churches in Chicago, a fancy banker fiancé, and a condo in Streeterville, Chicago's trendiest neighborhood. Not that the wedding or the fiancé had panned out for her in the end. Too bad, so sad.

No one had ever accused him of being the sentimental type.

He'd say this for Faith West, she didn't drive like a librarian . . . more like racecar driver Danica Patrick. Driving in Italy, especially around Milan, was not for wimps.

Yet here she was, weaving in and out of traffic, music blaring. Was she really that reckless or just plain stupid? Hard to tell at this point but Caine aimed to find that out . . . among other things.

• • •

Faith's knuckles were permanently white by the time she reached the small town of Positano. The infamous road of a thousand curves on which she'd been traveling clung precariously to the steep cliffs and was narrower than her parent's driveway at home. That didn't stop huge tour buses from barreling around blind curves, hogging the entire road and making her fear for her life and her sanity.

But she'd done it. She'd made it here. Alive. In one piece. Jane Austen would be so proud.

"Welcome to the Majestic Hotel, Mrs. Anderson." Huge terra-cotta urns filled with flowers bracketed the reception desk, which was adorned with colorful majolica tiles. The lobby, with its antiques and artwork, was a study of understated elegance. "We have the honeymoon suite all ready for you and your husband."

Her stomach clenched. This was no honeymoon and she had no husband. But she did have sunshine, breathtaking views, and the scent of citrus blossoms in the air. "It's Ms. West. Faith West. Not Mrs. Anything. I called ahead to explain the change . . ."

"Oh, yes, I see the note here. I'm sorry for the confusion Ms. West. If you could show me your passport please." He raised his hand and a uniformed bellman immediately appeared with her luggage. "Paco will take you to your room."

She'd spent hours over the past winter pouring over guidebooks and surfing websites trying to decide where to stay—the Grand Hotel in Sorrento or the Capri Palace Hotel on the island of Capri? But Positano had held her under its spell and, while she planned on visiting both Sorrento and Capri during her stay, this was her ultimate destination. The room didn't disappoint with its private terrace displaying a colorful bougainvillea-framed view of the pastel sunlit town nestled against the rugged cliffs that plunged down to the blue waves of the Mediterranean.

John Steinbeck was right. This place was "a dream."

The dream was interrupted by the sound of her stomach

growling. She needed to eat something and fast. The hotel dining room was serving for another hour Paco the bellman informed her in a sexy Italian accent, his liquid brown eyes gazing at her with Latin approval.

Faith was starving. But not for male attention. She handed Paco his tip and showed him the door.

She barely had time for a fast bathroom stop where she looked at the thick towels and large tub longingly before hurrying down to eat. Knowing that nearby Naples was the birthplace of pizza, she quickly ordered a pizza Margherite.

And waited. And waited. Other diners were seated on the sunny terrace dining area. Two guys in particular made a point of staring at her sitting all alone. She wasn't pleased to see their food arrive before hers. They hadn't even ordered Italian dishes but steak and fries. The skinnier of the two men gave her a leering look. He poured ketchup onto his plate and then dipped a fry into it, holding it up and taunting her with it before chomping into it with gusto.

Normally Faith would have looked away and ignored him but she wasn't feeling very generous toward the opposite sex at the moment.

Faith gave the man her best withering librarian look.

He responded by smacking his lips at her.

She made an eww-yuck face.

He dipped another fry in the ketchup and waved it at her before sucking it into his mouth in one go. An instant later the man grabbed his throat and started turning red then blue.

Before she could react, a man smoothly moved past her and gave the choking man the Heimlich.

Faith sank into her chair. She felt guilty that while trying to impress her, the idiot had ended up choking and nearly killing himself. Was there some kind of Italian curse that was reserved for brides who came to the Amalfi coast without their grooms?

Then all thought went out of her head as she got her first good look at the rescuer. Dark hair, dark eyes, stubble-darkened cheeks and chin. A dark knight. A man meant to get a woman's juices flowing.

He stopped at her table and stared down at her before saying with amusement, "I'll say this, you sure know how to make an impression on a guy."